Hattie Finds Trust

THE MAXWELL BRIDES SERIES: BOOK SEVEN

KRISSYANN GRANGER

Tug Hill Publishing
Company, LLC

Copyright

To request permissions, contact the publisher at krissyanngranger@google.com

ISBN: 978-1-955609-22-7 (Ebook)
ISBN: 978-1-955609-27-2 (Paperback)

First printing edition 2023

Tug Hill Publishing
Company, LLC

Published by:
Tug Hill Publishing Company, LLC.
West Leyden, NY 13489

https://www.facebook.com/KrissyannGranger

M ark pressed his back against the brick house. His breath collected in clouds and hovered in the night's stillness. His mind conjured images of brutalities seen since coming to Boston. Dread settled in his gut, a harbinger of the horrors awaiting inside. His heart raced as he fingered his pistol and waited for the sign. Taking deep breaths, he braced himself, nodding when Paul whistled.

He was ready as he was going to be.

He wanted to get it over with and leave whatever cruelties lie in wait to become another memory to torture his dreams. Paul pushed off the wall and kicked the door in with his pistol drawn. Mark pushed inside a second behind him. Mark scanned left and Paul scanned right. Their eyes adjusted to the darkness of the silent room.

Dean and Brian entered a moment behind, having taken a second to light lanterns for the search. They flanked Mark, and all four men studied the scene for danger in the darkness.

The air was stale, with traces of something rancid. No

one was there. If Mark had to guess, he'd say no one had been there for at least a day—maybe longer. The amber lantern light illuminated the true terrors in the dirty room and drove him closer to the madness that seemed to loom. He longed for the darkness, to block out the testimony of the soiled mattresses and shreds of women's clothing.

The room was sparse, as they always were. Pushed to one side was a small table with a couple of chairs askew. Their missing spindles smiled like toothless grins. White-hot anger burned away his dread as his eyes confirmed everything the Maxwell Group had suspected. He set his teeth and searched the corridor as he left the entry room.

"Is anyone in here?" Mark shouted into the dark. "There's no point hiding. We'll find you." He stomped up the stairs, but the place was a graveyard.

Their boots rattled the old wood floors and violated the deadly silence of the rickety house. The other men shouted as they searched, but there were no signs of life. There was nobody in the house to heed their warnings.

Mark rounded the corner from the upper landing to the first door. The handle jostled but wouldn't turn. Dean exited the adjacent room and stopped. Their eyes met and Dean sighed. A shake of his head confirmed Mark's greatest fears. They'd found a dead girl. Dean and Paul disappeared toward the last bedroom and Mark sighed at the door in front of him.

The flimsy wood gave way as Mark shouldered through the lock. Brian brushed against his back and they went in together. Mark's eyes swiveled about the dingy room, but stopped when they landed on the bed. The wraith-like body of a woman lay naked and tied to the bedposts. Mark's heart broke for the lady, but he checked inside the wardrobe and behind a threadbare old curtain for her captors. Brian scanned the closet, then got down to glance under the bed.

"There's nobody here." Brian sighed and stood with Mark.

"I don't know how much more of this I can take," Mark said.

Brian huffed again and squeezed Mark's shoulder.

Their next task was too sad for either of them, but after a moment, they moved in unison. Mark approached the bedside and pressed two fingers to the poor woman's neck. He had to restrain the desire to recoil from the icy shock of her flesh. Everything in him wanted to pull away and run. He owed her better than that, though, so he held his fingertips to her skin until he was sure there was no pulse.

"She's dead." It wasn't a surprise after what he'd seen in Dean's face in the hallway, but it still hurt. They were too late, and these women had paid the price.

Will this ever end?

Her skin was ghastly white, tinted with blues and purples. Some from bruises, others from the elements. Mark's heart and mind ached at the sight. His blood ran cold, and a shiver chased goosebumps up his spine.

She must have frozen to death.

He wanted to throttle someone, tear God down from his tower where he sat, and watched these evils unfold. Instead, he rubbed the tension from his eyes and swallowed the anger and pain. The visible damage to her body read like a book, relaying the horrors she had endured.

Her life had been torturous but in death, he would give her dignity. "Toss me that blanket," he said, pointing to a pile in the corner. The poor woman froze to death with a

3

blanket not five feet away. What was wrong with the world?

Brian handed the blanket to Mark and paced, his rage a palpable presence in the room. Mark shook out the rag and draped it over the woman, covering her lifeless face to block any judgment he might imagine there.

"Brian." Mark held up a hand to stop his friend from going off on a tirade. They would have time to rant later. There was work to be done.

Brian growled deep in his chest but nodded and joined Mark beside the bed.

"Hold up the light so I can see what I'm doing." Mark set to work on the knots at her feet. They would take both women to the undertaker and ensure they received a proper burial. It wasn't much, but it was all they could do. They would not be forgotten and faceless among the endless sea of women and children blighted by vile men.

No matter what we do, or how many women we save, it will never be enough.

Paul stepped through the doorway and to the bedside. "We found one woman. She was in the first bedroom across the hall." His quick fingers fumbled with the left wrist bond. "She was dead, too."

"What kind of monster would do this?" The flickering light trembled in Brian's anger-shaken hand.

Mark kept his eyes on his task. He wouldn't lose his cool now; there would be time for that later. "Someone pure evil," he whispered to himself as much as to the others.

"I don't know how much more of this I can take," Paul said. They'd seen too many dead or battered women, and Paul was ready to walk away.

"Mark here just said the same thing." Brian shifted the

lamp to give Mark better light. "Can't say I disagree. This is wearing on me something fierce."

Mark didn't blame him; he'd been ready to leave for a long time. These bodies would haunt them all for the rest of their lives.

Mark released the knot around the woman's left ankle and moved to her right.

"We don't even know their names for the undertaker." Paul tucked the limp arm he freed beneath the tatty blanket and moved around the end of the bed to free her other arm.

A faint moan trickled out of the woman.

All three men sucked in air and stared—frozen.

She couldn't be alive?

Mark hastened his efforts and jerked the rope in desperation. The woman's moan shattered into a sharp scream. She was alive and he'd hurt her. His heart raced as he reached up and pulled the blanket off her face. Mark locked eyes with the terrified girl.

For a moment, nobody moved.

"We've got you now," Mark said. "We won't hurt you. We just want to get you out of here."

Instead of responding, the blue eyes fluttered closed.

Mark moved more cautiously, examining her ankle; it was bloated black and blue. "This ankle is broken," he said, looking at Paul and then at the woman, who began wheezing.

"I can't believe she's alive!" Paul hurriedly tucked her other arm under the blanket and stepped back.

"Brian, find Dean and get the carriage," Mark ordered.

Paul—usually a rock under pressure—looked shaken. "I need to check the other girl again. We'll meet you outside." A spark of hope glistened in his eyes.

Brian set the lamp on the dresser and bolted from the room. Paul left a moment later. Mark untied the last knot and eased the broken ankle to the bed.

Mark stood beside the unconscious woman and watched her chest rise and fall under the blanket. He was sure she'd been dead when he entered the room. What miracle had revived her? He searched for something to splint her ankle, but aside from the bedframe holding the threadbare mattress, there was no furniture to break up.

Rather than wasting time, he removed his coat and draped it over her for extra warmth. He then pulled the blanket off her and tore it into strips. He bound her ankle as well as he could. Each tightening of the strip or manipulation of the joint drew whimpers and cries, and she rolled her head from side to side, but she seemed too weak to scream again.

Her pale face pinked as the warmth of his jacket seeped into her body. He imagined the cold had burrowed down so deep inside her bones it would take weeks to feel warm. She was small beneath his enormous coat, with only her feet and head stuck out. They had a half an hour ride to get back to the mansion. If he got her that far, everything would be okay.

He just needed to get her out of there alive and she'd survive.

Mark stepped to the window and watched for the carriage. He didn't want to move her before they were ready—the less she was jostled, the better.

He couldn't have another dead woman to carry around in his head. Her pale face was angelic in its vulnerability. His thought melted at once into guilt and shame. What kind of man finds a dying woman beautiful?

Maybe he just found the life inside her beautiful. She was a miracle.

After five agonizing minutes had passed, the carriage rolled into the yard. Dean stepped down from the driver's bench and said something to Brian. Brian slapped his shoulder and then Dean mounted his horse and rode away. He'd get everybody ready for their arrival. It was nice to work with such organized and intelligent men.

Brian mounted to the driver's bench and stared at the house.

Mark turned back to the bed, "Okay Miss, here we go."

"Brian's waiting in the carriage," Paul said as he returned wearing a solemn look rather than the hope he had gone off with. Mark didn't need to ask about the fate of the other woman.

"Let's get you out of here," Mark crooned. "You'll be safe with us."

"Give me your coat," Mark demanded.

Paul nodded and removed it; not seeming miffed by Mark's tone. With Paul's coat draped on her, Mark scooped her up and held her tight. Even with the two heavy coats, she didn't weigh nearly enough.

"We'll get you to a doctor. Just hold on a little longer."

The woman moaned. Her eyelids fluttered, but she didn't wake. Mark continued speaking, not caring if she heard him. Over and over, he assured her she was safe and no one would hurt her again.

Mark turned sideways to clear the door. "Watch that ankle," he said. "I don't want to make it worse." Paul followed and guarded her swollen foot as Mark carried her downstairs and out of the house. Her silence in the transition unnerved him and though he hated the sound of it, her whimpers would have been better than deathly silence.

Mark longed to get her to the big house. The doctor and the women would take care of her. Mark shuddered as the cold seeped through his shirt. He pulled the woman closer to his body, hoping to give her as much of his warmth as possible. He crossed the yard and stopped beside the carriage.

Paul ran up behind him and pulled the door open. He held the door and guided the woman's injured limb as Mark climbed awkwardly inside.

"I'll take care of the body and bring your horse back to the house," Paul said, and then closed the door. He slapped his hand twice on the side, alerting Brian that they were ready.

Mark shifted his weight to settle the woman across his lap, taking care to keep her broken ankle clear of the carriage wall. "The doc will be waiting for you at the big house." She shivered in place of a reply, and he gripped her closer to his chest. Using himself to not only keep her warm but to still her body against the rocking carriage. She probably couldn't hear him. Still, he kept speaking to soothe himself, if not her.

"We'll be there soon, I promise. No one will ever hurt you again. You'll be safe and warm. Mrs. Fritz will feed you silly. You'll be okay. Everything is going to be okay."

WHITE HOT PAIN JOLTED HATTIE INTO CONSCIOUSNESS. She'd been in a nightmare. No, it was real. It was all real. Someone was touching her, hurting her. A scream stuck in her throat as agonizing pain ripped through her. She wanted it to end, to go numb like the rest of her body.

Oh please God, no. Not another man.

The pain was too much. She opened her eyes, but couldn't focus enough to see; she could have been blind. Summoning the depths of her strength, she squeezed her eyelids shut to shield herself from whatever he would do to her. The words 'please stop' formed in her mouth but came out in raspy breaths.

Death was coming, but something inside her turned on, driving her to fight.

Her skin tingled and itched as warmth was restored to numbed flesh. She regained some mental focus. Was the weight over her a blanket? No one had so much as offered her a handkerchief, let alone draped a blanket over her before. Her thoughts drifted in and out of focus. When lucid, she believed they were playing a cruel trick. Would they let her recover only to undergo more torture? Would they dispatch her like a broken plaything? Her will to live and fight wavered.

Words murmured around her, their flutter like butter-flies always just out of her reach. The voice was warm and comforting in a way she wasn't used to. Then pain erupted from her ankle. It was more than she could bear, and she prayed once again for mercy. But between explosions of pain came slivers of warmth and comfort. Was she dying? Were the warm moments glimpses of Heaven? Was that soft voice God?

Her throat was ablaze and an intense heat rose out of her as she lay there, waiting for her body to die. She went from freezing to feverish in what felt like an instant. Why couldn't she just die? Hadn't she suffered enough?

Hattie whined again as her ankle pulsated with pain.

The warmth returned as she was squeezed tightly against a comforting heat. Was it her mother? Embracing her in death, ushering her to the other side? But no, there was a man. He smelled of soap and horse. He cradled her and crooned to her. Whenever the pain came, it was chased away by the warmth and that soothing voice.

Hoofbeats pounded the road, and they rocked from side to side? Had he moved her to a carriage? Where would he take her?

Hattie managed to heft her eyelids and stared into a man's face hovering inches above hers. He looked like the Roman Gods she'd seen in picture books. His square-cut jaw and strong brow gave the impression of Zeus. The pain faded as she studied his blue eyes and the gentle drape of his blonde hair. His strong arms held her steady, and she imagined for a moment that he was God, and she was in heaven. The warmth of his body and the clean cedar smell of him made him real, though. He was just a man, and men were dangerous.

She wanted to believe his whispered words. She wanted to trust that she was safe. Still, her body tensed, unforgiving like stone, unable to bear the touch of any man. She doubted she could handle even the touch of God.

Before her eyes closed again, she read the suffering on his face and softened. She could never see another person in pain without feeling for them. Something tormented him. She suspected it was her. Hattie lifted a weak hand and cupped his beautiful face. Gratitude for her bringer of peace crossed her mind as she fell deep into a fevered sleep.

~

THE CARRIAGE HAD BARELY STOPPED BENEATH THE PORCH when the front door flung open. Dean was ready and Mark shifted to the seat's edge. The woman rested like a child in his lap.

"Watch her ankle."

"I've got it." Dean supported the woman's limb with one hand. She did not react to his touch and a fearful look grew on his face.

Mark crouched and clambered down with hesitant movements, afraid to jostle her. Together, they ushered her inside.

Dr. Aaron Green rushed to escort the injured girl to a room upstairs. "Go straight up," he commanded. He turned to the housekeeper. "Mrs. Fritz put on a weak broth for the girl. She won't be able to drink it for a while, but it will be best to have it ready." He followed Mark up the stairs and pointed him into a bedroom.

"We readied this room as soon as Dean arrived," Elizabeth said as Doc waved for Mark to make haste. Doc Green was a good-humored man under most circumstances, but he was quite focused when he had a patient to tend to.

"Bring her here," Doc barked as he drew liquid from a vial. He held the needle upright and flicked it. A substance resembling water streaked out of the end. "We heard about the ankle. Have you noticed any other major injuries?"

Mark shook his head from side to side as he carried the woman to the bed, careful not to jostle her. Out of the corner of his eye, Opal Smith whispered something to her sister-in-law, Abigail, before they entered to help. Abigail's face was white as a sheet, but she stepped to the side of the bed and pulled a basin of water close.

"Lay her down," Opal squeezed Mark's elbow. He

found it hard to let her go, but he followed directions and stepped back out of the way.

Doc injected the solution into the woman's ankle, but she didn't flinch. He worked steadily on the ankle while Opal and Abigail removed the coats and tossed them over a chair. Once the woman was divested of the heavy garments, he was again confronted with her gaunt form, and Mark immediately turned his head away, his heart burning for her.

"Mark," Opal laid her hand on his shoulder, "It's okay. She's safe now."

Why was it so hard to let her go?

Mark didn't want to leave the room, losing contact felt like it would kill him. She shivered and moaned when he laid her down, and he was sure he didn't imagine her reaching out for him. His body was cold where hers had been against him, and he wished like hell he could lie in the bed and keep her warm and safe.

Elizabeth took Opal's place beside the bed and Opal stoked the fire, gathered the coats from the back of the chair, and then pulled Mark from the room like a little boy by the hand.

She said nothing when Mark winced at a cry from the other side of the closed door. Instead, in a far more intimate manner than he was sure she intended, she put her arm around his waist. Mark shifted his weight to settle right back against her and they walked together to the meeting room. She was warm and strangely comforting. This is what it must feel like to have a sister, and for a moment, he let her be his sister.

Daniel stepped into the meeting room with a tray full of tumblers and a decanter of whiskey, Brian right behind him. He poured a double measure into each glass before handing them out. Mark nodded gratefully and sank into a chair, his eyes locked on Dean.

"Paul isn't back yet," Daniel began as he took a seat. "What the hell happened to that poor woman?"

Mark shook his head and lowered his eyes to the floor.

THE WARMTH WAS GONE.

Hattie missed the warm arms, the God-like voice, and the gentle thump of a heartbeat against her ear. She hadn't realized she'd been listening to it until it was taken away.

In its place was cold, pain, and too many voices. Her head throbbed as she struggled to hear and understand what was going on. Her body was pulled in every direction and warm water cleaned her. The warmth was glorious, but as soon as the cloth moved, it left freezing skin behind. The cacophony overwhelmed her, and she drifted off to a fitful sleep.

Chapter Two

H attie Thompson's eyes flew open, and a strangled scream stuck in her mouth, like the death rasp of an animal. After a moment of panic, she relaxed back into the pillows.

She was at The Rose Dunn House.

She was safe.

It had been seven months since the rescue, but every night it came to her in waves of trauma and pain interspersed with warmth and comfort. It was always that night, but she could never quite remember what happened. The visions were flashes rather than scenes. Freezing chill and then warm muscular arms holding her tight, agonizing pain, and then glimpses of his Godlike face.

She knew his face well enough after sharing a dinner table with him for the better part of a year, but that night his eyes were wide with pain in a way she hadn't seen again. She hoped never to see him like that again. His eyes tortured her dreams every night, and the steady beat of his heart never stopped drumming in her ears.

Mark Webb.

Hattie shook off the dream and stretched. Then she climbed out of bed and pushed the dream away by running through her list of chores for the day. Getting on with it was the only way, or she would be crushed beneath the weight of anxiety.

As she dressed, she organized the day ahead. It would be much the same as the day before—breakfast, cleaning, lunch, cleaning, dinner, cleaning. Life at Rose Dunn had taken on a familiar rhythm that she found comforting. She was occasionally restless, but that was okay. She could handle the restlessness. At least she was safe.

"You're up so early," Elizabeth yawned. She sat up in the bed on the other side of the room and pushed her quilts away. "Was it the dream again?" Even with her dark hair mussed and her blue eyes swollen from sleep, Elizabeth was striking. Hattie was pale and invisible beside her.

Not that being invisible was a bad thing.

Hattie nodded.

Elizabeth climbed out of bed and pulled the covers up and tucked them in. "Maybe today you can speak to him." She always made her bed first thing in the morning. She told Hattie once that she didn't feel right all day long if she didn't make her bed right away. "If you talk to him, you might get him out of your dreams."

Hattie shrugged and crossed to her bed before Elizabeth could make it for her.

"It's nice that you can be in a room with the men, but at some point, you'll have to speak to them." Elizabeth patted her pillow and centered it on the bed. "Mark is a good man to talk to." Elizabeth crossed the room and picked up the corner of Hattie's quilt. Together they finished making Hattie's bed.

"I don't know what to say."

"Say what you told me last night," Elizabeth said. "Tell him that his sad eyes haunt you. Tell him he rouses confusing feelings in you." Elizabeth wiggled her eyebrows and then centered Hattie's pillow.

Hattie gasped and squirmed like she didn't fit in her own skin. She needed to keep a lid on her midnight chats with Elizabeth—she'd confessed far too much.

Elizabeth laughed. "Hattie, just talk to him."

"Mrs. Fritz will need some help in the kitchen, I'm sure," Hattie murmured as she ignored Elizabeth and laced up the stays on her dress.

She'd gotten into the habit of rising before anyone else and doing her share of the chores early. It was the best way to avoid most of the daily hustle and bustle. Even though she had become used to the other girls and enjoyed their company, she still liked to do things at her own pace.

Hattie was closest to Elizabeth and found her forthright protective nature comforting. While she didn't completely trust her, she was grateful to share a room with her. Sometimes when the nightmares were too real, Elizabeth would utter words of truth to ground her. On the first night they'd shared a room, Elizabeth had tried to hold Hattie, but it only increased her panic. After that, Elizabeth would just talk to her until the memories fell into the shadows and Hattie eased back into sleep.

Sophia was the opposite of Elizabeth in most ways. Sophia was shorter and voluptuous, with flowing blonde hair, whereas Elizabeth was tall and thin and wore her black hair slicked into a tight bun on the back of her head. Elizabeth was bold—sometimes quite aggressive—and preferred the company of the women. Sophia was quiet and insecure with the women and forward and flirty with the men. Now and then, Sophia slipped into a maternal mood, though, and Hattie liked her best during these periods.

Hattie and Angela had an immediate kinship. Angela was a quiet woman and struggled with the chaos of the house, too. She had spent many peaceful hours beside Hattie's bed. She didn't talk incessantly like Opal or Elizabeth, and she didn't fidget and fiddle with things like Sophia and Mrs. Fritz. Angela was present, but peaceful. She would sit beside Hattie and play a silent concert on an imaginary instrument. Watching her fingertips dance in the sunlight had a calming effect, unlike anything else.

Shortly after New Year, Angela and Paul were married and left The Rose Dunn House for a life in Hope. The Maxwell Group owned the biggest ranch in Montana Territory, and all the men shared a piece. Paul was ready to leave the city and Angela was happy to escape with him to a quieter part of the world.

Time had a way of slipping by in this place. Angela had been away for five months and was expecting a baby in the fall. Since her departure, Angela had written several letters and everyone relished reading about her success in Hope, especially after the awful business with her father.

Hattie had wanted to be married once. She'd had dreams of white dresses and bouquets of flowers. It was cruel that at only twenty years old, she was already ruined. Part of her tried to believe that matrimony could be in her future, but the rest of her had given up all hope. Her weariness around men was improving but performing any sort of wifely duties still seemed impossible.

Her future came more and more to her mind as the

months passed. Both her own concern and the well-meaning prodding of Mrs. Fritz. She couldn't stay at the rescue house forever—living off the charity of the Maxwell Group—and she had no other prospects or skills to fall back on. Before long, she would have to figure something out.

Everyone seemed to wait for the other shoe to drop. Roger Benson was dead, and the guards of Rose Dunn didn't seem to know what to do with themselves. Opal and Daniel returned to the ranch ahead of Paul and Angela. Dean had talked about heading West, and Hattie recognized the look of longing on Mark's face. He wanted to go, too, but something held him back.

Hattie would need to move on, but to what?

Hattie finished dressing and drifted to the door—lost in her thoughts—only coming back to herself when Elizabeth called after her. "Tell Mrs. Fritz I'll be down soon to help with breakfast."

"I will," Hattie smiled and shut the door behind her. She would be glad of the quiet before Sophia and Elizabeth came down. Dean, Brian, and Mark were probably pulling themselves out of bed and getting ready to head down for coffee. They would spend the first few hours of the morning in the barn, only returning to the house for breakfast. Hattie had discovered another benefit to being up first. She could make coffee and have a reason to spend a few quiet minutes each morning with Mark.

As she walked down the stairs and made her way toward the kitchen, Hattie's stomach twisted at the sound of his voice mingling with Mrs. Fritz's.

"There's nothing you need help with? More wood maybe?"

Hattie paused, longing for him to look at her the way

he did sometimes, like she was precious and made of glass. At the same time, she wished to be invisible. She wished she could watch him and be with him, but without him seeing or interacting with her.

A warm flush rose as she scanned his tall, powerful frame. He had one hand in his pocket, with his hip cocked like he hadn't a care in the world. Something hid beneath his casual façade, though, a sadness she felt in her own heart. Mark was the most sensitive of all the men, and he had a tenderness about him that drew her. Hattie had once believed she was good at reading people, but everything changed after her parent's death.

The betrayal of a trusted friend had thrown her into the hands of Roger Benson. A man made infamous for atrocities against women. Human trafficking, they called it, but torture is what it was. No matter how kind people seemed, Hattie had learned the hard way that she couldn't afford to give them her trust.

Now everyone flickered with suspicion and threat. Even those she cared for. You can never be too sure.

Even Mark Webb.

Regardless, he called to her like a lighthouse to a lost ship. She longed to feel the safety in his arms that she relived in her sleep. Her memories of that night weren't clear, but the warmth and safety of his embrace was crystal. Angela stood in the shadows of the hallway and watched Mark run a hand through his thick, sandy hair. Her hand tingled with the memory of touching his face, and a ripple of longing zipped through her.

She quashed it as a wave of panic followed. Everything made her anxious and edgy. Physical touch was still an uncertain domain. Sometimes she could spontaneously throw her arms around one of the women, and other times, a pat on her arm could send her into a self-contained fit of emotional turmoil. No rhyme or reason dictated her reactions, and she longed for the day when she was free of fear and panic.

Mrs. Fritz shooed Mark away, looking annoyed.

"If I need help, I'll ask for it," she said. "Get on with you. I've got breakfast to prepare. If you want to make yourself useful, give the girls a shout."

Mark shrugged and turned away, freezing at the sight of Hattie in the hallway. She flushed. It was obvious she had been watching him.

"Good morning," she said, her voice coming out as a whisper. Mark nodded to her, a sad smile playing at the corners of his lips.

"You're up early," she said, echoing Elizabeth's words and then feeling foolish for stating the obvious.

"I've been restless. There's not much to do since uh—," He cut himself off, nobody ever wanted to say Mr. Benson's name around her. Their eyes locked, and neither could speak. The air between them was charged. Or maybe it was only she who felt it. Was he also remembering the night he held her in his arms?

The memory of that made her—almost—trust him.

"Well, I guess I'll see you at breakfast," he said when she didn't reply and Hattie nodded, stepping aside for him to pass.

He slipped by, but as his body towered over her for a split second, she flinched, and he almost jumped down the hallway, looking horrified.

"I'm sorry," he said, holding his hands up.

"It's okay," Hattie reassured him, but her heart was pounding in her chest.

Would it always be like this?

She turned away from him and fled into the kitchen to join Mrs. Fritz.

~

BRIAN PACED BACK AND FORTH, EVEN MORE RESTLESS THAN Mark. "We've been on the edge of our seats with Benson and now we're cooling our heels." He shook his fist at an imaginary enemy. "It feels all wrong." Brian dropped his fist onto a table and flopped into a chair.

Mark, Brian, and Dean had taken to meeting in the conservatory. Mark upended an English Ivy and separated the roots. The fresh scent of soil comforted something in his soul. He'd discovered the conservatory after arriving at the rescue house, and he'd cleaned it up and restored the plants to life. It was one of his few joys in life. He repotted the ivy for the second time since finding the poor near-dead thing months earlier. Watching something grow and thrive made it easier to survive the horrors of their days.

At first, they'd come to the greenhouse to discuss rescue missions. They had closed the last Benson case, though, and now they were floundering.

So, Mark tended to his secret garden while Dean and Brian pondered their futures. Not just theirs, but the women and The Rose Dunn House, too. The Benson case had felt endless. It had started for them when Jeni— Caleb's wife—had come to Hope. After years of fighting, they hadn't prepared for life when it was over.

"I can't sit on my hands forever." Brian jumped to his feet and resumed his pacing. He was like a lion Mark had seen in a cage when he was young.

"Maybe we don't have to," Dean suggested, his face creased in thought.

"What do you mean?" Mark asked. Although he'd been the one to start the conversation, he was only half listening. He kept his hands busy, but his thoughts were on Hattie's reaction to him that morning. The way she'd been looking at him, all wide-eyed and beautiful, but so, so fragile.

Then the way she had shrunk back from him, her whole body jerking with fear. Nausea and fury swirled inside of him when he'd frightened her.

Benson and his cronies might be dead, but they would never have justice, and Mark hated it. Death was a mercy compared to what Hattie had gone through.

"Well, there are other women out there who need a safe house," Dean pointed out. "Whether it's from men like Benson or even their own fathers—or husbands." They both glanced at Brian.

"We offer them a place at Rose Dunn—" Brian nodded. The wheels in his head were turning, and he looked happier than he had in a long time.

Dean nodded, "It's called The Rose Dunn Rescue House for a reason." He fingered a rose, and shrugged, "Nobody said it was only for victims of the Benson organization."

Mark nodded, "I like it."

"We don't have to go out looking for another big operation. We just need to keep our ears to the ground and let women who need help know we're here," Dean said.

Dean caught Mark's eye and raised a dark eyebrow at him, sensing his displeasure.

"What is it?" He stepped beside Mark and scooped the soil into the new pot. "I thought you'd welcome the change of pace," he sighed.

Mark lifted the foliage to let Dean fill the pot. "I need

this to be over for me," Mark said, in a fiercer tone than intended. "I never want to see another battered woman in my life." He pressed the soil into place and picked up the watering can.

"It sounds like time for you to go home," Dean suggested.

"Growing crops and mending fences sounds pretty damn good to me," Brian said.

Mark didn't reply. He set the Ivy on a shelf and grabbed a beautiful Rex Begonia to repot. He fingered the green and burgundy leaves for a moment and stared out the window. New buds were forming on the trees and glowed in the sunlight.

They were right. He needed to go home.

After his family had died from cholera on the Oregon Trail, he'd stumbled into a job at the Maxwell ranch. He'd grown up with the Maxwell brothers, with Scott, Hank, Will, and Daniel, too. Then later, Brian and Dean joined the group. They'd been through it all together, including Scott's death and losing Caine's first wife, Amy.

He considered them brothers, but he never set himself equal to them. When Rose and Iris Dunn would have moved him into the big house and mothered him, he'd insisted on staying in the bunkhouse with the hired men.

They let him know they loved him, and the feeling was reciprocated, but he couldn't let himself show it. The death of Rose Dunn had hurt him as deeply as losing his own mother, and he couldn't cope with losing another family.

"You're right," Mark said. He set the begonia aside and leaned against the workbench. "It's time for me to go home."

Brian and Dean looked satisfied, but Mark's thoughts went straight to Hattie. What would she do when he went back to the ranch? They'd barely exchanged more than long glances since her rescue, but he had cast himself in the role of her protector. The memory of carrying her from that godforsaken house was branded in his mind.

He'd known then that he'd have to let her go. But now that it was time, he didn't know how.

Chapter Three

The porch door of the midtown home was hanging on one hinge when they arrived on horseback. Mark stared at it for a moment before he slid to the ground and tied his horse to a post. Damn. Not again.

Dean whistled, pointed to the alley between the houses, and started walking. He'd need a minute to check out the back of the house. Brian cursed and shook his head, mirroring Mark's feelings. They climbed the few steps to the porch and eased the half-hung door open enough to enter. The porch creaked and groaned under their weight. Cobwebs hung thickly in the corners and the place wreaked of filth.

The front door was also smashed open, but at least it hadn't been torn from the hinges. The hall inside bore signs of a break-in or a fight. With all the windows covered, it was dark, and Mark couldn't see much beyond the foyer.

Mrs. Fritz had given them the tip-off. Reverend David Chambers said he'd been visited by several ladies in the congregation, and he hadn't seen the Duggans since he'd married them. The women reported concerns that Isabel Duggan was being abused by her new husband. The Rev said that the neighbors reported screams coming from the house at night.

Nobody bothered to call the police. What was the point? As long as he didn't actually kill her, they wouldn't do anything about it. A man had a right to discipline his wife; a view that Mark had always found abhorrent. His parents had respected each other; that's how love should be.

"We need to go in," Brian murmured. Mark nodded, his hand going instinctively to the handle of his gun.

They'd gone to the house to talk to Mrs. Duggan and let her know about the safe house. Mark hadn't prepared himself to visit a crime scene. He took a deep breath and stepped inside. They could stumble into anything.

"She's a tiny little thing," Mrs. Fritz had told them. "She'll not be able to defend herself against Bert."

Mark couldn't help thinking of Hattie. He'd never forget the sight of her tied up—more dead than alive. Even now, seven months later, he awoke nightly in a cold sweat.

He didn't want anyone else to go through that. That was why he had to get the word out to the women in town about The Rose Dunn Rescue House.

His heart said it was too late to save Mrs. Duggan. He wanted to turn and run. He could disappear, get a job on a farm somewhere and spend the rest of his days plowing fields and bringing in the harvest.

"Stay low," he told Brian.

He took a step into the dark hall and stopped dead. Brian moved to the window and jerked the curtain open. Mark stared ahead of him. What the hell happened? The place was a disaster. Glass glittered on the floor, coming from several broken lamps, dishes, and a mirror in the hallway. The furniture was askew, and the walls were marked up as if something had been dragged across them.

Something like a body? The morbid thought sent a shiver through him.

Dean entered through the backdoor.

"This way," Brian said quietly from behind him. "The kitchen is through that door. These houses are all the same."

Pistol raised, Mark crept toward the closed door. Intuition said there was someone behind it. Isabel Duggan, or her brute of a husband?

The boards creaked below his feet. It didn't matter; he wasn't worried about Bert Duggan. If it came to a fight, he, Dean, or Brian could take him. A good fight might be just what he needed. Mark bubbled with anger and his desire to pummel the bastard who would beat his own wife.

But what he didn't want to do was scare Mrs. Duggan if she was hiding somewhere in the house.

Glass scraped and clattered as he pushed the door open. The kitchen floor was overtaken with broken dishes and the contents of the cupboards, topped with an overturned table.

But where was the woman? Had Bert Duggan taken her with him? Or maybe she had managed to get away? Mark prayed that she was safe.

"No sign of them outside." Dean entered through the back door and blew out a frustrated breath.

"Isabel!" Brian called out. "Mrs. Duggan!"

There was no reply. "Let's check upstairs," Mark said. He held his breath as he took the stairs two at a time.

They found Mrs. Duggan sprawled across the bed in

the master bedroom. Her clothes were torn and bloody, and her face was swollen. The stench of death hung in the air, and Mark shuddered.

"Mrs. Duggan?" Brian said as he approached, feeling for a pulse, even though the effort was futile.

She was dead, and they all knew it.

The body was cold. Her eyes were open, staring without seeing. Barely an inch of her exposed flesh was unbruised. She might have been beaten by a group of men, not just her husband, by the way she looked. What kind of man could do such a thing?

"God," Dean murmured behind him. "She must have fought back hard. Look at her hands."

Mark stared down at the dead woman, his heart sick with anger. Is that what happened? Had she fought back when Bert Duggan came for her? Perhaps Duggan hadn't meant to kill her, but Isabel had finally tried to defend herself and that sent him into enough of a rage to do... this.

Mark wanted to kill the son of a bitch.

"She won't be needing our help now," Brian said quietly, sounding stricken. "The best we can do for her is bring her killer to justice."

Mark nodded, but rage and torment rose up inside him. Bert Duggan was a monster, and Isabel was dead. He closed her eyes; the unseeing gaze would haunt his dreams for a long time to come.

It was time for him to go. He couldn't be part of this any longer. Not because he didn't want to help, but because he did—but too often couldn't. It was time to let someone else take over.

That was it. The thought struck him with the force of a revelation. It was time.

Every time they went out on a case, every time they

found another dead girl's body, it chipped away at his soul, grinding the broken pieces to dust, until he was hollow and empty. He hadn't been the same since they found Hattie.

He couldn't forget the way that she flinched when he passed her in the hall. He never missed the sudden look of fear in her eyes at the loud noises, or if one of the men entered the room when she was alone. Her ordeal had scarred her, and there was nothing that Mark could do to help ease her wounds.

"You want to go after him?" Brian said. "The bastard who did this?"

Mark swallowed, and for a moment, he wasn't sure if Brian was talking about Bert Duggan or the men who had hurt Hattie. He dragged his mind back to the present.

"Yes. Let's get the police in, and offer to help with the manhunt. They'll take us up on it."

Brian and Dean nodded. The police never refused their help. They had honed skills over the years of working together; so when they offered their services, the police accepted.

If his neighbors found him first, Bert Duggan would be lucky to escape with just a lynching. The community would be outraged to hear of what had happened. Mark contemptuously curled his lips. People only cared once it was too late, and they didn't have to take any actual responsibility.

Mark said a prayer for the victim and left. He'd catch up with the police later. Dean and Brian could handle everything there, he needed to get away. Far away.

They didn't try to stop him.

∽

AFTER THE DISHES WERE DONE, HATTIE WANDERED THROUGH the big house, leaving the others to talk. The busyness didn't bother her as much, and she even found the house oddly quiet now that most of the group had gone back out west. But sometimes she needed to be alone.

Alone with her thoughts and fears.

Her nightmares were fading and less common. She'd slept three nights in a row without waking from a bad dream, and that was a big deal. The sudden flares of panic didn't interrupt her day-to-day life as they had done. The soothing rhythms of The Rose Dunn House had slowly helped to heal her.

She had a way to go on her healing journey, but it was time to think about what her future might hold.

She'd been in residence there for more than half a year. The Benson investigation was over. Most of the Maxwell Group had returned home, and even Angela and Paul were gone. There were just six of them now.

Including her and Mark.

She didn't know why she put their names together, but somehow, Mark was hers. It was no secret to anyone that Dean and Elizabeth had some sort of magnetic push-and-pull between them. And Brian was madly Sophia's—he didn't hide his feelings at all. So, if they coupled up, then that just left her and Mark.

A little tingle shot through her. Desire or fear? Both?

Mark rescued her. He found her, wrapped her up, and carried her out of hell. She was, of course, grateful to the entire Maxwell Group—but Mark was her hero.

She just wished it was easier to speak to him. She wanted to, but her reflex was to freeze up around men. Their deep voices reminded her of the torture and abuse she'd suffered.

She pushed the memories away and sneaked into the conservatory. When nobody was around, she sometimes went in and tended the plants. Something about healing the dying plants eased her heart.

Except the greenhouse wasn't empty as she'd expected. Mark sat on the floor with his head buried in his hands. He looked so miserable that Hattie immediately went toward him, natural compassion overriding fear. Her footsteps made him look up, and she stopped, gnawing at her lip with sudden nerves.

"I'm sorry, I didn't mean to interrupt you..." Her stomach flipped with terror. She turned to leave, but something in Mark's anguished eyes pulled her back.

He was hurting, and badly. The raw vulnerability in his face extinguished her fears. She took another step forward, her hand instinctually flickering by her side, wanting to reach out to him.

"Is everything alright?" she asked softly. "I heard about today."

Mark shook his head and crossed his arms over his knees.

"We caught the husband quick enough and brought him in. He'll hang for what he's done, but it won't bring her back."

He looked up and the plea in his red-rimmed eyes melted Hattie's heart. She forgot her anxieties and sat on the floor beside him.

"It won't bring her back," she said. It was the saddest truth in the world. He looked down at his boots again, and then back up at her face.

"She reminded me of you," he breathed. " Just an innocent woman. She couldn't have done anything to deserve... that."

Hattie swallowed, trying to fight back the tears that had sprung to her eyes. She wouldn't cry for herself. Not when Mark so obviously needed support. And in a way, it was nice to be the helper for change. Before her life had fallen apart, she had always been the listening ear in her family. Her father always said she had a natural intuition for others' feelings. He'd meant it as a compliment, but Hattie wasn't sure it was always a positive thing. Now, though, her heart broke for Mark. His pain was so fierce it was almost tangible in the room. "I'm alive, Mark." She grazed a timid hand across his arm but couldn't bring herself to hold his hand.

But when Mark didn't answer, she assumed he'd rather be left alone.

"I'm sorry," she mumbled. "I didn't mean to interrupt."

She rose, but Mark reached out and caught her hand. She stiffened, but didn't pull away. Mark dropped her hand quickly.

"I didn't mean to do that," he apologized. "Forgive me. I'm just... struggling." It was difficult for him to admit his vulnerability, but his weakness made her more comfortable with her own.

Hattie lowered herself back to the floor by his side, trying to ignore the way her hand tingled where he had touched it.

"It's okay. What you guys do... I can't imagine."

"I bury the feelings all day, but I probably need to talk about them. But..." he shrugged, looking for a moment like a lost child, "... where do I even start? There is such evil in this world." He scrubbed his face with his hands and sighed. "I don't need to tell you that."

"There is such good, too. Look at you." Hattie chanced

another arm graze with her hand. "You're a good man, Mark."

"Am I?" He shook his head. "I can't do this anymore. I'm going home. I feel guilty leaving with so many women out there who need help."

Mark's departure from The Rose Dunn House filled her with dread, but Hattie tried to ignore it.

"Your lantern is out of oil," she said. "And no wonder. You've been burning it nonstop for months. There will always be people who need help, but you can't save them all. It isn't all on your shoulders."

"What if I'd quit before I'd found you?"

Hattie shook her head and dropped her hand to the floor beside her hip. "I've never forgotten that day."

"I haven't either." Mark dropped his hand to the floor beside hers. "I thought you were dead, you know—you came back to life right in front of me." Mark's fingertips grazed hers and a spark flew up her arm. "You're a miracle."

They stared at each other for a long moment. His gaze melted into hers. Waves of his emotions crashed over her. The silence said more than their words and the intensity between them swelled.

Hattie traced her fingertips over his in an almost imperceptible touch and her hand came alive with electricity. "I've never thanked you properly."

"There's no need." His eyes were still locked onto hers, and he slid his fingertips across her palm and wrist. Her pulse fluttered, but it wasn't her usual anxiety. She wanted him to touch her so badly.

So badly, it frightened her.

Panic flooded, and she needed to escape. She jumped

to her feet with her heart hammering against her ribs like a bird in a cage.

"Mrs. Fritz will be looking for me," she said, even though her chores were finished for the day. "But...it was nice to talk to you. You really are a good man, Mark," she insisted, wanting him to believe it.

"Thank you, Hattie," he said, his voice sad and sincere.

She smiled before she hurried off, her mind a dervish with confusion. She didn't want Mark to leave The Rose Dunn House. But he clearly needed a break. She was just being selfish.

His presence had become an anchor for her, and she feared that without him, she would be washed away by the waves of anxiety.

She wasn't ready to think about the other reason she couldn't let him leave.

Her hand still tingled where he'd stroked it. For once, Hattie hadn't flinched with fear. No, it was something else. Something a lot like desire.

That was something she never thought she'd experience again.

Chapter Four

A week later, Mark strolled down the familiar hall to the conservatory, his eyes trailing the neat lines of the floorboards. There had been no fresh cases since the Duggans' and the lack of action was both a problem and a solution for him. Pressing the door open, he spotted Hattie at the workbench. As the quietest room in the house, it was a good place to go when he needed time alone with his thoughts. He wasn't sorry to lose his solitude to her, though.

Hattie reached across the bench for the clippers and a lock of blonde hair escaped her ribbon. It trailed over her arm and she shrugged it behind her shoulder. He couldn't see what she was working on, but she dropped clippings on the floor and hummed to herself as she worked.

He leaned against an old workbench and admired her from the side. She was angelic with her delicate movements and peaceful expression. The slightest bit of color rested on her cheekbones.

Her expression was thoughtful and focused, turning up the corners of his mouth. He liked seeing her like this, free from her frayed nerves. She smiled and sang and communed with her plants. As soon as she saw him, she would flinch, her shoulders would tighten and her eyes would dart around, checking the exits. So he kept quiet and let her have her peace.

If life had been kind to her, surely she would have been long married and a mother. She would be a wonderful mother. His imagination soared away, and he pictured the possibilities. Hattie with a baby in her arms, laughing at something and cradling her precious bundle. She would have been happy.

Could that have been him? He imagined other circumstances where their paths could have crossed. He might have seen her at the market. He would have commented on the weather. She would have smiled and flashed the sweet dimple on her cheek. Mark smiled. It would have been sweet for both of them.

Coming back to the present, his heart warmed, remembering the way she'd drawn him out. She'd comforted him after the Duggan case. He looked at the place they'd sat and he felt her hand in his. She'd pulled him from the depths, like a breath of air, to a drowning man.

Who was rescuing whom?

But they weren't innocent strangers meeting at the market. They'd both seen horrors, and they weren't the sweet people they might have once been. Not wanting to interrupt her serenity, he backed out of the room, but she looked up, startled at first, then smiled. She looked glad to see him.

"Hello," she said. "I was just trimming Esther."

Mark smiled, "Esther, huh?"

Hattie chuckled. It was the first time he'd heard her laugh. "Orchids are my favorite, though I've only seen them in books before now." She traced the edge of a delicate petal. "This one is Esther. This one is her best friend Penelope."

Mark laughed. That might be the cutest thing he'd ever seen. "I came to work on the roses. They're coming along." He couldn't stand there and stare at her, so he cleared a space on the workbench near her and retrieved the roses. "I didn't think they would come back when I started, but look at them now." He spun a pot on the table and admired his work.

Hattie smiled and hummed an approving sound in her throat.

Mark breathed the scent of soil and flower and basked in the quiet company of a beautiful woman. Then he laughed, "This one is Bob and the one over there is his best friend Arnold."

Hattie's laugh was magic.

They trimmed and tied and watered in comforting silence for a while. Mark moved Bob back to his place beside a bench on the path and retrieved Arnold.

"How are you doing?" Hattie eyed him and then returned her attention to the next orchid in her lineup. "Feeling better?"

Her concern moved him—embarrassed as he was. It was hard to be open about his feelings. But with Hattie, it felt wrong to be anything less.

Mark shrugged. He wanted to sit with her and talk to her again. He wanted to hold her hand. His hand still tingled whenever he thought of the fire that had shot up his arm at her touch. He'd never imagined she would get to a place where she would reach for him, even in such a small way, and it set his imagination wild every time he remembered.

Maybe with time...

But he didn't have time. He was leaving.

Hattie changed the subject. "I've written to Angela."

Grateful to be off the hook, Mark smiled. "You must miss her." He handed the trimmers to Hattie and picked up the twine she'd set between them. "The two of you seemed close."

"I do. Very much." Hattie slid the orchids to the back of the workbench and pulled a small potted rose close. "It was nice to see her last month, even though it was brief and under less than pleasant circumstances." Hattie spun the pot several times, studying the plant before continuing. "I appreciate the other women in the house, but Angela had a lovely, quiet way about her."

Hattie glanced up and Mark was lost in the blue depths of her kind eyes.

Hattie blinked twice before she went on. "I miss the music." She had the voice of a songbird and he'd missed the music as well. Because without Angela to accompany her, Hattie had stopped singing.

"Of course. Sophia and Elizabeth are good to me," she blurted. Did she think she sounded ungrateful?

Mark chuckled. "They're good women. Elizabeth's independent spirit can be a little much." He smiled at Hattie.

"Perhaps... At times." Hattie smiled. "Sophia's too quick-witted for me. The two of them get to bantering and it makes my head swim."

"They are quite a pair." Mark spun his pot a few times, searching for any dead leaves to pluck, and then returned Arnold to his spot beside Bob. He brushed his hands off and returned. Instead of grabbing another plant, he crossed his arms and leaned on the workbench.

Hattie often faded into the background—but not to him. To him, she shone brighter than any woman he'd ever met.

He swallowed hard. He had to stop thinking about her like that.

"I'm glad you've settled in," he said.

"Yes," Hattie said, her voice soft. Those big blue eyes searched his face. "But you haven't answered my question. I asked how you were, after finding that poor woman?"

She was too perceptive. Why did she make him want to pour his heart out?

Because she would understand. She was the only person who would. He answered his own unasked question with a sigh.

"I had a couple of bad nights but I'm okay," he admitted, shaking his head to clear it of the image of poor Isabel Duggan's lifeless gaze and battered body because the image that followed would be of Hattie, as near to death as he'd ever seen anyone. It was a miracle she'd lived. He cleared his throat. "It helped—talking to you the other day."

"I'm glad," she said. Her eyes were pools he wanted to drown in. Could she see right into his soul? He'd be okay with that; it would save him the trouble of fumbling for words.

"How about you?" he asked. "Do you talk to anyone about what you've been through?" He couldn't stand empty hands, so he moved the orchids to their place on a shelf for her.

Hattie drew back. He'd said something wrong. "I'm sorry. That was intrusive, I don't know why I asked that. I just meant..."

Hattie held up a dirt-covered hand to stop him. "It's

okay. I know what you meant and I'm not offended," she reassured him. "And yes, it's good to know I'm not alone. We all have very different stories, of course, but in some ways similar, too." She paused and the look in her eyes was very far away. Mark regretted mentioning anything. What was wrong with him? He lost his wits around her.

All he wanted was to see her smile again.

"I don't want to remind you of anything." He avoided her gaze by moving Esther and Penelope.

"It's not as if I can forget," she said with a sigh that was so sad his heart broke. "Sometimes I wonder if I will ever be normal." She shrugged and pinched off a dead leaf. "I still limp a little, you know," she added.

"You are normal," he said, taking her hands. "You're perfect. The men who did that to you were monsters."

Surprised by his outburst, Hattie blinked rapidly. She didn't pull away. Instead, she studied her hands in his and blushed. "You think I'm perfect?"

Mark's cheeks went warm. "Yes, I do," he said. He grazed the backs of her hands with his thumbs. He'd never bared his soul to a woman before, yet he was naked in front of Hattie.

"Thank you," she said, then dropped his hands and turned back to her work. "I suppose I have to hope I will find someone who agrees with you." She began pinching dead leaves from another rose plant. "Mrs. Fritz keeps hinting that we need husbands. We can't be alone in the world, and we can't stay here forever." She tossed the clippings more forcefully. "I suppose she's right. I can't hide forever."

Mark couldn't think about it. He shouldn't have brought it up. He grabbed a broom and cleared the mess they'd made on the floor.

"Mrs. Fritz thinks our best chances are with the mail-order bride agency." Hattie slammed the trimmers down on the bench and then wiped her hands on her apron. She shook her head, "I can't imagine traveling to marry a stranger."

Mark's stomach twisted. Surely, she wouldn't want that. Mrs. Fritz shouldn't be talking about such things to Hattie, of all people. But she was right, in a way. It was dangerous to be a woman alone in the world. Especially a woman as beautiful as Hattie.

Did she have a family? Apart from the way he found her, little was known about Hattie. She'd told them her parents had died, and she had no one to return to. He didn't know how she'd ended up falling into Benson's clutches, and he wasn't about to ask.

"You don't need me to tell you the world can be a cruel place," he said. "But there are good men in this world, Hattie. Ones you can trust." He hated to think of her alone out West, feeling scared and unsafe.

"I can trust you, can't I?" she asked, her eyes clear and full of innocence. Mark ached to hold her. Protect and shield her from the world.

"Always," he promised. He'd never meant a promise more. "I'll do whatever I can to protect you."

"Thank you," she said. Then she smiled, a genuine smile that lit up her entire face. "It's nice talking to you like this," she said.

"It is. I'm not like this with anyone else," he admitted.

"Because you're a man?"

"Partly," Mark shrugged. "But also, I just don't talk about myself much. It's easier with you."

"We're friends," she said, and Mark nodded and held his hand out. "Friends," he said, and Hattie laughed as

41

they shook on it. That was the third time she'd taken his hand without flinching. That was good.

Mark grumbled. "I'll leave you to the quiet," he told her. "But maybe we can do this again? If you need someone to talk to, I mean? I come here a lot when I need peace."

"Me too," she giggled. "As big as this house is, sometimes it's just too full."

Mark grinned, nodded, and left with his heart beating just a little too fast in his chest.

It may not be a good idea, but he couldn't wait to spend more time with her.

Getting too close to people was dangerous. He'd learned that from experience. He'd lost everyone he ever loved, and he was teetering on the edge, ready to fall for Hattie. It wasn't fair to her, it just could never work.

Could it?

Hattie trusted him. He was her friend, the man who had rescued her. He was a heel for thinking romantic thoughts about her. She deserved better than him.

Plus, he was leaving.

He fingered the letter in his pocket. They wanted him to come home to the ranch and take his place. His offer to work as a ranch hand had received an indignant reply. He would have his share of the ranch and live in Scott's old place. Caine said he would send men over to fix it up. They wouldn't let him wriggle out of the brotherhood this time. Not after the things they had seen together.

He looked forward to going home. The only blight on his anticipation was the idea of leaving Hattie behind. Before he left, he had to make sure she was okay. He'd promised to protect her.

But he couldn't help Mrs. Fritz find her a husband. For

reasons he didn't even want to think about, the idea made his blood boil.

❦

"HELLO AGAIN." HATTIE LEANED AROUND THE DOORWAY AND breathed in the fresh air and flowery scents. Mark sat on the bench and stared at the little water feature. It had become a habit for them in the past few weeks, meeting there at odd moments and talking about nothing and everything.

They had both lost their parents from fever. His on the Overland Trail to Oregon. Hers in their impoverished tenement in the city. Sharing their pasts bonded them. Hattie found comfort in their shared histories.

She hadn't spoken about her experiences after losing her parents. She didn't know if she would ever share that.

"Hello, yourself," Mark snapped a book closed and smiled. His obvious pleasure at her appearance made her fluttery. "Have you finished your work for the day?"

"For now. I'm sure Mrs. Fritz will find something for me to do. Although I shouldn't complain; I enjoy being busy," Hattie sat on the bench beside Mark. "Mrs. Fritz has taught me a lot of new dishes to make. She is a lovely cook. I'll be quite the housekeeper—or wife—by the time she's through with me."

Mark's face pinched, and the slight smile on his lips flattened as he turned his attention back to the water.

What had she done wrong?

He spoke before she had long to dwell on it.

"She's still pushing you girls to get married, then?" His tone was tensed with a forced casual playing on the surface. Hattie's heart sped.

Did it bother him she was talking about marrying someone else? She hoped so.

Because Mrs. Fritz was right, Hattie didn't want to make her way alone in the world, but she didn't want to marry a stranger, either. If Mark offered... she would say yes and do everything to be a good wife who loved him.

He had to ask first, and so far, he'd shown no sign he was thinking about it. Maybe they were just friends.

But he had called her perfect. Men didn't do that unless they liked a woman?

"Yes. She's invited a woman to speak to us tomorrow, although I'm not sure what about? Sophia thought it might be for deportment lessons," she giggled.

"You don't need them. You're already graceful," Mark said, looking surprised at his own words. He did that a lot.

"Elizabeth thinks it is the matchmaker," she added.

Mark took a deep breath and blew it out. "There'll be no one left at The Rose Dunn House if you all go," Mark said, leaning forward and bracing his elbows on his knees. Hattie wanted to rub his back and make him feel better, but she kept her hands to herself.

"You're going to Montana, then?" she asked. Mark had told her a few days earlier about his plan to accept his shares of the ranch. Her heart squeezed every time she thought about it and she prayed he would ask her to go with him.

"In a few weeks. Brian and Dean will probably head that way too if they don't make other plans," he said. Hattie watched his shoulders rise and fall. What would she do without him?

She fell silent, thinking about the possibility of being there without Mark. He was her anchor, and her safe place, but everything was changing again. If only he would ask her to go with him. She wished she dared to hint at it herself.

Instead, she changed the subject. "Sophia won't be happy if Brian goes," she said. "Her flirting campaign has stepped up. Have you noticed?"

Mark grinned. "She's as subtle as a stick of dynamite."

Hattie giggled. He had a way with words.

"Do you think he likes her?" She stared into the water and played with the ruffle on her apron. "Sometimes I think he does, and sometimes I think he doesn't."

Mark shrugged. "He has a lot on his mind."

"It would be lovely if they all ended up on the ranch together," she said.

Pretty high-handed hint, she scolded herself.

What would the ranch in Montana be like? It would be busy with all the Maxwells and their wives. She'd met most of them when she was first rescued, and although she'd not been speaking much then, she'd heard the stories of how Jeni and then Sarah went out to Montana as mail-order brides. Of how Opal and Daniel had got together after being friends for years.

Hattie wanted a love story like that, and she wanted to believe that even after everything that had happened to her, she could still have it one day. With Mark. Because while some men might consider her damaged goods, Mark had said she was perfect.

"I suppose it'll get crowded, especially if they keep having kids," Mark said, not seeming to take her hint at all.

Hattie sighed. Before her abduction, she'd always assumed that one day she would meet someone, get married, and have children. It wasn't something she'd thought about for a long time, but she loved children.

Did Mark want children? He'd make a great father. She

glanced at him, imagining him with a little boy with the same wavy honey hair and hazel eyes, teaching him to ride a horse and chop wood.

Hattie looked away as Mark caught her watching him. There was another awkward silence, and she wished she knew what he was thinking.

Would he ever ask her to go with him?

What if he didn't?

Chapter Five

Hattie trained her focus on picking at the ruffles on her skirt. She couldn't bring herself to make eye contact with the other ladies. Mrs. Fritz had taken it upon herself to invite the matchmaker to tea. After morning chores, she'd called Sophia, Elizabeth, and Hattie into the parlor to wait for the woman who came with the offer of husbands.

The normally chatty threesome silently awaited their doom. It was like a judgment after a long trial. Only, none of them would be granted freedom. One way or another, a life sentence was in store for each of them.

Sophia stood in the window and stared into space. Sophia released a sigh so deep Hattie felt it to the bottom of her soul. Elizabeth sat erect, with steel in her spine and no-nonsense on her face. Hattie dipped her head to hide a smirk. It would be a cold day on the sun before Mrs. Fritz got her to agree to a mail-order marriage.

Hattie sat up and turned when a throat cleared in the doorway.

Ready, or not...

"Ladies, this is Mrs. Philips," Mrs. Fritz said, introducing a lovely older woman with a neat gray topknot and pink cheeks. "Please listen to what she has to say. She's been a friend of the Maxwell family for a very long time."

"That's right," the woman said cheerfully, looking around at Hattie and Elizabeth. Her eyes settled on Sophia and she stopped. Her direct stare served her purpose, and Sophia joined the others around the coffee table. She smiled and took a seat as Mrs. Fritz joined Sophia on the settee. "I'm very happy to meet you all."

She seemed to be waiting for them to express their joy at meeting her, but after a moment, she moved on without any such welcome.

"As Mrs. Fritz said, I have known the Maxwell Group for years. I brokered marriages for both Jeni and Sarah," she said proudly. She shrugged and smiled, then added, "Jeni's marriage went a little sideways for a while there, but she's nicely on track now."

Elizabeth made a very unladylike snort but maintained her polite posture and expression.

Mrs. Fritz tutted loudly and glared at her.

"I'm sorry," Elizabeth sighed. "I intend to find my way in the world without a man."

Mrs. Phillips clasped her hands in front of her and sighed. "This is hard for all of you. I know." She shrugged. "I wish we lived in a world where women didn't need husbands, but we don't." She held her hands up in surrender. "The best I can do is try to find you the best husbands I can."

Hattie's heart sank and her pulse pounded in her ears. The conversation unnerved her, even though she knew it was coming.

"If I can settle Sarah Forbes, I can match anyone." Mrs.

Philips chuckled. Despite her rising anxiety, Hattie managed a weak smile. "That girl struts around with her man pants and wears a gun. She was no one's idea of a proper wife. And yet, her husband penned me a letter himself—thanking me for sending him that bullheaded twerp." She chuckled. "He called her a bullheaded twerp in his letter."

Mrs. Philips seemed lovely and very genuine. She smiled fondly as she talked of the brides she had sent to their happily ever afters. Hattie couldn't help but like the matchmaker.

She pressed her nails into the palms of her hands.

You always trust people and then it blows right up in your face.

Hattie curled inward and reminded herself over and over not to accept Mrs. Phillips' proposition too easily. There could be no guarantee with a strange man in the West. No, she would follow Elizabeth's lead and remain guarded.

"There are plenty of single young men out West," Mrs. Philips continued, "and a shortage of young women for them to marry. I will find you solid men, just like I have done for dozens of other ladies."

Mrs. Philips was eager to help, and Mrs. Fritz was more than a touch pleased with herself, but Hattie cringed. A mail-order bride? To be sent off like a package to a man she'd never met?

Sophia was more than keen. She clapped her hands together with excitement. "Well, if you can find me a man as good-looking as the Maxwell brothers, I'm willing." She sighed dramatically. "It's better than sitting around here waiting. I'll have grey hair and a squint if I have to wait any longer."

The others all laughed, even Elizabeth, but although Hattie tried to join in, her strained smile was more of a grimace.

She wouldn't be bought and sold like cattle again; she'd rather die.

"I'm not doing it," Elizabeth announced mutinously. "I don't know why you all are so eager to get married off. First Angela and now you, Sophia. We have a good life here and we're independent. I don't want no man telling me what to do, ever again."

"But how will you support yourself, Elizabeth?" Mrs. Fritz asked in a gentle tone. "The Rose Dunn House is here for you, but you must want more out of your life."

Elizabeth's eyes were dark with frustration. "I'm not going. I will find myself a job, but I won't sell myself to a stranger." She glared at her hands. "If you'd been a prisoner, you wouldn't be so keen to become one again."

Although not quite so aggressive about it, Hattie felt the same. She picked at her fingernail and begged God to show her an alternative. Shame overwhelmed her. Nobody would want her after what she'd been through. A stranger might be her only option.

Without a husband, and without the kindness of the Maxwells, most women in her position would find themselves with nowhere else to go but the nearest brothel. She could never cope with that kind of life.

Perhaps one man would at least be better than a hundred. But how could she leave this safe place and put herself into the hands of a stranger?

"No." Hattie shot to her feet with her hands clenched into fists. "No, I won't do it. I can't," her voice broke into a sob as she turned and fled, leaving the others in the parlor.

Hattie ran to her room, shaking from head to toe, and

bolted the bedroom door. She threw herself onto the bed and sobbed into her pillow. A crowd of memories assailed her, and she clutched at her temples as though that would somehow push them out of her mind.

What had she done to deserve so much trauma? All she wanted was a quiet life with a sweet man. But all she had were scars and memories of how she'd received them.

"Hattie?" Sophia's voice came through the door, sweet and reassuring, and it grounded Hattie a little. "Can I come in?"

Hattie swallowed sob after sob until she could breathe. She wanted to talk to Mark, but she wouldn't want him to see her in such a state. Sophia was sweet, and she only wanted to help.

After a few moments, Hattie had settled enough to sit up. She wiped her eyes and went to the door. Sophia closed the door behind herself and sat on the bed, taking Hattie's hand in hers. Hattie wanted to rip her hand away, but she didn't. She couldn't blame Sophia. Physical touch was her first instinct, it was the way she showed she cared. Hattie focused on the love and comfort of her friend and the urge to pull away dimmed.

"I'm sorry," Sophia said. "I shouldn't have jabbered on all excited like that, not when I knew you were upset. I just didn't realize how much...you've never really told us what happened to you, but I know it must have been terrible..." Sophia paused.

"I can't talk about it..." Hattie scrubbed her eyes but couldn't rub away the images that haunted her.

Sophia squeezed Hattie's hand. "It's no surprise you wouldn't want to go near a man, especially a stranger. Mrs. Fritz and Mrs. Philips are just looking out for us. Nobody is going to force us to go, but Mrs. Phillips won't send us off to marry men she isn't sure about."

Hattie shook her head. "How do we know we can trust her?" Hattie snapped more sharply than she'd intended.

"Well... she's a friend of the Maxwells," Sophia protested. "I didn't always trust them, but they've proven themselves to be reliable."

"I thought I had a reliable friend once," Hattie said before she told Sophia a part of her story she'd not yet shared with anyone. "The woman who took me in after my parents died, Mrs. Chadwick... she was like a grandmother to me." Hattie smiled sadly. "I was lost and alone, and she held me while I cried. She fed me and protected me and I trusted her. Then she sold me to Mr. Benson. I'd seen the man who came to take me before. I don't think I was the first girl she'd sold to Mr. Benson."

Sophia's mouth dropped open. "A woman did that to you? I don't know what to say. It seems like even more of a betrayal coming from a woman." Sophia's hands rubbed frantic circles over Hattie's. "Hattie, I am so sorry for you."

Sophia's distraught face was more than Hattie could handle. Instead of Sophia comforting her, Hattie tried to soothe Sophia.

"If I've learned anything at all," she said, her voice so quiet that Sophia had to lean in to hear, "it's that you can never trust anyone."

"You can trust me," Sophia exclaimed, and she pulled Hattie into a quick, tight embrace before standing. "You don't have to do anything you don't want to do. Come back downstairs with me. I still want to hear what Mrs. Phillips has to say, but I'm afraid, too."

"I suppose. I'll come down for you," Hattie said. Now that her panic had subsided, she regretted her rudeness to their guest. "I'd rather keep what I said between us. I don't want everyone to know."

"Of course," Sophia nodded. As they walked back downstairs, she slipped her arm through Hattie's. "We're in this together, you know."

Then why do I feel so alone?

Hattie followed Sophia into the parlor and sat beside her on the settee. "I'm sorry for my outburst." She fussed with her skirt and stilled her hands. "Trust doesn't come easily to me."

Mrs. Fritz fussed around her like a mother hen. "Perhaps I should have approached this differently, my dear," she said.

"I know you're only trying to help," Hattie assured, "I just don't know how I could ever face going to meet a stranger."

Elizabeth passed Hattie a cup of tea but remained otherwise stiff and unemotional, however when she clasped her hands in her lap, they were trembling.

Mrs. Phillips cleared her throat. "Traveling west as a mail-order bride is a frightening experience for any woman. It's a trip into the unknown with no guarantees of success." She adjusted herself in her seat and patted her hair. "I'm sure that women with your experience must be even more anxious. I only accept suitors with two or more letters of recommendation, and one must be from their minister. I also promise that if anything goes wrong, I will pay for your return ticket and board you at my own home until I can find you a safe place." She held eye contact with each of the ladies and then nodded. "I'll leave you to think about it."

Without pressing further, Mrs. Phillips rose and left the room.

As soon as she'd cleared the doorway, Elizabeth wilted. Her posture melted, and she leaned back in her chair. "How can anyone make a living by selling women to men and try to convince us it is a good thing?"

Hattie nodded. My thoughts exactly.

"Oh, I don't know..." Sophia started.

Elizabeth cut her off with a sharp look. Sophia abandoned her place on the settee and walked over to stare out at the gardens in her usual fashion.

Exhausted after the tidal wave of emotion that had swept over her, Hattie wanted to turn her memories off. It would be lovely to trust Mrs. Phillips. She wanted the happily ever after that Jeni and Sarah had found. Who wouldn't want to believe there was a beautiful future waiting for her?

Not long ago, she'd believed there was no future. She'd expected to die in that room, tied to that bed. There were even times when she'd hoped for it.

But then Mark had swept her away. Doc Green had nursed her, and she'd recovered. Now she wanted to live. She wished to be a mother. She'd started dreaming of a future, of her own fairy tale.

It wasn't all sunshine and rainbows. The thought of lying with a man made her shudder. Her time with Mark had proved that, given enough time with a patient and gentle man, she could overcome her anxiety.

Overcome with the urge to see Mark, she excused herself and wandered toward the conservatory. She'd seen Brian and Dean go out earlier and Mark hadn't been with them, so there was a chance she'd find him alone.

Spending time alone with him had given her more than just friendship. It helped her grow in confidence. His words healed her. She carried them around with her, and they emboldened her around others. From his words, she drew strength to explore things in her mind she had closed herself off to, but what was it all for?

He was leaving soon to return to the Montana ranch. A wild hope inside her expected he would ask her to go with him.

He'd called her perfect. That had to mean something.

The anticipation grew when she recalled his reaction to the mail-order bride idea. Would he try to talk her out of it? Perhaps it would be what pushed him to declare himself,

Hattie's heart was in her mouth as the scent of dirt and flowers reached her. She slowed her steps, ready to just spill out all her fears and hopes to him in a way that she couldn't with anyone else.

Maybe he would feel the same. Perhaps she could have a happy ending, after all.

But he wasn't there. He was nowhere to be found.

Chapter Six

Mark practically bounced down the hallway to the conservatory. He'd been trying to connect with Hattie all week, but their paths hadn't crossed. He saw her at meals, but long glances and secret smiles weren't enough. He wanted to speak to her. He missed her.

At the end of the hallway, his smile faded, and he sighed, crestfallen. The conservatory was empty. Mark kicked a bucket and slammed his hand down on the work-bench. He grumbled and then got to work. He needed to keep his hands busy. Sinking into a brood wouldn't do any good.

A fresh case in town had tied him up for days on end and all he'd thought about was clearing it up so he could tell Hattie about it. The Maxwell Group had answered a call about a kidnapped girl—but she turned out to be a runaway. The spoiled young lady was discovered installed at a local hotel. Her plan was to pout until her father gave in to whatever whim she was going on about. Thankfully, this one had a happy ending, and they returned the girl home with no harm done to her.

The temperature in The Rose Dunn House had changed, though. The atmosphere seemed to cool with each visit from Mrs. Phillips. Instead of rousing arguments about chores at the dinner table, the women whispered to each other.

The men were being left out of the discussion, and both Brian and Dean had expressed the same frustration that he felt. They were pretty sure the secrecy and excitement centered on finding husbands for the women. That's what Mrs. Phillips did, wasn't it? She sent women west as mail-order brides.

Could Hattie want such a thing? She was still so uncomfortable around men.

Except him—maybe. She didn't seem to be afraid of him anymore. Mark wrapped twine around a twig and pictured Hattie sitting beside him on the bench, holding his hand.

Sometimes, lying awake at night, Mark allowed himself to imagine what life on the ranch with Hattie would be like. Now that he was going to have his own place, he had something to offer. He could support a family. The thought of Hattie's body swelling with his child made him hot and full of protectiveness.

It wasn't a bad feeling.

But he was the man who'd rescued her. He would forever be a reminder of the worst time of her life. How could he do that to her? She deserved a fresh start with someone who hadn't seen her half dead.

He sat on the bench and stared at the water, wondering if she'd turn up. This was the usual time of day that they were likely to 'bump into' one another. But half an hour passed and there was no sign of her. A stab of disappointment came as the truth hit him.

She wasn't coming because she didn't want to.

Idiot. He'd allowed himself to fall into this routine with her and now here he was expecting her to show up as though they had some kind of courtship. Mark's disappointment turned to anger with himself. He'd always been so certain that he didn't want romance; never wanted to lose another family the way he'd lost his parents and sister, and now he'd made a fool of himself. Trying to play protector to Hattie when he couldn't even protect his own heart, never mind hers.

Safely tucked inside the soothing rhythms of The Rose Dunn House, he'd forgotten reality. Even if Hattie wanted him, he'd be terrified of losing her. He lost everything important to him.

He needed to leave her alone. Since she could come into the conservatory at any moment, he got up, brushed the dirt from his hands, and left. If he couldn't have her, he'd best avoid her altogether.

But he wasn't fast enough. As he walked past the kitchen, she found him barreling into him as she came running down the stairs.

"Oh! Mark, I'm sorry." She flushed as she straightened and Mark put out a hand to steady her. Unlike weeks ago, she didn't flinch at his touch but smiled up at him. Her soft, full lips were just inches from his and his mouth went dry. She was so beautiful...

Mark swallowed hard and stared into Hattie's eyes. Her breathing became shallow, and she leaned forward. Going against all warnings he'd been telling himself; Mark drew a fingertip across her ivory cheek and pressed a hair behind her ear. His breath shook with his control, but he couldn't stop himself from following his pounding heart toward her. He leaned forward and closed his eyes.

A sharp intake of breath stopped him halfway to Hattie's lips. She breathed rapidly and Mark stepped back, removing his hand from her shoulder where it had landed.

Asshole. What the hell was I thinking?

He was about to flee when he caught sight of a paper shaking in her hand. Her eyes followed his to it and she clutched the letter to her chest and her cheeks flushed a delicate shade of pink.

She cleared her throat and gave Mark an apologetic smile. "Mrs. Phillips has been here today," she explained.

Mark smiled, but he wanted to run away. "Have you decided to go as a mail-order bride, then?" It was a struggle, but he kept his voice low. Thank God they'd run into each other in the dim stairway, so she couldn't see the blush that heated his face.

Hattie would be mortified if she knew what he'd been dreaming. The image of her running around the Montana ranch, pregnant with his child, was never far from his imagination.

Hattie turned and sat on the steps with a sigh that sank all the way to Mark's heart. "I can't decide on anything."

Mark smiled and sat with her. Even though he perched two steps below her, they were eye to eye. He leaned his back on the wall and studied her fingers, toying with the edges of the letter. "What do you want?" he asked.

Something flashed in Hattie's eyes. Fear? His stomach tightened. But of course, she would be afraid. What woman wouldn't be terrified about marrying a stranger thousands of miles away? Mrs. Fritz and Phillips shouldn't be pushing her forward like this. Hattie was too sensitive.

Precious.

"Well, I can't live here forever. The Maxwells are generous, but I'm only 20 years old. I can't stay here for the rest of my life." She leaned against the banister and sighed. She'd been doing that a lot more lately.

Joy bubbled up in Mark because, in that instant, he knew what he needed to do. He opened his mouth to ask her to come to Montana with him. He would keep her safe.

He would love her.

But Hattie's next words stopped him in his tracks, and he nearly choked.

"Well, this letter is from a rancher named Quinn Fletcher, from someplace called Silent Creek." She swallowed and rocked back and forth. "Mrs. Phillips says he's a wealthy gentleman, a widower with a young boy, Harlan. His minister sent a reference letter and described him as kind and gentle." She listed his traits with no feeling at all. Her eyebrows scrunched as if she was trying to be okay with the words she spoke. "He goes to church and doesn't drink." Her fingers ticked each positive comment. "I have to consider it, right? I might never get another offer."

Mark hated Quinn Fletcher and his minister for writing those letters. He hated Silent Creek, and he hated himself for being such a coward.

Hattie's anxious eyes flicked to him, and he squashed his feelings.

"What do you think?" She peered up at him with the same wounded eyes she'd first looked at him with. Only this time, he was certain she was afraid his words would hurt her—not his fists.

She was right, she couldn't stay at The Rose Dunn House forever. Mark wanted to be selfish and keep her to himself. No matter how many times he said he couldn't do it, he would never shake her. But Mr. Fletcher had more to offer than Mark. He had wealth and position and stability. Hattie deserved those things. "I think you should reply to the letter."

"Really?" Hattie's eyebrows raised and her eyes searched his.

Mark nodded. "You deserve better than this," he said, waving a hand around, meaning better than himself. "You deserve a good man who can keep you safe and look after you." He cursed himself for encouraging her to do the very thing he least wanted.

Why couldn't he just tell her what he felt?

Hattie blinked, then her face smoothed into a careful smile. What was she thinking? He wanted to know, but didn't feel as though he had the right to ask.

"I thought you would try to talk me out of it," she said in a quiet voice. Hope flared for a moment in Mark's heart, before Hattie added, "You've always looked out for me, Mark... You've been like a brother to me since I've been here."

Mark clenched his jaw and forced himself to smile.

She saw him as a brother. Damn.

"I just want you to be happy," he said. "You deserve happiness, Hattie."

Hattie nodded and lowered her eyes to the paper wrinkling in her grasp. She pressed her lips together and continued to rock.

Mark didn't tell her he'd heard murmurings about The Rose Dunn House around town. The rumor was that if he, Brian, and Dean left, the girls would be sitting ducks for every man in town with ill intentions. They had no plan to leave the house unprotected, but the rumor haunted him when he thought about Hattie staying behind without him.

If she didn't want him, the best he could do was to encourage her to pursue Quinn Fletcher, the man with the security she needed. "I think you should consider the handsome rancher." He made himself look straight into her eyes.

Her eyes glistened in the dim light. She looked everywhere but at Mark for a moment and then seemed to screw up her courage to voice her fear. "What if he's not what he seems? Mrs. Phillips is so sure, but how can she know?" She chewed on her lip and Mark wanted to take her into his arms and comfort her, but he couldn't.

"Hattie," Mark took her hand into his, "you will always have us. At the first sign of trouble, we'll be there to help. Silent Creek is less than a day's ride from Hope." He squeezed her hand and dipped his head to get her eye contact back. "We're always going to be here for you."

Hattie smiled, looking more reassured.

"Just think about it," he mumbled. "Tell him—and Mrs. Phillips—that you need time. Don't throw yourself into anything just because..." He trailed off, unsure what to say. Or how to say it.

"Because what?" She pressed. The atmosphere between them shifted as they both held their breath.

How do I say this?

"I just mean, you deserve to be happy," Mark said, unable to put words to his true feelings. After weeks of being open with her about everything else, he still clammed up when it came to talking about love.

Because he didn't want to have those feelings. He couldn't bear to have her and then lose her.

He was so confused.

"Would it make you happy?" he asked, pushing the

mysterious rancher out of his mind. "To be married, I mean. And maybe a mother?"

She blushed and stared at a spot on the step above her hip. He'd embarrassed her. But she answered before he could apologize.

"Yes," she said, not looking up. "I've always thought I would have a husband and children."

"Then find out more about him," he suggested. "He might offer the life you dreamed of."

They squirmed through another loaded silence, and then Hattie looked up with a smile on her face. He was sure it was more than a little forced, but said nothing.

"You're right!" she said gaily. "I'll find Sophia and have her help me write a reply. She'll know what to say."

Though she smiled, her eyes were sad. "Thanks, Mark." She patted his shoulder as she slipped past him and almost ran off down the hall. Mark watched her go with his insides twisted.

He couldn't stand between her and a great match like this. Not when he couldn't get his act together to offer for her himself.

Besides, he was sure she'd say no. Pouring his heart out to her now and having her rebuff him—albeit as gently as possible because this was Hattie—was more than he could handle. He'd rather drink snake poison and try to saddle a mule.

The echoes of Hattie's anxious voice came floating down the hall with Sophia's giggling response. Mark's hands clenched into fists at his side. He'd never wanted to punch anyone as much as he did Mrs. Phillips's wealthy, God-fearing, perfect prospect of a husband.

He stomped upstairs to his room and found Brian sitting on the end of his bed, cleaning his boots with more gusto than the leather required. Dean was there too, leaning against the back wall with his arms folded, staring out the window.

Damn, these guys know how to brood.

"Hey," Dean said. He turned from the window and shoved his hands into his pockets. "We were talking about the ranch."

"It would be good to have the group together again." Brian dropped his clean boot and grabbed the other. "I just want to spend some time ranching like when we were young."

Mark dropped into an upholstered armchair and rested his elbows on his knees. "Yeah." He couldn't seem to rustle up any enthusiasm for the plan that didn't include Hattie.

Brian and Dean exchanged glances.

"I saw that." Mark blew out a frustrated breath and sat back.

"What rattled your cage?" Dean crossed his arms and resumed his task of holding up the wall and watching out the window.

"Forget about it." He'd never been one to talk about his feelings, and he wasn't about to start. "I'm just tired," he lied.

He'd known them long enough to know they didn't buy his explanation, but also that they wouldn't push him to talk if he didn't want to. The three men sulked in their own personal quicksand for a few minutes. It was nice to have friends who let you wallow from time to time.

"Mrs. Phillips was here again." Mark pushed to his feet and paced. "She just won't back off."

Brian nodded. "Sophia found me earlier and waved a letter in my face." Sophia's favorite person to tease was Brian. Whenever she had a spare minute in her day, she sought him out. She flirted with every man who came into her company, even the old guy who brought the groceries. But Brian was the only one she searched out and the one she teased the most. Brian's feelings were more difficult to read. There was a bond between a rescuer and the victim they saved.

Look at him and Hattie. How else could he explain their connection?

"Elizabeth won't go for it," Dean said.

Mark and Brian both laughed, and Dean's frown cracked. Mark joined Dean and looked out the window. "I don't even think Mrs. Phillips is bothering Elizabeth," Mark said.

Dean chuckled. "Unless she gets a letter from a groom looking for a woman who will wear the pants in the relationship."

All three men sighed in unison and then laughed again.

"Hattie's carrying around a letter too," Mark said. "Of all the women we've rescued, she has to be the most vulnerable." He sat on the edge of his bed and scratched the stubble on his jaw. "You saw what she was like when she arrived. How can they think it's a good idea to send her off to an unknown man a thousand miles away?"

Brian and Dean exchanged glances again. Mark groaned. They knew each other too well.

Dean shoved his hands back into his pockets and paced. "She's come out of her shell. I passed her yesterday, and she didn't even flinch." He picked up his hat from the dresser and spun it in his hands. "We can't treat them like China dolls forever. I'm sure Mrs. Phillips knows what she's doing."

Brian chuckled and dropped his clean boot to the floor.

"I can't say anything for Mrs. Phillips, but Mrs. Fritz isn't sending her chicks off unless she's sure they will be safe."

Mark laughed. "That's the damn truth. But just because Mrs. Fritz trusts the matchmaker's judgment doesn't mean I do."

"If you're worried," Brian ventured, "you could offer to marry her yourself? You've got a place to take her."

Mark groaned.

Hattie had been too eager to accept his encouragement to write to her wealthy suitor.

"I'm not interested in marriage," he snapped. "I'm just looking out for her, is all."

He lay back on the bed and closed his eyes. Dean and Brian may believe it as easy as asking, but they weren't the ones facing rejection from the sweetest woman alive.

Chapter Seven

With Sophia's help, Hattie's letter to Mr. Fletcher was quickly dispatched. They'd decided that it was a good idea to detail some of her history so they could gauge his response. Upon Elizabeth's suggestion, Hattie included a request that her groom agreed to wait a minimum of thirty days before consummating the marriage. It was a sensible addition, and Hattie was glad she'd consulted with Elizabeth. She almost hadn't—Elizabeth turned a disapproving eye upon anyone who dared to mention mail-order relationships in her presence.

The pace of the mail delivery was a fresh torture. Hattie haunted the foyer each afternoon, waiting for the messenger to come in with the mail. No matter how many times she told herself that the wait would be at least a month, she couldn't help looking every day.

"Mail," Jonah called as he closed the door with his hip. He laughed at Hattie as she flew down the stairs. "I think I have the letter you've been waiting for, Miss."

It took an eternity for Jonah to find the right one in his

bag, but he pulled it out and handed it to Hattie. "Good luck, Miss."

Hattie flashed him a soft smile and then rushed to the conservatory. She lowered herself onto the bench and ran her fingertip over the neatly scrolled address. Now that she had the letter, she was afraid to open it.

What if he rejected her? She'd shared some very personal tidbits.

What if he didn't?

She wasn't sure which was worse. So, she sat with her letter but couldn't open it. She reached down and ran her fingers through Arnold's soft leaves and smiled. She turned and looked at his best friend, Bob. Mark had been teasing her when he named them, but the names still tickled her.

The sun began to set, and Hattie couldn't put it off forever. Instead of reading the letter to herself, she decided to ask Sophia to read it to her. Her disappointment would be mitigated coming from Sophia's soft voice.

Hattie found Sophia in the front parlor window. She stood with her arms crossed and her feet planted. The glow of the setting sun silhouetted her hourglass figure and made her appear quite ethereal.

Hattie cleared her throat.

Sophia smiled as she turned around. "What did it say?" She rubbed her hands together and settled down on a couch. "I saw Jonah, and he said he'd given you a letter." Sophia patted the seat beside her. "Come on, spill it."

Thank God for Sophia.

Hattie sat beside her and held out the letter. "I couldn't bring myself to open it." She took the deepest breath she could manage and blew it out. "I don't know what I want it to say."

Sophia shoved her hand out and nodded. "Give it." She tore the letter open and held up one finger to keep Hattie quiet while she read through the letter herself.

Hattie tried to speak, but Sophia's finger just raised higher and shook a few times. Hattie smiled and held her questions until Sophia finished.

Sophia dropped both of her hands to her lap and grinned. "He assures you that your history has no bearing on his decision, and he would like to offer you his hand." Sophia squealed, but Hattie just slumped back against the sofa.

Sophia cleared her throat and read from the letter. "It starts out with a bunch of blah blah—his name and town and all that stuff you already know." She rolled her eyes and gave the paper a snap. Then her tone became very formal as she held the letter straight in front of her face. "I am impressed that you dared to share such painful details with me. Your letter has encouraged me, and I believe our marriage will be blessed." Sophia lowered the letter and beamed. "There! You see, I told you. Your marriage will be blessed."

Hattie banged her head against the wood detail on the back of the sofa and rubbed.

Sophia squealed as if the words were for her.

Hattie held up a hand before Sophia could continue reading. "Shh...," she said, embarrassed and not wanting to draw attention, "you'll have Mrs. Fritz in here if you don't keep it down." Hattie sat up straight, still stinging where she'd hit her head. "I don't need her in here fussing and trying to find out what's going on."

Sophia nodded and stood. "Let's stroll through the garden and I'll read you the parts that are most interesting." She whispered conspiratorially. Hattie obliged and looped her arm through Sophia's.

Mr. Fletcher's letter eased some of Hattie's insecurities. He accepted her as she was, damaged and all. And he agreed to Elizabeth's suggestion to delay consummation. He described his ranch and the more Sophia read; the more Hattie was able to accept that this man might be her future. She couldn't muster excitement as Sophia did, but she felt something akin to gratitude for his understanding.

It was one thing for Mark—who knew her—to be so forgiving of her past, but Mr. Fletcher was a stranger. She read the letter repeatedly throughout the day. One by one, she shared the missive with the other women and asked for their opinions. No matter how many times she was encouraged to accept the suitor, she couldn't overcome the fear of traveling such a distance to marry a stranger—even a kind one.

The only person Hattie couldn't bring herself to discuss the letter with was Mark. Late in the afternoon, she'd gone to the greenhouse, but when she saw him at the workbench, she'd turned and run away.

Without any arguments against accepting her suitor, Hattie made the decision to take a chance on the man in the West. Her heart raced every time she thought about it and tears sprang to her eyes whenever she saw Mark, but she couldn't stay at The Rose Dunn House forever, and Mr. Fletcher was offering a fresh start.

Waiting would only prolong the anxiety, so only one day after receiving the letter, Hattie asked Mrs. Phillips to telegram her acceptance to Mr. Fletcher. By the end of the week, Hattie had received a reply with a dress allowance and instructions for travel.

Hattie couldn't breathe. She'd just begun to feel

secure at The Rose Dunn House and now her whole world would turn upside down. And she'd have to adjust to her new life without Mark's comforting presence.

There was no time to worry because the women of Rose Dunn were in a flurry of preparation for her new life in Silent Creek. They sewed and knitted and embroidered and worked tirelessly to create a wardrobe fit for a new wife.

Hattie groaned as Mrs. Fritz handed her a third dress to try on.

"Watch your manners, young lady." Mrs. Fritz folded a garment and patted it neatly into place at the top of a nearly full travel trunk. "I'm not sending you to your groom in ill-fitted clothes."

Before she could get the previous dress off, Sophia breezed into the room with her signature squeal. She held aloft a long white satin gown and danced around the room with it.

"Quick, take off your dress." She didn't wait for Hattie to obey. Instead, she laid the gown on the end of the bed and went to unlace Hattie herself. "I found this in the wardrobe a while ago and set it aside for the first of us to get married." Sophia made quick work of the stays and then retrieved the gown as Mrs. Fritz helped Hattie step out of the dress. Mrs. Fritz took one side of the satin gown and Sophia held the other. They hoisted the dress high and brought it down over Hattie's head.

In a matter of minutes, Hattie was laced in. She'd never seen such a beautiful gown in her life.

Hattie twirled in front of the long mirror, hardly able to believe her eyes. The long white dress fit her slender frame perfectly. Sophia brushed her hair until it shone before curling it and threading it with ribbons. A bit of rouge on her cheeks and lips transformed her.

"I look pretty," she gasped at her reflection.

Elizabeth rolled her eyes. "You've always been pretty, you dolt. Now you look beautiful. A blushing bride."

Sophia sighed, looking down at her own curvier frame. "I wish I was as slender as you."

"No, no," Hattie insisted. "I'd love to have your curves." Although the thought of how much attention those curves drew from men changed her mind.

"You are lovely," Mrs. Fritz said. "Leave it on for a few minutes until Mrs. Phillips is here; she'll want to see." Mrs. Fritz continued folding garments and placing them into the trunk, but now she had a smile on her face. "We've made good use of that allowance." Mrs. Fritz seemed quite pleased with herself.

Mrs. Fritz had insisted on taking all the girls shopping. None of them felt that they needed lessons, but they were happy to accompany her nonetheless. Boy, were they wrong because Mrs. Fritz certainly knew how to drive a hard bargain at the haberdasheries and milliners. There was no chance of her getting done over by the shoddyocracy.

Even Elizabeth looked impressed.

The knocker echoed up the stairs and Mrs. Fritz nodded, "That'll be Mrs. Phillips." She waved a sock at Elizabeth. "Go on and let her in." Turning to Hattie she added, "you just stand there a minute."

"Of course," Hattie said, smoothing her hands over the delicate white lace. It was the nicest dress she'd ever seen.

A shadow fell across the doorway.

"Mark!" Sophia cooed. "Come and see Hattie's wedding

dress. Isn't she a beautiful bride?" She squealed and danced circles around Hattie.

Hattie's face heated and her heart raced. The idea of Mark seeing her in a dress intended for another man was unbearable. Luckily, Mrs. Fritz ran across the room and slammed the door in his face.

"It's bad luck for a man who isn't family to see her in her dress before her own husband," the older woman announced.

"What about the tailor?" Elizabeth asked as she entered, with Mrs. Phillips trailing behind.

"He doesn't count," Mrs. Fritz said firmly.

Hattie laughed, but Mark's appearance had dampened her spirits. Being separated from Mark by a single wall while dressed in a gown meant for another man made her heart ache anew.

The prospect of being settled comforted her, and the idea of belonging to a good man—of being safe—was reassuring. But when she pictured those things with Mark, her heart soared, and she became excited. No matter how she tried, she could not get excited about her marriage to Mr. Fletcher.

Her mind circled around the challenging aspects of marriage. The others assured her she was not used and broken, but the idea of being touched even by her husband sent her stomach into knots. Hattie was grateful for the month-long delay, but she dreaded the conclusion of that month.

She vowed to hide her discomfort, and, over time, she was certain she could get used to it. The thought flip-flopped from sadness and fear to firm resolve. No matter what she'd been through, she planned to live her best life.

The memory of her rescue came back to her. It was

mostly fragments—her body trembling to cope with the pain and flashes of blackness. But she remembered Mark holding her close. She remembered his strong arms pulling her into his hard chest. She remembered his steady heartbeat, giving her the strength to carry on. His touch was gentle, and his eyes were tormented.

The idea of physical touch was not as frightening with Mark. Hattie wanted his love, his warmth, his heartbeat in her ear. She imagined what it would be like to go to bed beside him. He'd pull her close, and she'd let his heartbeat lull her asleep.

Mark understood her in a way her future husband never could.

"Hattie?" Mrs. Fritz asked with concern.

Hattie feigned a chuckle. "Sorry. You caught me woolgathering." She looked herself over once more in the mirror and hoped the lie would seep into her and become the truth.

MARK TURNED AND PRESSED HIS BACK AGAINST THE WALL. The image of Hattie in her wedding dress would haunt him for the rest of his life. She was the most beautiful thing he'd ever seen.

And now he was too late. Nothing could have hammered the point home as efficiently as the vision of her wrapped in white satin.

They would have one last journey together as he escorted her West to her betrothed. As his plans and hers fell in line, it made sense for him to take her, but the thought of handing her over hurt his heart. Thank God he wouldn't have to lay eyes on her future spouse. Her train stop was several hours earlier than his, and she would take a stagecoach the rest of the way to her new home.

He could bask in her silent company once more before they both took their chances at a fresh start. Mark needed the familiar comfort of the ranch. He needed the labor, wide open spaces, and brotherhood.

He craved it.

He was not made for city life. Hank expressed it perfectly when he described it as a cesspool. Why would anybody want to live all crammed together like that?

Mark pressed his hand to the wall with his heart somewhere just on the other side. Always out of reach. He thought about the day they found her, the amalgamation of dread and joy when they discovered she was still alive. How she felt in his arms while he prayed and pleaded for her to live.

She would roam the halls in the early days. She'd seemed untethered, like she was looking for someone to direct her to where she needed to be. He wanted to be that person now, but he was too late.

He would forever regret not expressing his feelings sooner.

He balled his fist and pushed away from the wall. He'd stay as far away from her as he could until it was time for them to leave. He stomped down to the greenhouse. He'd be safe from Hattie down there for a while. Mrs. Fritz wouldn't let her move a muscle as long as she had that gown on.

Brian and Dean were just getting in from giving their statements to the police about a recent case when they found Mark.

Brian scooped a handful of soil and gently shook it over the seeds as Mark planted. "Why ye acting the maggot?" He never minced words. "Just ask her to marry ye. It's not too late."

Mark shook his head, not sure how to reply. They hadn't seen her twirling in front of the mirror in that fancy dress, so they didn't know what they were talking about.

Dean crossed his arms and leaned a hip on the workbench. "I don't know about maggots." He shot a quizzical look at Brian, "But the Paddy's right. Just ask her." He shoved his hands in his pockets and shrugged. "Worst she can do is say no and you ride west in silence." Dean's mouth turned up in one corner. "It's not like either of you are real conversationalist, anyway."

"Who're ye callin' Paddy?" Brian said, mock offended. His Irish accent was exaggerated for effect.

Mark grinned. He'd miss these two until they joined him on the ranch.

"Brian, focus," Dean said sharply. He turned to Mark again. "If you don't ask, you will regret it for the rest of your life." And as if he'd run out of words, he walked away.

"He's a pain in the ass, but he's right. Ask her, it'll be grand." Brian flashed him a tired smile and clapped him on the shoulder.

Then Mark was alone again.

A flood of giggles from the hall caught his attention. Elizabeth and Hattie walked arm and arm, whispering to each other. Hattie looked happier than she'd been since he'd known her. How could he interfere with her happiness by smothering her with his own feelings? He didn't have it in him to be so selfish.

Not wanting to be found, he dusted his hands and slipped out of the conservatory. He let himself into the office and settled himself behind the massive desk with a bottle of whiskey. The slight smoke scent of the office reminded him of their old days at the house. The time when they were on a mission, and they were all working together to meet a goal.

He missed Opal and Daniel. Without them, the group lacked leadership. The three men naturally took turns leading when the situation dictated it, without a sense of competition or animosity between them. They all knew when they needed to take charge and when to follow. This type of camaraderie was rare, and he appreciated it—but he missed having a direction and purpose.

This melancholy would soon be relieved upon his return to the ranch. Mark tried to relax, but he couldn't convince himself that his problems would end with his return home.

He poured himself a large measure of whiskey from the crystal decanter, then leaned back and propped his feet up. Normally, he preferred to find respite in the conservatory, but he was avoiding Hattie. He'd gotten into the habit of viewing the greenhouse as their place. It was where they'd met so many times. If he went in there and she didn't find him, he would feel dejected.

Better to hide in the office where she would never look for him than to sit like a dog waiting for its master to return. He held the golden liquid on his tongue and enjoyed the smoky warmth.

He settled his head on the back of the chair, closed his eyes, and imagined his life on the ranch—this time without a pregnant Hattie puttering around. A hollow feeling swelled in his belly.

You're not going to be happy without her.

Going home meant he could put the trauma behind him, but that wasn't all he wanted. His time with the sweet woman had encouraged feelings he hadn't ever expected to have. She made him want a wife. She made him want a family.

His pre-dinner whiskey rendered him a bit loose at dinner. Voices fluttered around him, but he couldn't follow the conversations. He was happy to drown them all out because all they seemed to want to talk about was Hattie's upcoming wedding. That was the last thing he wanted to think about.

He tried to recall the last time they spoke. How long has it been? She'd been so busy with her new prospects; he'd fallen to the wayside.

What did he expect?

Hattie raised her eyes to his and held his gaze. There was something almost pleading in her eyes, but he couldn't discern her feelings. They stared into one another, and his heart left his body, and ran to embrace her.

If only his body could follow.

The longing to throw his arms around her was an ache in his bones. He wasn't sure who broke eye contact first, but he missed it the moment it was gone. The cold emptiness resounded like it had the day of her rescue. She had branded him that day, and he would bear her mark all his life.

When dinner was finished, Mark waited in the conservatory. He sat on their bench with his elbows on his knees and cradled his face in his hands.

He couldn't let her go.

If she came, he would ask—no, beg her to have him.

Footsteps passed and his heart skipped, but no one entered. He waited for the better part of an hour before storming out of the room.

He collided with Hattie in the doorway, and they

nearly fell to the floor together. He grasped her around the waist and pulled her body against his to steady them both. With their bodies pressed together and their faces mere inches apart, Mark couldn't think.

They stared into each other's eyes. Mark's gaze was drawn to Hattie's mouth when she licked her lips. She released a shaky breath and Mark came to his senses.

He released Hattie and did his best to pull himself together. "Are you okay?" he stuttered, "I'm so sorry. I didn't see you."

The look on Hattie's face was indiscernible. She stared for the space of a heartbeat and then fled. He watched her form disappear around the corner and winced.

Her flight confirmed his worst fear.

WHAT MUST HE THINK OF HER NOW?

Surely Mark had read the lust in her eyes. She hadn't believed herself capable of such feelings, but when he grabbed her, his hands sent shivers of excitement up her spine. She'd breathed in his scent. Their mouths had been so close. If she'd followed her impulse and risen just an inch, she could have kissed him.

But then he'd broken the magic. He'd once again shown her he had no intentions toward her. In a fortnight, they would leave for their trip, and it would be too late for her to convince him she wanted him.

A fortnight.

Her groom had arranged everything, and she wished she could be as excited as the other ladies. Instead, Hattie tossed in bed with her thoughts turning over in her mind. During the day, it was easy enough to pretend all was well, but in the dark, there was nothing but anxiety and fear to berate her.

Mrs. Fritz had taken over her days. Hattie was kept on a strict schedule of guidance at the direction of that sweet woman who seemed to enjoy the employment a tad excessively. A sudden thought made Hattie giggle aloud.

"What's funny?" Elizabeth murmured and rolled over to face Hattie's bed.

Hattie bit her lip, considering what to say. The darkness freed her from shyness. She could be honest. "I was just thinking that Mrs. Fritz is enjoying the bridal festivities so much, perhaps she should go to Silent Creek, and I will stay on as a cook.".

"Could you imagine?" Her giggle elongated into a full-blown fit of laughter. When it died down, her tone became more serious.

"You know you don't have to go, right?" Elizabeth raised up on one elbow. The white moonlight streaming in through the open curtains highlighted her sharp features. "If you have reservations, it's not too late to change your mind."

Hattie rolled to her side and tucked her hands together beneath her cheek, facing Elizabeth's bed.

"Do you promise to keep it a secret?" She spoke just loud enough for Elizabeth to hear, but still feared others might be listening.

"Of course."

"I wanted it to be Mark." This was the first time she'd said it out loud, and it felt good.

Elizabeth made a noncommittal sound and asked. "Did you tell him?"

"I tried to." Hattie flopped onto her back and stared at

the ceiling. "I, well, I don't know. Sometimes it seems like he cares for me, but then he pushes me away."

"You're not the most direct speaker, Hattie. If you want something from him, tell him in no uncertain terms how you feel." Elizabeth rolled to her back and stared at the ceiling as well.

"What if he feels sorry for me and marries me out of pity?" Silent tears rolled down Hattie's face. "Can you imagine anything worse?" Hattie wiped her cheek and sighed. "I want him to love me, not to save me again."

"I think we can both imagine worse." Elizabeth scoffed. "But I hadn't thought about it like that. I don't think he would marry you out of pity, though. I've seen the way he watches you." Elizabeth turned on her side again. "I think he loves you, too."

The silence squeezed between them, and Hattie considered Elizabeth's words.

"I'm going to miss you, Hattie."

"I'm going to miss you, too, Elizabeth."

Chapter Eight

H attie could count on one hand the words she and Mark had exchanged since their encounter outside the conservatory.

Inspired by her conversation with Elizabeth, Hattie began to entertain bold thoughts. Unlike Elizabeth, her courage was limited. She desperately sought him out, but he stayed scarce. She only saw him at mealtimes, but he never returned her gaze. Her heart cried for him to look at her, for him to see her, but he couldn't hear it. He was out of reach.

Now the fortnight had ended and time had run out.

Hattie snapped the latch into place on her trunk with a sigh. There was no turning back. A telegram had been sent to Quinn Fletcher with confirmation of her travel plans. He'd sent a response, ensuring her that he would be there when the stage arrived in Silent Creek.

Hattie caught her reflection in the looking glass. A stranger stared back. Her new cloak fit well. The navy blue fabric was richer than she was used to. And the cut of her dress suggested more curves than Hattie possessed.

Hattie was weary of the shorter, modern collar, but Sophia assured her of its style. She fingered the pearl-like buttons and admired herself.

Brian knocked on the frame of the open door. "All set? I'll take it out for ye."

She smiled and nodded. Hattie stepped away from her trunk and picked up her hat and traveling gloves from the vanity table. Brian must have seen her hands shake because he stopped beside the trunk and gave her a sweet smile.

"It's goin' ta be alright. Nae, it'll be grand. The future always is." His words were warm and comforting.

Hattie hadn't spent much time with Brian. She hadn't even had a conversation with him before, but he didn't make her uncomfortable the way everyone used to. The two of them stood alone in her bedroom, and she didn't have the urge to run away. Maybe she really was going to be okay.

"Thank you, Brian." Her heart didn't race, and her palms didn't sweat—at least not more than they already were. She really had come a very long way since she first been installed in the bedroom upstairs with Elizabeth.

The epiphany restored her, and she walked a little taller, chin poised, ready to see what life held for her in Silent Creek. After all, her life was worth more than the decisions of men. Elizabeth was right, her life was her own. She'd made her own decision to be a mail-order bride.

Her hands continued to shake, but Hattie did her best to squash her nerves. She might not be calm, but she could fake it for appearances.

Hattie cast a glance over at the bed where she'd been brought back to life. She ran her hand over the lilac-colored quilt she'd clung to while Elizabeth had whispered words of hope and soothed her night terrors. A bitter-sweetness pulled at her heart, but she did not let it slow her momentum.

She would press on for herself and for the women who didn't make it out of the house with her that day. With a deep breath, she put some starch in her spine and left the room ahead of Brian and her trunk.

"Atta girl," Brian said behind her.

Elizabeth greeted Hattie at the bottom of the stairs. They clasped hands and for once Hattie didn't wish to pull away.

After a long embrace, Elizabeth said, "I'm going to miss you, Hattie."

Hattie wiped a tear from her eye and nodded. She tried to form words, but she was too choked up to manage.

After a moment of meaningful silence, Sophia skipped up and threw her arms around both of them. Hattie laughed through her tears and with a little struggle she untangled herself from Elizabeth and pulled Sophia close.

Elizabeth smiled stoically over Sophia's shoulder, and Hattie grinned back. Hattie's fondness for the two and their differences swelled.

In true dramatic fashion, Sophia clung to Hattie's hands and begged. "You'll write to me, right? Like you and Angela?" She dabbed at her eyes with a handkerchief that Hattie had embroidered for her. "I don't know what we'll do without you."

Hattie pulled Sophia close again and promised. "I will write as often as I possibly can."

Looking at them both, she drew from Elizabeth's straightforwardness. "I'm grateful to have had this time with you. I don't know how I could have gotten this far without both of you."

The words did not fully express her feelings of gratitude, but it would have to do. A shadow in the doorway saved Hattie from babbling more effusions of appreciation for her friends. Mark's eyes were glazed with something wild as he leaned on the doorframe and took deep breaths.

Had he been running?

Sophia giggled and clapped her hands. "Elizabeth, let's go get Mrs. Fritz so she can say her goodbyes." It was an obvious ploy to leave Hattie and Mark alone. They all knew Mrs. Fritz was packing up food for Hattie and Mark to eat on the train.

Elizabeth rolled her eyes but obliged.

When she could no longer hear their footsteps, Hattie turned to Mark for an explanation of his state. He'd caught his breath, but the wildness remained in his gaze.

Mark took a step forward and his mouth opened, but a knock at the door stole his words. He made a grumbling sound at the back of his throat and blew out a breath. His brow cocked as he opened the door to a tall woman in a straw bonnet.

Sunlight poured around her slender form and she could have been an angel. The vision clutched a brown carpet bag in her delicate hands. She raised her head and revealed large gray eyes and a shock of fiery hair. Her features were fine and porcelain. Hattie was in awe of the stranger's beauty. Not an angel. She was a faerie.

Mark dipped his head. "Good morning, Miss. How may I help you?" he asked. The wildness seemed to flow out of him as he addressed the lady.

She stood tall and swallowed hard before she answered. "Good morning, Sir." She hugged her bag to her chest. "Pardon my forwardness." She swallowed again. "I'm sorry if the information I have been given is mistaken, but I was instructed to seek lodgings here." A look of pain tightened her sweet features.

Mark stepped back to make room and swept his arm in a welcoming gesture. "No apologies are necessary. Please, come in." Mark held out his hand, and she reluctantly released her carpetbag to him. He set it on a bench beside the door.

Hattie was about to introduce herself when Mrs. Fritz and the others came jabbering down the hall. All three women spoke at once, and Sophia bounced in her childish way.

Their conversation was silenced at the sight of the stranger. Tension buzzed in the air until the clock chimed and reminded them that they had a train to catch.

Mark rubbed the back of his neck. "I'm Mark Webb. I hate to run out, but Miss Thompson," he gestured to Hattie, "and I have a train to catch. Miss, uh?"

"Mrs. Campbell, Florence Campbell." She said. Her voice was sweet and clear but a little shaky.

Mark nodded. "Mrs. Campbell, we must be leaving, but Mrs. Fritz, Miss Snyder, and Miss Cooper will get you settled."

Mrs. Campbell nodded and sent Mark a gracious smile. The way Mark and this woman gazed at each other rubbed Hattie wrong. Her stomach twisted and her pulse beat faster.

Mark was a handsome man and any woman with eyes could see it. Sharp tears pricked as the image of Mark with another woman intrusively flashed through her mind. It was especially painful because the vision now had red hair and big gray eyes.

Mrs. Fritz pushed forward and ended the uncomfortable scene. "Excuse us, dear, for just one moment." She nodded to Mrs. Campbell and then turned her attention to Hattie. "I'm going to miss you so very much, my dear." The sweet woman dabbed at her eyes with the hem of her apron. As Mark and Brian loaded her trunk and carpetbag into the wagon, Mrs. Fritz fired last-minute bits of advice and encouragement.

When Mark returned and cleared his throat, the motherly lady ran out of words. She gave one last embrace and kissed Hattie's cheek. Then Mark took Hattie's elbow, gave one last long glance and nod to Mrs. Campbell, and guided Hattie out the door.

"Florence, dear, I'm Mrs. Fritz—" The door closed with a soft click, and just like that, Hattie left The Rose Dunn House behind. She didn't depart in chaos as she'd arrived, but with a quietly closing door—as another woman took her place.

As Mark escorted her to the carriage, Hattie imagined Mrs. Campbell sleeping in her bed and sharing late-night conversations with Elizabeth. Mark handed her up into the conveyance and she pictured Sophia fussing over their new housemate like a mother hen. She'd tell her secrets and ask questions of a far too personal nature.

A tightness took hold of her throat and she forced herself to look forward and not back. So distracted in her thoughts, she paid no mind to Mark's hand in hers as he helped her into the carriage. A thing she would normally have thrilled in.

The carriage rolled forward. The click-clack of the horses and rumble of the wheels drowned out all other sounds. As the seconds passed, her heart squeezed and she turned to look back. Her gaze swept over the big house one last time until the earth swallowed her former home as they crested the hill and started down the other side.

The carriage jostled, and they bumped into one another. The shake-up broke the tension and Hattie laughed. She was on her way and she wouldn't spend her last few days in Mark's company with a head full of worry.

They hit another deep rut in the road and clung to the sides of the carriage to avoid being unseated. As they bounced down the road, they both laughed. Hattie's eyes met Mark's, and they smiled openly for a moment. There was something in his eyes that she didn't recognize and she remembered that he'd been about to speak when Mrs. Campbell had arrived.

"I—" Hattie began, but Mark had started at just the same moment. Exchanging laughs, Hattie urged Mark to speak with a wave of her hand.

"I was just thinking about how strange it is to be leaving Rose Dunn." Mark leaned back in the now steady carriage but didn't loose his hold on the window frame. "I've been here quite a long time."

Hattie nodded and blinked away tears. "I was thinking the same." She stared out the window for a moment. "I'm going to miss Elizabeth, Sophia, and Mrs. Fritz. They all made such a difference in my life."

Mark nodded.

"With the sudden arrival of Mrs. Campbell, I feel a bit replaced." Hattie shrugged and stared out the window. "I know that's not fair to her." A moment later, she added, "I wonder what brought her to the house."

Mark opened his mouth a few times before he spoke.

His voice was filled with a familiar hesitancy. "You could never be replaced, Hattie."

She'd heard that tone in his voice anytime he'd been vulnerable in front of her. Hattie took his hand and squeezed it. She wasn't the only one leaving Boston with a heavy heart.

His words quelled the jealousy that had risen when he'd gazed at Mrs. Campbell. He'd called Hattie perfect once and she would cling to those words for the rest of her life. The bittersweetness of her thoughts multiplied as the carriage rolled into the train depot.

This really was the end for Mark and Hattie.

The train steamed and snorted like a raging bull at the platform. Its sleek black body cast an ominous shadow over the boardwalk like a herald of bad tidings rather than her ticket to a new life full of possibility. Hattie's nose crinkled at the odor of burning coal mingled with the tobacco smoke of men waiting on the platform. Her senses were overwhelmed with a nauseating dread.

Thankfully, Mark knew where they needed to go and Hattie didn't have to navigate the busy station on her own. He wrangled porters to handle her trunk and then guided her to the train.

Hattie bore her eyes into Mark's back and followed mutely as he walked toward their compartments. Unpleasant images of arriving to discover Mr. Fletcher, not what he described in his letter crept up, but focusing on Mark kept them at bay. The porter put her luggage in her sleeping compartment, "Do you need anything else, madam?"

Her heart quickened. She'd been unprepared to talk to strangers, but Mark saved her from having to respond.

"We're fine. Thank you." He tipped the porter and waved Hattie into her room.

Mark's quarters were adjacent to hers, identical in every respect with two sleeping bunks. Their wooden frames were freshly polished and shining. The far wall had two windows side by side with small drapes wide open to invite the bold spring sun.

Hattie watched Mark enter his room and closed her door. She sat on the beige and brown topped quilt on the bottom bunk and collected her thoughts. For a few days, she would occupy the small compartment by herself. During the days she expected to ride in the open seating at the front of the car, and she'd take her meals with Mark in the dining car. But at night, she would sleep by herself and the prospect frightened Hattie. Her heart ached for Elizabeth's company.

Her mind had just turned to the stranger at the end of her journey when a knock made her jump out of her skin. She restrained her scream and managed to get through with nothing more than a flinch.

Hattie cleared her throat and straightened her skirt before she took the two steps to reach the cabin door.

Mark beamed at her from the hallway. "How do you like your sleeper?"

"It's lovely." Hattie shuffled her feet, uncertain of the etiquette for an unmarried woman to be greeting an unmarried man in her private train compartment. "I'm grateful to have my own. I don't think I could have slept a wink in the communal sleeping car." The idea of sleeping amongst strangers made her shiver.

Mark remained in the hallway and spoke across the threshold. He ran his hand through his hair. "Awful nice of

Mr. Fletcher to put me up as well." The words came out awkwardly, as if they didn't fit in his mouth.

Hattie didn't know how to respond, so she nodded and fussed with the pleats on her skirt.

An awkward pause concluded when Mark cleared his throat. "I want to check your lock." He rattled her door. "Make sure it works."

His concern warmed Hattie to the soles of her feet. She hadn't thought to check the lock, and she didn't want to consider the repercussions of such a mistake.

Mark slid the door closed between them and Hattie turned the bolt. He jiggled the locked door and then bumped it several times. "Okay," he said. "Open it again."

Hattie slid the door open and her breath caught in her chest. Mark's smile held her captive, and she never wished to be free.

Mark tapped the lock. "Seems fit to me."

Hattie returned his smile. "Thank you, Mark; for always keeping me safe... and everything." Their eyes locked and a million unsaid words charged the air between them.

The whistle blew and the wrought-iron clacked slowly. The train lurched forward and threw Hattie off balance. She clutched the wall, embarrassed but amused.

Mark chuckled. "Ever been on one of these things before?"

"Not once."

"Let me show you around, and then we'll get some coffee and something sweet."

Mark held his arm out in a show of escorting her down the aisle, but the train rocked, and Hattie's balance abandoned her again. Before she could catch herself, she fell right into his arms.

The hallway was crowded with strangers, and Hattie had no question of the appropriateness of being in his arms with so many onlookers. Her eyes darted left and right as she extricated herself as quickly as possible from his embrace. "Excuse me. Thank you. I'm sorry." She blurted whatever came to mind and righted herself with one hand on the wall and the other on Mark's arm.

Such closeness would only make their separation more painful. Hattie vowed to keep as many chaperones around as she could manage. The last thing she needed was to be alone with the man she adored.

"We can't seem to quit knocking each other over," he said with a laugh that turned Hattie's tumultuous stomach to butterflies.

"I've always been clumsy. Maybe I'm not made for train travel."

Mark shrugged. "You just haven't got your sea legs yet."

Chapter Nine

" Is this your card?"

Hattie gasped and covered her mouth in delighted shock as Mark revealed her King of Hearts with a flourish.

"Yes!" She bounced and clapped her hands, much as Sophia was known to do. "How did you do it?"

Mark cocked his eyebrow at her. "A showman never reveals his secrets." He smiled slyly and bumped her with his elbow. After showing Hattie around the train and grabbing a bite to eat, they sat in the public car, side by side, with a narrow table in front of them. The rock of the train jostled Hattie into him and they giggled as she straightened. Mark didn't try too hard to prevent himself whenever the train rocked him into her, and he didn't think she was trying either. Their knees bumped and her faint scent of lavender washed over him. At one point, their thighs absentmindedly rested together. Mark relished how she didn't seem to mind.

Mark tapped the cards on the table and cleared his throat. "Okay, long train rides are an excellent time to develop a gambling habit. I know the perfect game for you. It's called Colonel, basically—" He was about to teach her how to play the western man's version of a Spanish card game taught to him by Paul when an older woman sitting in the row across from them turned around.

"Congratulations! You're a beautiful couple." She smiled sweetly and clasped her hands together at her heart.

Hattie flinched beside him and Mark was compelled to set the woman straight.

Mark rubbed the back of his neck and shifted in his seat. "Thank you, kindly ma'am. I mean no disrespect, but we're not a couple." Mark's face heated, but he didn't lower his face as he wanted to do.

The woman eyed them suspiciously and wiggled her eyebrows mischievously. Mark smiled thinly, and she turned back around, whispering into the ear of an equally aged man, whom Mark assumed to be her husband. The man turned around and eyed the two, his expression not as lighthearted as his wife's.

Hattie stiffened and slightly shifted away from him, but said nothing. He decided that it was better not to give it too much of their time. So, he cleared his throat, tapped the deck on the table, and started to shuffle. "Okay, where was I?" He snuck a side glance at Hattie and smiled. When she smiled back, he continued. "I was going to teach you how to play, Colonel. Paul was obsessed with this card game. He's not much of a talker, so he liked to play with me instead of Brian." He smiled, thinking of the time spent playing cards with Paul. It would be nice to see Paul again. He imagined more of these nights lying ahead of him in Hope.

Brotherhood was what he needed, not a wife. But then

he looked at her, her big eyes taking him in and he almost forgot everything. He'd made up his mind to ask her to abandon her plans and marry him when he'd returned to the house that morning. The arrival of Mrs. Campbell had interrupted him and then there just hadn't been a chance. And now they were settled into compartments paid for by her betrothed. He could hardly ask her now.

Shuffling was harder with sweaty palms.

Mark pulled himself out of his brief melancholy and turned his attention to the game. "Alright, this isn't really a lady's game, but I'll make an exception for you. Just promise not to tell Mrs. Fritz."

"Oh, how thoughtful of you," she said with just the slightest bit of sass. They shook on it, her small pale hand delicate in his rough paw. He gently slid his thumb across the back of her hand, but the hitch in her breath reminded him of his place.

HATTIE AWOKE WITH HER HEART POUNDING AND TEARS streaming down her face. She'd had upsetting dreams many times, but this was not a nightmare.

She was alone and confused in the dark sleeping compartment, wishing she could unburden herself to Elizabeth. She sniffled and laughed at herself. Elizabeth was bold, but there was no way Hattie could have spoken to her of the dream. Sophia, perhaps, but nobody else.

The train swayed, and she bunched herself up in her bunk, her eyes fixed on the wall that separated her from Mark. She covered her face, embarrassed, but something else too. She couldn't place the feeling exactly, but something akin to relief tinged with fear and uncertainty.

After everything she'd been through, intimate relations were a topic she'd tried not to consider. With her impending marriage, it had been on her mind a lot because one month after her nuptials, she would need to fulfill her wifely duties. How would she ever give herself to a man?

She'd warned Mr. Fletcher that she had been abused. She'd even warned him that the memories returned to her at inconvenient times. She could only hope that he would honor his promise to treat her with patience and understanding.

She flopped onto her back and stared at the stars outside her window. The last thing she'd expected was to have such a—dare she say pleasurable—dream about Mark Webb. Hattie experienced traces of the familiar fear and anxiety that accompanied any thought of relations with a man. But during the dream, she had none of those nerves.

Hattie pulled the pillow from beneath her head and pressed it over her face and gave a silent scream. She crushed her embarrassment and replayed the dream in her mind. Something about her naughty thoughts delighted her, and in the dark of her compartment, she didn't shy away.

The dream had begun as their day had ended. Mark had walked her to the door and bid her goodnight. That's when everything changed. Rather than shooting her a sad smile and leaving, Dream-Mark stroked her cheek and told her she was perfect. The subtle roughness of his calloused finger sent an exhilarating shiver through her body.

She didn't recoil. She leaned into his touch and let his palm cup her face. She clasped his hand with hers, brought it to her mouth, and kissed each knuckle one by one with her eyes locked on his.

Mark groaned and goosebumps sprung up on Hattie's body.

He'd leaned forward to kiss her, but she'd stepped back and pulled him by the hand into her room. Mark's gaze was intense as he slid the door closed and flicked the lock.

She'd licked her lips and shuddered.

Hattie turned face-down on the bed and quietly screamed into her pillow again. Her body was on fire, just replaying the dream in her mind. She closed her eyes and continued.

Mark had moved slowly toward her, and pulled her body tight to his. She couldn't bear the suspense, so she rose up onto her toes and kissed him long and hard. Her mouth opened to the press of his tongue and she moaned all the way up from the bottom of her feet.

He'd walked her backward until she was pressed up against the wall. Her body came alive when he lifted her up. She'd wrapped her legs around his waist and her arms around his shoulders. His lips ravished her neck and mouth, and his hands cupped her bottom.

Hattie took a deep breath and blew it out. Next was her favorite part. She squeezed her thighs together and let the scene play.

Mark had pulled back far enough to gaze into her eyes. He'd pressed the softest kiss to her mouth and then whispered, "I love you," low and breathy in her ear.

She squealed into her pillow again and again as her body experienced feelings she had never known before. Desire heated her center and quickened her pulse.

Hattie'd burned for him. Her body had arched and

ached. She'd needed to feel his flesh on hers. She'd taken his kiss deeper and deeper until he was as frantic and desperate for her as she was for him.

Hattie couldn't help peeking out from under the blankets. She turned her back again and made sure nobody could see or hear her. She smiled to herself. She was alone. Truly alone. Not even the shadow of shoes blocked the faint light under the door.

With a serving of apprehension, and perhaps a bit of shame, Hattie remembered a particularly horrifying conversation she'd had once with Sophia and grinned. She finally understood. Hattie slid the hem of her nightgown up her thighs. She imagined Mark's hands instead of her own. Her body radiated with her need and she squeezed her legs together—but nothing could relieve the pressure of her desire.

Hattie closed her eyes and remembered how she'd slid down Mark's body and tugged at his shirt. She could still feel the heat of his skin on the palms of her hands. When she couldn't reach over his head, he'd pulled the shirt off himself and revealed a broad, muscled chest with a sprinkling of hair.

He'd kissed her and worked the laces on her gown until he just slipped it from her shoulders and dropped it to the floor. Hattie's breath quickened and her heart soared.

In the dream, they'd finished disrobing and slid into the bunk. Hattie skipped forward a little in her imagination until the part where Mark had crawled down her body and taken her breast into his mouth.

She glided her hand up and cupped that breast, then moved her other hand up and cupped both. As she imagined his mouth, she squeezed and tugged at her nipples. Heat pooled in her center, and she trailed her right hand down, following the path of his kisses until she reached her core.

Hattie remembered her hands fisting his hair as he suckled and licked until she exploded. Her fingertips worked at her little spot until she cried out and trembled. She slowed her fingertips and gentled her hand on her nipple.

The rest of the dream was a blur, and Hattie was sated from her release. She went limp in the bed and slowly caught her breath.

If only the dream could be a reality and she could fall asleep to the sound of Mark's heartbeat.

The remainder of the night was peaceful. Once Hattie drifted back to sleep, her dreams were full of joy and possibilities. Unfortunately, her dreams centered around Mark, and not Mr. Fletcher.

Hattie bolted upright and smashed her head on the upper bunk when a sharp knock at the door awoke her from a sweet dream. Then Mark's deep voice came through to her. "Mornin', Hattie. Ready for breakfast?" Hattie rubbed her head and then scrubbed her eyes with her hands.

"Good morning. Yes, just one moment." She flung the bedding off and climbed out of the bunk. She stretched and then dressed in a coral-colored frock with white lace trim. The dress was one of Sophia's favorites, which made Hattie miss her friend. She dressed quickly and arranged her hair. Hattie shrugged at her reflection and then draped a shawl across her shoulders.

As she went to open the door, she realized her bed was unmade, and she rushed to make it. Then she missed Elizabeth. She hadn't bargained for the homesickness she'd feel upon leaving The Rose Dunn House.

When she finally opened the door, Mark stood on the other side with a wide grin on his handsome face. "Someone slept in." Mark laughed, "I'm teasing you. Did you sleep well?" He reached around Hattie as she entered the hall and slid her door closed behind her. He took the key from her and locked the door.

Hattie was grateful for his moment of distraction because her cheeks burned when she considered how to answer his question. Her heart fluttered and, whether real or imagined, warmth seemed to radiate from him.

He handed her the key back and raised an eyebrow.

"I slept fine." Hattie couldn't look at him, so she distracted herself by putting the key into her reticule. With that done, she took Mark's arm and let him lead her to the dining car.

Breakfast was a quiet affair. Clinking China and sipping coffee were the only sounds that passed between them. The silence was peaceful. It was nice that they could just be together without filling every second with idle chitchat.

Hattie hoped she could have the same comfortable companionship with her betrothed. She nibbled at a slice of toast and stared out the window. The train blurred by trees and blue sky; the beautiful spring day pulled a smile from her lips. "It's beautiful, isn't it?"

Mark followed her gaze out the window and smiled, too. "It is. Wait till we get further west. It's like nothing you've ever seen." Mark grew whimsical, and Hattie slid her plate away from her and smiled. "Wait till you see prairies that stretch on for miles and miles, wide as the eye can see. Or mountains that disappear into the clouds." He pushed his plate away too, but didn't release his coffee cup.

He'd told her many times how badly he wished to be back on the farm, but it was something else to hear him speak of it outside of their little conservatory. "I suppose you'll never fancy yourself a city dweller."

"If anything, my time in the city made me more of a cowboy. There's nothing wrong with city folk. I just don't like all the noise and everyone all packed together like that." He shrugged and sipped his coffee. "I like wide open spaces. I want to lie down and have the sky at my fingertips."

Hattie nodded. What a beautiful sentiment. "I like that idea." She took a breath and tried to imagine it. "I hope Silent Creek is like that."

Mark nodded, but the wonder in his eyes flickered out at the mention of Silent Creek.

Rather than ruining the last few days she would have with Mark talking of the stranger who would be her husband, Hattie continued their friendly discussion and pretended she hadn't brought up her future home. "Do you think the west is safer than the city?"

"There are good folks and bad folks everywhere." He leaned forward and rested his elbows on the table. Mrs. Fritz would have a fit, but his gaze was so intense Hattie couldn't be bothered to correct him. "It's the human condition, isn't it? We're good and bad creatures. After everything I've seen, I sometimes think we're more evil than good."

She'd been trying to avoid that truth. She'd read the papers and dime-store novels. She had heard of the dangers of life in the Wild West, but she'd tried to ignore the risk. If she allowed herself to really think about it, she would have already said goodbye to Mark, and she'd live at The Rose Dunn House forever.

She knew the risks, though. Better than anyone.

AFTER BREAKFAST, THEY AMUSED THEMSELVES BY STROLLING up and down the cars. Mark liked the way Hattie clung to his arm in the gangways, but also the way she seemed to enjoy those little crossings between train cars.

By mid-afternoon, they found themselves seated in the public car. Hattie read from a tattered copy of Jane Eyre. Mark pulled a soap bar from his pocket and began carving it.

Hattie looked up from her book. "What are you making?"

"You'll see." He worked slowly, using just the tip of the knife. Small flakes of white soap curled on the floor. He liked the way Hattie watched him work with her book forgotten in her lap.

Mark focused for a moment to get a small detail just right and then spoke again. "We never had soap growing up, not like this anyway." He didn't look away from his task. "I remember the first time I saw soap in a bar. I thought it was a candle." Mark laughed and glanced up to see the sweetest expression on Hattie's face. "Now, it's everywhere"

Hattie watched him for several minutes before she resumed reading, but Mark caught her glancing over her book to view his progress from time to time.

Two hours later, when dinner was called, Mark held the figurine to his mouth and blew. "This is for you."

Hattie took the soap and turned it over and over in her hands. "It's lovely."

"It's a buffalo."

"It's beautiful, but you should keep it." She held it out for him to take back. "You worked so hard on it."

Mark pressed it back into her hands and smiled. "I want you to have it. For good luck and protection."

"Protection?"

Mark turned his attention to sweeping the shavings into his hand to hide the darkness he suddenly felt. "Buffalo are strong and protective creatures. As long as you have this, you'll be safe."

She brought the carving to her heart and then, with a sob, she threw her arms around him. At the dinner bell, the public car had emptied so the two of them were alone. Every part of him said it was wrong, but Mark let himself indulge in her affection. He wrapped his arms around her and pulled her close. His face settled into the crook of her neck, and he breathed in her scent.

They parted slowly with a million unsaid words hanging in the small space between their mouths. Their eyes locked, and neither moved. He could do it—bridge the gap—connect their lips and tell her everything he'd been dying to say without making a sound. But the car rocked, and the spell was broken.

Chapter Ten

Mark awoke, and for the millionth time, he studied the striped wallpaper separating him from Hattie. How would he let her go? The weight of their separation was like an elephant on his chest. He pressed his fingers to the wall between them and tried to picture her.

They had sat longer than usual in the public car the night before. He couldn't bring himself to leave her, and she didn't make any indication that she'd wanted to retire. So, they'd ridden in silence until Mark became increasingly aware of her against his side. Then she'd fully relaxed and fallen asleep against him. Her beautiful head had rested on his shoulder and her breathing had evened out.

That's what he wanted for the rest of his life. He wanted to watch her eyelashes flutter on her cheeks and listen to her breath while she slept. If only she didn't have a fiancé waiting for her at the other end of the day.

He sighed. By nightfall, Hattie would be married to another man.

Mark tossed the covers aside and sat on the edge of his bunk. He let his elbows rest on his knees and dropped his face into his hands.

He exhaled deeply and rose. Nothing would be accomplished from the bunk in his cabin. As he washed at the basin, he made up his mind. No matter what happened, he would put it all on the line and ask Hattie to change her plans.

Dean was right; what did he have to lose?

Once his mind was made up, he focused on getting ready for the day. He took extra care with his appearance because if all went well, he would be a groom before the sunset.

He didn't let himself consider the consequences because then he would only talk himself out of his new plan. In his haste to pull on his pants, his foot betrayed him and he fell.

God telling you it's a bad idea.

Mark sat on the floor and laughed. He said a quick prayer and then pulled himself up and finished dressing. When he was satisfied with his appearance, he left his compartment with a measure of excitement he hadn't felt in a long time.

He considered knocking on Hattie's door, but before his fist caught wood, he decided that it would be better if he could get a cup of coffee into him and organize his thoughts before he spoke to her. With an extra bounce in his step, he headed toward the dining car.

Luck was not on his side because the first thing he saw when he crossed the gangway was Hattie sipping tea at their usual table. He watched her through the window for several minutes.

She wore a lovely blue dress with little white flowers

on it and she'd taken extra care with her hair. She must've risen quite early and put a lot of effort into her appearance. Her face was bright—glowing, even—like a bride.

Mark's heart sank. She'd taken extra care because she was going to meet her husband. Her expression was peaceful as she stared out the window and absent-mindedly ran her fingertip around the edge of her cup.

He let go of the last of his hope and grabbed the door handle. Hattie caught sight of him three steps before he reached their table. She turned a brilliant smile on him and he had to avert his eyes. The sight of her happiness conjured by another man was like gazing into the sun—it was beautiful, but it hurt.

"Good morning, Mark." Hattie poured coffee from a carafe into his cup. "I asked the waiter to bring coffee."

The coldness that had come over him upon the reality of his crushed dream faded. How could he take his disappointment out on her? Mark lowered himself to his seat and smiled. "Thank you."

Hattie slid the cream across the table and then poured a bit of coffee into her own empty cup. "I couldn't sleep." She shrugged.

Mark winced at the first hot sip of coffee, but the second felt good. He set his cup on the table and spun it around in his hands. "You're pretty excited, huh?"

Hattie lost the blush on her face and turned to stare out of the window. It was as if the wind had left her sails a bit. "I'm not sure excited is the right word." She swallowed and then cleared her throat. "It's just a big day."

Mark studied her profile but couldn't read her emotions. "It is a big day."

Rather than speaking, he picked up his menu and hid his face behind it. "Have you eaten?"

"No, I waited for you."

Mark tipped his menu to look at Hattie, but she was now hidden behind her own menu. The words were a blur, but Mark stared at them and debated once again if he could be selfish enough to ask her to change her plans.

The main problem, as far as he could see, was that Hattie had the softest heart. If he asked her, she would say yes because breaking his heart would kill her. But then she'd forever torture herself for having disappointed Mr. Fletcher. In time, she would grow to resent him for taking her off the course she'd set for herself.

How could he do that to her?

It took them twice as long as usual to order their meals, and then they both silently stared out the window. Their comfortable companionship was not quite so soothing, though. Tension flowed between them and when their food was delivered, they ate like they were having their last meal.

Hattie cleared her throat and dabbed the corners of her mouth with her napkin. "Will we have time for one more game of Colonel?" He looked hopeful but nervous.

Mark checked his watch, though he didn't need to because the minutes were ticking down in his head. "The train will pull into the station in about thirty minutes from now." He wiped his mouth and downed the last of his coffee. "We should probably get your things together. There won't be much time before your stage departs."

Hattie fidgeted with her cuff and swallowed hard. She nodded and took Mark's arm when he offered it.

Mark stood in the open doorway and watched Hattie prepare to leave. She slipped something into her carpet bag and then smoothed the ivory silk dress and settled it neatly on top. His heart squeezed when she ran her hand so softly over the fabric to keep away wrinkles.

"Five minutes," the Porter shouted from the end of the car. "Livingston Station," his voice boomed. "Five minutes."

Hattie and Mark stared across the threshold. The buzz between them tingled on his skin. When the porter returned to call out their arrival at Livingston Station, Mark's heart skipped.

Hattie's eyes were wide and her hands fiddled with the ruffle at the bottom of her sleeve. Mark swallowed his emotions and vowed to make the transition as easy for her as possible. He reached around her and picked up her bag. Then gave her a smile. "Here we go."

Hattie took a deep breath, straightened, and closed her eyes. When she opened her eyes again, she nodded and followed Mark to the exit.

Livingston swallowed them up as the train rattled and hissed its way to the platform. Mark disembarked and then took Hattie's hand to help her down. He wrangled two porters and gave them instructions for her trunk. He tipped them and told them to be quick, as her stage wouldn't wait. The young men were happy to oblige and bounced away immediately.

The smile Mark flashed was sad, but he was tired and couldn't do better—even for her. He watched them disappear into the baggage car and turned back to Hattie. He tried to convince himself that once she was gone, he could start over.

He couldn't fool himself, though. The pain would remain, but the joy would be gone. He wouldn't have the ebb and flow of her presence to keep the tide of trauma at bay.

It's going to rot inside of you.

Mark offered his arm and turned. Every step toward the stagecoach was a fresh stab to his heart. He would be torn apart by the battle waging inside of himself, but he put foot in front of foot and escorted her to his heart's demise.

Tell her, let her break your heart.

But instead, he resigned himself to the fact that their time had expired, and whatever had passed between them was simply his imagination. They were friends with a connection unlike any other and he shouldn't mistake it for love.

The inevitable conclusion of their walk arrived, and they stood beside the stagecoach. Mark gave Hattie's ticket to the driver and settled her carpet bag under her seat. Then he motioned for the two porters to be quick with her trunk.

The only thing left to do was bid her goodbye.

Mark swallowed hard and turned to Hattie. Her eyes were full of tears, and she furiously tugged at her fingertips. Mark took both of her hands in his and stared down into her eyes. "Will you be okay from here?" He glanced inside the stage at the passengers. "It's good that you won't be alone with anyone. There are men and women already inside."

Hattie cleared her throat and nodded. "I made something for you." She pulled a cloth from inside her sleeve and handed it to him. "It's not as impressive as your buffalo, but I wanted to give you something to express my appreciation."

Mark choked up when he ran his fingertip across his name. She'd embroidered it in blue along the bottom edge of one of her handkerchiefs. "Thank you, Hattie." His breaking heart stopped him from further speech.

The driver shouted a warning and climbed to the top of the stage.

"If the ghosts come back to haunt you, I hope this..." she pointed to his name on the cloth in his hand, "reminds you of the good you have done. I am alive because of you."

Then her tears began to fall and Mark couldn't hold back any longer. He cupped her cheek and wiped her tears with his thumbs. "I'll miss you." He took a breath. "Please write to Abigail or Opal and let me know you're safe. If you ever need us, The Maxwell Group will always be there for you." He pressed his lips to her forehead.

The driver broke the moment with a loud whistle and a cough. "We're burnin' daylight." He made a show of checking his watch, and the last of the passengers climbed into the coach.

Mark took Hattie's trembling hand into his and helped her into the coach. Then he closed the door, slapped it twice, and stepped away. As soon as he was out of the path of the wheels, the coach jolted into motion.

He watched the coach until the dust cleared and did the math in his head. It would take three hours for the stage to arrive in Silent Creek, and within the hour after her arrival, she would be married. Mr. Fletcher had detailed their plan in his letter, so Mark had the unfortunate luck to be able to know exactly what time Hattie would arrive at her new home, eat her dinner with her new husband, and retire to her new bed for the night.

Every moment alone was a fresh torture. The dust scuffed up around him as he returned to the train platform.

One more stop and it's all behind you.

Hattie's absence was like a piece of himself had gone missing. He didn't feel right in his own skin.

"HE DITCH YA THEN, DID HE?" A GRAVELLY MALE VOICE broke Hattie from her trance.

"I beg your pardon?" Her muscles went rigid, and she clutched her handkerchief to her chest.

She scanned the coach and looked over each of the five other passengers, relieved to see that most of them were women. Three older women were escorted by a strapping young man. They seemed to mother him and it was cute how he allowed them to fuss over him.

And then there was the speaker. Of course, the only person to acknowledge her with more than a nod would be a filthy, wild-eyed miscreant. Hattie wished she hadn't responded to him because he appeared happy to have gotten her attention.

"Yer man back there." He licked his lips, and Hattie's palms went clammy. "He ditch ya? Yer lookin' a mite heartbroken." The speaker was traveling alone. His gray hair was a chaotic nest about his head, and his long wispy beard bobbed back and forth as he spoke. He shot Hattie a menacing smile that revealed a mouthful of speckled teeth.

She forced herself not to cringe at the sight of him.

"No," she said.

Elizabeth's advice rang in her ears. "Share as little information with strangers as possible."

That's precisely what she planned to do, but the old codger wouldn't let her be.

"Looked like you was sweethearts to me." The man

scratched his head like a flea-ridden dog. "What'd he do?" He leered and grinned. "Spoil your virtue, then send you away, did he?

The other passengers seemed to be as affronted by this man as she was. The woman sitting beside him asked their young escort to change places with her. The shifting of people inside the busy conveyance gave Hattie an excuse not to respond. The ladies shot her comforting expressions, and she found solace in the camaraderie.

Boredom overtook them an hour into their journey, and the ladies became more chatty. They talked between themselves for a while and Hattie learned that they were sisters, and the young man with them was their nephew. He had come to Livingston to escort them to Silent Creek, where their other sister was expecting her first grandchild.

The woman who had exchanged seats looked across the aisle at Hattie. "Pardon us for all the silliness. This will be the first grandchild in the family." She clapped her hands. "I am Mrs. Byrd," she pointed to one sister and then the other, "Mrs. Drummund, and Mrs. Leslie. And this..." she smiled and patted the strapping man's knee, "is our Bobby."

The tall man grinned at his aunt. "Robert White." He held his hand for Hattie to shake but pulled it back when she flinched. They all reacted to her reflex but said nothing.

The dirty man across from her perked up, though, and studied her with beady little eyes and a disconcerting grin.

"Excuse me," Hattie said. "I'm Hattie Thompson." She extended her hand to Mr. White and smiled graciously when he took it.

Mrs. Drummund leaned forward and gave Hattie a motherly smile. "You are pretty as a picture, dear."

The attention made Hattie shift uncomfortably in her seat. "Thank you."

Mrs. Leslie sat beside Hattie and rubbed her hand. "Where are you going, sweetheart?"

"Silent Creek." Hattie didn't like the glint in the stranger's eye. He was the only one who hadn't given his name, and he seemed to delight in the discomfort of those around him.

Mrs. Drummund leaned across her sister every time she spoke to Hattie, but Mrs. Leslie didn't seem to mind. "Oh, good. We'll be able to help you find your way."

Hattie smiled at the sweet woman. "How kind."

The chatter turned to reminiscing between the sisters, with Mr. White giving little updates on changes to the town. The ladies had grown up in Silent Creek and moved to Livingston with their husbands when their children were little. They told Hattie stories about the town in its youth and tossed in a bit of gossip about people she might run into—just to spice it up a bit.

Mrs. Byrd wriggled her eyebrows at Hattie when the ladies had gotten themselves quite riled up. "Who was the handsome young man that left you on the Stage?" She squealed and her sisters joined in. "He reminded me of my dear departed Shep."

Mrs. Drummund kicked her sister's foot and laughed. "Your dear departed Shep never looked like that a day in his life." She let a hearty laugh out and Mrs. Leslie joined in.

It was fun to watch Mr. White try to hold a straight face with all of his aunts giggling like schoolgirls. He looked at Hattie and finally cracked. "Uncle Shep wasn't more than five and a half feet tall," he chuckled when his aunt elbowed him, "and he was at least as big around as he was tall."

Mrs. Byrd waved a handkerchief and dabbed her eyes. The tears she dried were tears of joy because she continued to giggle. "I meant the sweet look on his face reminded me of my dear old Shep." She sighed. "So, was he your sweetheart?"

Hattie's heartbreak must have shown on her face because all three women exchanged their jolly expressions for sympathetic frowns. Hattie faked a smile. "Mr. Webb was only my escort."

"Why not escort ya all the way, huh? Let a pretty little thing like you travel three hours by yerself," He tutted, "the west is a dangerous place."

Hattie shrunk into herself and prayed the man would stop speaking to her. Her mind went to the bison in her reticule and she calmed herself.

He watched her with a keen eye until she settled and then addressed her again. "Want me to escort ya? I'll keep ya real safe," he laughed again, and Hattie's heart nearly left her chest. Visions of dark rooms and other leering grins overwhelmed her, and she covered her face.

Mrs. Leslie made a crude shushing sound at the man. "You stop that right now." She glared at him under disapproving eyebrows. "You leave this poor girl alone or I will have our Bobby get the driver to stop and put you out right here in the wilderness."

The man shrunk into his oversized coat and glared, but he didn't address Hattie again. The company grew quiet and Hattie was certain they were all thinking about what would make her react in such a way.

She stared out the window and miles of nothingness stretched to the horizon. She'd never seen such desolation in her life. Her insides matched the outside. It hadn't been long, but she desperately missed Mark.

Hattie was relieved the old man had exited at the first stop. She regretted telling him her stop, but was glad nothing malicious had come of it.

The sisters chattered with their nephew chiming in from time to time, but Hattie let her mind drift. Before she knew it, the sisters were gathering their reticules and straightening their hats because they were rolling into Silent Creek.

The coach rocked to a stop and Hattie's heart quit beating.

Chapter Eleven

No amount of deep breathing would settle Hattie's nerves when the Coachman pulled open the door and announced their arrival in Silent Creek. Her knee bounced and her hands shook as she waited for the others to disembark from the stage.

When there was no possible way to delay any longer, Hattie closed her eyes and took one last deep breath. She pulled her carpetbag close to her chest and said a prayer for safety.

Then Hattie stretched out a trembling hand and accepted the coachman's support. The gracious man didn't rush her, and when her feet were on solid ground, he offered a reassuring squeeze before releasing her. Hattie tried to smile, but her face twisted into what felt like a grimace. He tipped his hat and then turned to help unload the luggage. Hattie's skin was slick with cool sweat when she finally raised her head and glanced around.

The sun seemed brighter than in Boston, and the air was cleaner. She shielded her eyes as they adjusted. Mrs. Byrd was henning over another woman that could only be her other sister. The lady had the same face as Mrs. Leslie and Hattie wondered if they were twins. The group smiled and waved to Hattie.

"If you need anything, dear," Mrs. Drummond called over her shoulder as she walked away, "come and find us."

As they rounded the corner, one of the ladies shouted a promise to keep Hattie in their prayers. They were a bright spot in her trip, and Hattie was happy to have met them.

Hattie wished she could stall forever. One distraction after another would be wonderful because then she would never have to meet and marry a man who was not Mark Webb.

Every second added to her anxiety though, and finally, Hattie's heart was beating so fast that her entire body vibrated with nerves. She scanned the depot for Mr. Fletcher.

No men approached, and no one appeared to be searching for her. What if he didn't come? Her vision see-sawed and she went weak in the knees. The coachman and a stranger righted her and sat her upon her trunk.

"Miss? You all right?" The coachman patted her on the back and then stepped away without waiting for an answer. "Just sit there a minute and you'll be jus fine."

Hattie swallowed and tried to breathe deeply. "Thank you. I'm sorry." She straightened her hat and smoothed her skirt. "I'm weary from travel." She looked around again, but not seeing any wealthy-looking ranchers coming her way, she added, "I'm looking for Quinn Fletcher. Do you know him?"

The stranger who had helped the coachman catch Hattie clapped his hands and rubbed them together excitedly. "Quinn ain't comin', Hattie."

Hattie stuttered over syllables but couldn't form words. What man could pay her train fare and then abandon her? It was her nightmare.

The stranger pulled the straw hat from his head and pressed it to his heart, but there was no sadness in his expression. Instead, he appeared to be quite excited.

Hattie took in the measure of this man who not only took joy in her abandonment but had just had his hands on her. He was too tall and broad. She hadn't noticed before, but as he hovered over her, his size was oppressive. Mark was a tall man, but he'd always respected her space. This man forced her to crane her neck to look at him.

His mud-brown hair hung in greasy tangles around his shoulders, and he had a large scraggly beard that could double as a home for woodland creatures. He must have enjoyed her study of him because he grinned widely, revealing thin teeth with more missing than present. Dirt darkened the skin of his hands and face, giving his eyes a feral and menacing stare. While his appearance was unpleasantly equal to his odor, what frightened her most was his casual usage of her name.

Hattie stood and braced herself on a railing. "Excuse me, sir, please. How do you know my name? Are you a friend of Mr. Fletcher's?"

Hattie was relieved to have given herself some space, but then crushed when he rounded her trunk and stood too close again. "You talk so sweet... Oh, excuse me, sir." He raised his voice in a high, mock female tone.

Hattie stepped back, and he didn't follow. It wasn't enough space, but she was grateful for every inch between them. She searched the street for an escape. If Mr. Fletcher wasn't coming, she needed a new plan.

"Sure, I knew 'im. He was my brother. I got his estate

when he died." He grinned that abhorrent grin again and snapped his suspenders with his thumbs. He didn't seem upset about the loss of his brother, only proud of his inheritance.

"Are you saying he's de—dead?" She could hardly get the words out. Hattie struggled between horror and subtle relief. She wasn't engaged. She could marry Mark. There was nothing in her way. She scanned the street again and tried to decide where to start.

The stranger reached for Hattie's hand, but she pulled back. "Let's go," he said with a wave of his arm for her to follow him.

"Go?" Hattie's mind had turned to thoughts of Mark. She hadn't even considered that the dirty mountain man would be more than just a messenger. "Where do you want me to go?"

He raised his eyebrows, as if to suggest that she was daft. "To get married 'course."

"Wait, no. What?" Hattie jumped away from him and clutched her carpetbag. "I was to marry Mr. Fletcher, not, um." She didn't even know the name of the man who was trying to marry her. It was absurd, like the moment when a dream distorts from reality and the dreamer realizes they are dreaming.

"I AM Mr. Fletcher." He took a step forward, and Hattie retreated again. He extended his hand, but Hattie couldn't take it. "Name's Travis, Travis Fletcher." He shrugged when she didn't take his hand. "You'll still be Mrs. Fletcher." He laughed and slapped his knee. "Shew-wee, we're gonna have fun."

"I cannot marry you, sir." Hattie's voice shook, but she remembered Elizabeth's advice to stand up for herself and not be pushed to do anything she didn't want to do. "I don't know you."

"You ain't know Quinn neither. I got Quinn's ranch. I got Quinn's money. And now I get you." He ticked items off on his hand and then pointed his beefy finger at Hattie. He stepped forward and crowded her again. "My brother's money paid for you, so now you're mine."

The words were too familiar and Hattie stumbled backward. Her legs hit the edge of her trunk and she plopped down. She'd been sold again. Her vision wobbled, but she bit back the tears that threatened. Elizabeth had told her to be prepared for anything, and she thought she was.

She thought wrong.

The world around her teetered on its axis and she gripped the side of her trunk to steady herself. The only thing she knew for sure was that she couldn't marry Travis Fletcher. Everything about the man made her skin crawl, but fear of his reaction to her rejection paralyzed her.

After an eternity of searching for the right words, Hattie said, "Surely, you understand that a lady needs time to consider these matters?" She spoke slowly and lightly, hoping Travis was more reasonable than he seemed.

"I don't see no reason to waste no time." He wiggled his eyebrows at her and her biggest fear was that his brazen demeanor could turn violent. "I like what I see."

Hattie stood and smoothed her dress, trying to buy herself time and space from Mr. Fletcher. "Is there a boardinghouse? I have enough money to pay my own way while we sort this out."

"No." The instant she reached the limit of his patience was obvious. His face went from a leering smile to a dark scowl. "We're gettin' married right now." He lunged for her arm.

Clouds of dust kicked up around her feet as she dodged him. He chased her around her trunk once but stopped when Hattie yelped and people seemed to take notice. The muscles in his jaw ticked and his nostrils flared as he stood and glared at Hattie.

Hattie drew on a well of hope she'd filled at The Rose Dunn House. She had people and possibilities, and she had a man who loved her only a few hours away. There wasn't a doubt in her mind that Mark would come if she asked, and she had no reason not to ask now. She just needed a way to get away from this, Mr. Fletcher, long enough to send a telegram and buy a little time.

Hattie held up both hands. "Please. I know it seems as if I didn't know Mr. Fletcher, but I corresponded with him before I accepted his proposal. I had a letter from his minister. I read references written on his behalf. I did know a little of him." Hattie had no idea where her words were coming from, but she was glad they were there. "I cannot marry a man I don't know at all."

Mr. Fletcher blew out a frustrated breath and growled. "Ah alright. But this ain't over. My money paid for you." He pointed to a rickety wagon attached to a donkey. "Jeremiah will take your belongin's." He walked over and climbed on the wagon with his back to her.

Hattie looked around, but no explanation was coming. "I'm sorry. Who is Jeremiah?"

Travis spat a brown glob onto the ground, and Hattie's stomach turned. He looked over his shoulder with a roll of his eyes. "Jeremiah's my ass."

She had never heard of someone giving an animal such

a name before. She glanced between the donkey and the man, then back at her luggage.

"Come on, I ain't got all day."

It was then she realized he was not going to help her with her things. She placed her small trunk on top of the larger one and dragged them to the cart. It was by pure luck or the help of God that she managed to lift the larger of the two trunks into the wagon bed. The feeling gave her some semblance of pride and confidence. Drawing from the stories she'd heard of Sarah, she tried to picture herself as a real Western woman.

"Hurry up!" He barked at her.

Hattie dropped her carpetbag onto the wagon beside her trunks. Travis snapped the reins and everything she owned in this world, including her money, bounced out of reach.

"Follow this road. Boardinghouse is all the way at the end." He sparked the beast of burden into motion and didn't look back. "Hi-ya Jeremiah. Move on ass!"

THE MILES FLEW BY OUTSIDE THE WINDOW, BUT MARK DIDN'T care. He had no excitement about arriving home. He only had heartbreak. The older couple he'd seen a few times laughed at something he couldn't hear. The happy sound hurt because he would never hear Hattie's laugh again.

He watched them for a while. It would have been sweet to grow old with Hattie. He would have loved to see her through life. They could have raised children and then watched grandchildren together. He'd lost an entire lifetime to his damn honor.

He turned once again to stare out the window.

The steady clack of the wheels suddenly exploded into a screeching scream. The train car jolted, bounced, and then the world outside the window spun. Mark's shoulder crashed into the corner of a lantern before he hit the ceiling, and then in an instant he was on the floor. There was no making sense of anything as his body was thrown around. His arm hit the edge of a seat and Mark grabbed hold. He clung to the cushion with all of his strength and when the train stopped sliding and rolling, he dropped down to the ceiling.

The impact knocked the wind out of him, and Mark gasped for air. He shook his head and tried to clear the overwhelming nausea. Mark groaned and rolled over. Every part of his body hurt, but after a quick evaluation, he didn't think anything was broken.

Mark looked out the window and watched people scattering like ants. Some ran toward the overturned car, but most were trying to get away. The smell of smoke and copper filled his nostrils. That's what finally got him moving. He needed to get everyone off the train.

He pulled himself up too fast and leaned against the wall of the train to steady himself. He looked left and right and assessed the damage. The car was upside down and several men were crawling and calling to their loved ones. Several men were pulling at the jammed door and trying to get out. A woman wailed over the body of another woman who was clearly dead. He saw no flames to go along with the smoke he smelled. It was only a matter of time, though. He needed to get moving.

The elderly woman he'd been watching lay unresponsive beside her husband, so Mark made his way to them.

The old man gathered his wife into his arms and rocked her back and forth. "Clara? Oh Clara, please wake up." His voice choked with sobs. Her head had a large laceration and the pool of dark around her did not bode well.

"We need to stop the bleeding." Mark rushed to them and lay her back down. Then he pulled a lost shawl from nearby and pressed it to the wound. Mark placed two fingers on her neck and prayed. Her pulse was painfully weak and slowly flickered out as life extinguished.

His eyes met the man's and shook his head. "I'm sorry."

The older gentleman cracked, and he threw his body over his wife, pleading with God.

Mark had to move on; others needed help. He stood and, with a clearer head, took another look around. There was no order and nothing productive was happening.

"We all need to get out of here. It's not safe," he shouted. His sudden command silenced the cries of the injured and the wailing of the mourners. All eyes turned to him. With a pounding, head and aching body, Mark moved to the middle of the train car.

"All of you who are not injured need to help the wounded off. When it is safe, we will move the dead." Mark walked toward the door that was still jammed closed. "We need to work together." Mark's heart slowed as he took control of the situation. Later, he would be able to feel all the things he was repressing, but for now, he needed action.

"You two." Mark pointed to a middle aged man and a younger man.

"Help me get the door opened." The wood around the door had become pinched and splintered together. Mark pushed and pulled at the boards until his hands bled, but they wouldn't move. With the help of the other two men, they broke the leg from a busted bench and used it to pry away at the boards. After working on the task for a while, the door finally came free of the frame. Mark threw his shoulder into it and in a few minutes, they were able to make a clear and safe pathway out. Mark broke free first into the clear sunlight and prayed a quick thanks to God for letting them make it out.

A young boy walked up to him and tugged at his arm. "My mother needs help. Her leg is broken. She can't walk." He pulled Mark's arm and led him back into the train car.

Mark motioned to two young men from the crowd and they followed him. They helped the woman up and supported her between them. She screamed in pain as the two men each hooked one arm through one of hers. The boys were clumsy in their actions at first, but there was no better way to untangle her from the seat that had fallen on top of her. Once she was righted, she settled as they repositioned her and supported her leg.

The young men carried her between them and her boy bounced behind, shouting a never-ending stream of cautions and directions at them. Mark helped them through the door and turned back to the car to help others.

The old man still kneeled beside his dear wife. Mark gently pulled at the man's arm and he stood. His face was blank as he followed Mark from the train car.

Mark and the old man were the last to leave the car. The sun was bright, and the man squinted until someone came and took him from Mark. He watched the old man being led to a stump and then turned when it was clear he would be safe. The wounded were being tended to. Mark assumed the man was a doctor who had been on a part of the train that had not derailed. He carried a doctor's bag and stopped briefly at one patient after another, giving directions to whoever was taking care of the patient before moving on.

Mark turned his eyes back toward the tracks. Two of the three passenger cars had come loose from the track and were toppled in the field. One car was upside down and the other two were tipped on their sides.

The conductor came huffing down the length of the train and announced that men had been dispatched on foot to the next station to seek help. "The station is a two-hour walk. With any luck, they will have the wagons here by dark." The conductor was tall, thin, and neat. His voice was reassuring and Mark was glad to know help would arrive sooner rather than later.

It wasn't safe for anyone in these parts after dark. They would be vulnerable to gangs and looters. Not to mention wild animals.

The conductor waved people close and then pushed the group toward the two remaining cars. "It's not a good idea to stay out here in the cold." He pulled the door open to the first of the two remaining train cars. "Bring everyone inside and let's get them warm."

Mark pitched in and took the arm of a man with a badly sprained ankle. In a short time, everyone had been moved inside again and seated in the open cars. They were a sad, silent group of people trying to process the trauma of their shared experience.

A chubby, suited man walked around celebrating with whiskey for all. His red cheeks suggested he'd already helped himself plenty. Mark understood his relief, but his gleefulness was distasteful for those mourning. He scowled at the too-jolly man, but he didn't say no to the whiskey.

Mark was trying to escape the darkness, but it seemed to be following him. He pulled the handkerchief Hattie had given him from his pocket and pressed it to his lips. The faint lavender scent of Hattie lingered on the cloth. He imagined she was married by now or would be soon. Her life was already changing, and he was stuck, still surrounded by death and pain.

He downed the whiskey and raised his glass. The jovial man gladly poured him another measure. "That's the spirit!"

Mark smiled grimly, then his eyes landed on Clara's husband sitting alone with a stone face. They had moved the bodies into one of the overturned cars and covered them with linens.

He tucked Hattie's handkerchief into his pocket and went over to talk to the old man. Mark offered him a whiskey, but the old man declined.

"I'm more of a port man," he sighed. His eyes shifted to his hands, where he nervously picked at his fingers atop a walking stick.

Marked nodded. "Mark Webb." He offered his hand.

The old man shook it. "Bernard Dodge—Bernie's fine."

"I'm sorry, about—" He couldn't finish his sentence.

"We were married for forty years. What am I going to do without her?" He looked at Mark with tears in his eyes.

Mark hung his head and shook it. He couldn't imagine multiplying his feelings for Hattie by forty years and then losing her.

The old man sighed. "Forty years and we never left our hometown. I never wanted to. Never trusted these beasts." He banged on the floor with the metal head of his walking stick.

"Our son, our only son, Matt, moved out west and got

married. His wife just had our first grandchild. Clara begged me to move here, to be with them. I couldn't say no to her, could I?" His face begged Mark to tell him that he had done the right thing.

When Mark didn't speak, Bernie continued as if he had. "I wish I had told her no. She would still be here." He pulled a handkerchief from his pocket and wiped his eyes under his spectacles. "How can I live without her?"

Mark remained quiet. He had no words for this man. He swallowed the lump in his throat and put a reassuring hand on Bernie's back.

"Have you ever been in love?" Bernie asked.

"Uh—" The question caught Mark off guard.

Bernie smiled. "The young lady you were traveling with, what happened to her?"

"She departed for another town by stagecoach two stops ago."

"But you loved her?" His eyebrows raised, "Clara suspected you did. She fancied herself a bit of a match-maker back home." He laughed fondly, his eyes seeming to watch something play out in his memory.

"I always used to say, Clara darling, we shouldn't meddle in other's affairs. But she couldn't help herself. That was my wife for you, so vibrant and keen." Tears fell, catching in the lifelines on his cheek.

The man wiped at his face and took a shaking, deep breath. Then he looked at Mark again. "Was she right then?"

"Pardon?"

"Clara. Was she right? Do you love that young lady?"

Mark's eyes fell to the ground. "Yes." His emotions were too raw to deny the truth.

Bernie flashed a smile before falling back into a line. "Why did you let her go?"

"She was promised to another."

"Ah, I see." Bernie leaned his cane against his shoulder and leaned forward with his elbows on his knees and stared at the floor. "I was not a man of honor like you."

Mark watched his profile. Bernie smiled, but he seemed to be staring back in time. "What do you mean?"

The man propped his hands on his walking stick and rested his chin on top of them.

"When I asked Clara to marry me, she was set to marry another man." He chuckled. "I had waited and waited, talking myself out of it. The night before her wedding, I went to her bedroom window, which she shared with three sisters. I didn't care. I needed to ask her." He sat up and ran his hand through his hair. "Boy, did she think I was mad, but she didn't say no. Oh, the scandal we caused." Bernie wiped his eyes again. "See, her betrothed was the son of the mine owner. His father practically owned our entire town." He laughed and smacked his knee. "And she married me. I had nothing to my name. I wanted to be a tailor but worked as a logger until I earned up enough to open my own shop," He smiled.

Bernie patted Mark on the knee. "Do you think it's too late? Too late to go get her?"

Mark nodded, unable to speak.

"Well, that's too bad. I think she loved you too." Bernie tucked the handkerchief into his pocket again and banged his walking stick on the floor. "My Clara wasn't the only one with a keen eye." His smile quivered.

The two men sat together talking until help arrived. The passengers loaded in groups onto wagons to the next station. It was a long ride, and they required several trips to transport all the passengers.

Mark urged Bernie to go on the first wagon and they parted ways with a handshake.

Dawn was breaking when Mark finally arrived at the neighboring station. He had helped clear the tracks and moved the bodies onto a wagon to be carried to town.

He checked the station's clock. The early train headed east would arrive soon, but the engineer was rerouting it west while they repaired the damaged eastbound tracks.

Mark purchased a ticket for the stagecoach and sat down for breakfast at the boardinghouse. As the day came and went, he found himself in Hope with a heavy heart.

As long as he lived, he would never get over her.

Chapter Twelve

Hope grew larger as Mark watched out the stagecoach window. He normally would have ridden up top for fresh air but it was still quite nippy out, so he was jammed inside with five other people. It was a miserable way to travel and as soon as the coach stopped, Mark pushed the door open and stepped to the ground.

He groaned and stretched his back, and took a look around. Nothing ever changed. He smiled as his boots kicked up a familiar cloud of earth. Though spring had come, the rains would not grace the land for another month or two. It was arid but refreshing after the stale coach ride. Heartbroken or not, it was good to be home.

The sound of hooves trotting drew his eye and a grin spread across his face.

"Look what the cat dragged in," Will called down from the wagon with a laugh. "I thought maybe we'd lost you to the city forever." He set the brake, hopped off the wagon, and embraced Mark with a brotherly hug.

Mark held Will tight for a moment and then banged him on the back and stepped away. "It's good to see you, brother."

Will was a few inches shorter than Mark and he'd gained a few pounds around the middle since his marriage, but he was a sight for sore eyes.

"We expected you yesterday and when you didn't arrive, Iris was in a right state." Will took the hat from his head and banged it on his thigh. A dust cloud exploded around his legs. "I told her not to worry, but you know her." He patted Mark on the back and reached for one of the bags on the ground at Mark's feet. Will continued as he walked back toward the wagon. "She made me promise to come straight away this morning to check the wire."

"We derailed," Mark said. He grabbed his other bag and dropped it into the wagon bed.

"Shit! You seem alright though." Will looked closer and Mark shifted under the scrutiny. "Was it bad?" he asked.

Mark's lips formed a line and Will read his eyes. "Are there any good derailments?"

Will nodded sadly. "I guess not. How many dead?"

Mark shifted and leaned against the back of the wagon with his arms crossed. "Six." He sighed. "Could be more now. A dozen or so were banged up pretty bad." He shrugged in an attempt to minimize the experience and get away from Will's sorry expression. "I made it out by pure luck." He looked down, heavy with guilt for all the times he managed to survive while others didn't.

"You're here now." Will grabbed him by the shoulders and shook him. "Cheer up. Iris won't leave you alone if she sees your face like that."

Some of the weight dropped away and Mark laughed.

"We've got everything fixed up at Scott's place for ya." Will climbed onto the driver's bench and Mark pulled himself up on the other side. "Starting out at Scott's place is like a rite of passage round here; we all stayed there at some time or other." Will laughed and snapped the reins.

They rode to the sound of hooves and wagon wheels. Mark was lost in his old heartbreak instead of focusing on his new one. They'd lost their brother, Scott, years ago, but the hurt was always as fresh as the day he'd died.

Mark took in the town, rushed with memories, good and bad. Then Hattie crossed his mind. He wanted to ask if Will had heard anything from her but didn't want to give himself away. He'd get it out of one of the women later.

The forty-five-minute ride to the cabin seemed to pass in a moment. Will filled Mark in on all the recent ranch news as they followed the well-worn road, but Mark's mind was hours away with Hattie. He tried to make appropriate responses to Will's conversation, but in his head, he was wondering if Hattie's new husband was what she'd hoped for. Was he gentle and patient? Was he respectful?

Was she happy?

Before he knew it, Will pulled up in front of Scott's cabin and they both stared at it sadly for a moment. It would always be Scott's, no matter how many years passed. Iris stepped out onto the porch and Mark's sadness drifted away. At the sight of the men, she covered her mouth with her hands and squealed. Mark smiled and forced back a tear. He hadn't seen her do that since her twin sister Rose had died. He jumped down to the ground and met her on the porch.

Iris wrapped her arms around his middle and squeezed him tight. He hadn't realized how much he'd missed her until then. Mark held her and pressed a kiss to the top of her head. Iris finally stepped back and wiped her eyes with the edge of her apron. "I'm so glad you're home safe."

A warm sensation filled Mark; one he had not felt since he was a boy. When he had a nightmare, his mother would take him into her arms and stroke his forehead. She'd whisper in his ear that he was safe and run slow circles with her fingertip on his face. When she died, he thought he'd never have that again, but then he'd met Iris and she felt like his mother. "It's nice to see you too, Iris."

Mark turned to grab his bags, but Will already had both in his hands. Mark and Iris followed Will into the cabin, and Mark's stomach instantly growled when the aroma of food hit him.

Will laughed. "I can't stay for lunch." He set the bags on the side of the bed and turned around. "I'll let Maggie and the others know that you're here." He snickered. "I wouldn't be too surprised if you get a few visitors today."

Mark smiled and hugged Will again. "Thanks, brother."

Iris got busy in the kitchen, so Mark took a moment to find where everything was in Scott's house. He unpacked his bags and tossed another log on the fire while Iris set out lunch.

The cabin had only two rooms, but there was a food cellar under the kitchen. When they'd dug the cellar, they'd discovered an old cave leading away from the house. Scott had been so excited about the cave and the energetic young boys they used to be had dug and dug until the tunnel was cleared enough to walk through. It had been their shortcut to the creek until they'd dug the well, and then it was only used once after that. It was used the night Scott had died to get his new wife out of the house. The tunnel had saved her life. Mark was lost in his study of the trap door to the cellar that he didn't notice Iris waiting for him until she cleared her throat.

Mark looked up in surprise and then laughed. He stepped to the sink and washed his hands.

The dining table sat four, much smaller than the grand table in the dining hall of The Rose Dunn House. Iris set out cold cuts of chicken, beans, corn cakes, and fresh milk on the table and they sat across from one another. The smell of the warm corn cakes made Mark salivate, and he realized he'd missed breakfast. He had been too caught up with everything going on to think of eating. His stomach roared as he sat down.

Iris eyed him suspiciously as he made his plate. "You reek of a heavy heart, my boy."

He froze, a spoonful of beans suspended above his heaping plate. After a second, he relaxed again. "I'm fine."

"Unburden yourself before you see the others, otherwise those girls will eat you alive." Iris dabbed at her mouth with her napkin and then settled it into her lap. "Best do it now."

A slight laugh escaped him, and he took another bite. He bought himself a moment because he wouldn't dare speak with a full mouth in front of Iris. "You're too sharp, Iris."

She smiled, her eyebrows lifting, pressing him to continue.

Mark sighed. He wasn't ready to talk about Hattie, but

he knew Iris too well. She wouldn't let him go without baring his soul. Maybe she was right, maybe it was better for him to tell her than to be berated by one of the others.

He was too tired to mask his feelings. He was tired of bearing so much tragedy and pain. If not to Iris, then to whom could he entrust his feelings? He took a mouthful of corn cake, allowing its buttery sweetness to lift his spirits.

"Alright," he took another bite and savored it. Iris didn't rush him. That was the thing he loved most about her. "You've heard about Hattie?"

"The girl who wasn't dead?" She hit that nail on the head.

"Yes," Mark smiled. "The girl who wasn't dead."

"Sure." Iris waited patiently for him to continue, but when he didn't, she added, "You love her." It wasn't a question. Iris just knew things like this. Sometimes before he did.

"Yes." Mark restrained a smile. Iris could pick through his soul like a stack of old books. It certainly made unburdening himself easier.

"Did you tell her?"

"No."

Iris sighed and shook her head. "Well, then it can't be helped." She clapped her hands together and set them in her lap.

"What do you mean?"

"You missed your chance. Now you have to move on." She added coffee to her mug and then gave him a hard stare. "You know how to reach Mrs. Phillips." When Mark's head snapped up, Iris giggled. "It's time for you to find a wife, dear boy. You're ready."

"How can you be so sure?"

"Do you doubt me?" Iris raised her eyebrows in a challenge but couldn't hold the serious expression long.

They both laughed, and Mark felt a bit better.

"It makes sense for you to feel connected to Hattie, but God has a plan and he sent you on separate paths." Iris came around the table and stood beside Mark. She took him into her arms and pressed her cheek to the top of his head. "There is someone out there for you, my sweet boy."

Mark nodded his head, wishing to change the subject, but knowing he couldn't until Iris was satisfied. "I'll think about it." When Iris's eyebrows shot up and she tipped her head, he threw both hands in the air and laughed. "I promise."

Apparently satisfied, Iris began clearing the table. "Alright, enough of that." She waved a towel in the air as if to clear away the emotions. "Tell me about your trip. What held you up?" Mark told her about the derailment, leaving out the death toll.

They chatted about lighter topics as they cleaned up together and set the kitchen to right. Then Iris demanded a ride home and ordered him to go and visit his brothers. After all these years, it still felt good to call them his brothers.

TRAVIS HOPPED OFF THE WAGON IN FRONT OF THE boardinghouse. With his thumbs in his belt loops, he stood watching Hattie as she ambled down the street.

Silent Creek was quiet and Hattie found it unusual given the time of day. She would have expected to see women and children bustling about, but there was no one. The building facades were all new and freshly painted.

The air was clean and crisp, unlike Boston, where the air always held the ghost of dampness and sea. The boarding-house was a fine-looking place, and Hattie imagined the price would quickly eat through her money.

One look at Travis and she was happy to pay whatever it costs to be away from him.

The brisk walk left her slightly winded. Sweat curled and frizzed the hair around her forehead, and her cheeks burned with red. Hattie hated to make her acquaintance with the boardinghouse keepers in such a state, but Travis had given her no choice.

"I was thinkin'," Travis started the moment she was within earshot. "You don't be needin' to stay here. You can stay at my old place. No need to waste money."

The boardinghouse door opened and a man and woman stepped out. They were young for keepers of such an establishment, Hattie guessed they couldn't have been much older than five and thirty.

"Travis." The man said, his tone unwelcoming.

"Don't Travis me like that. I ain't done nothin'." He put his hands up in the air, touting his innocence.

The woman stood with her arms crossed behind the man. They both glared at Travis and Hattie's already pounding heart sped up. What kind of man inspired such a reaction from his neighbors?

"Look, I ain't here to cause no trouble. 'Sides, we both know if I'm wanting trouble—I know how to find it." He puffed his chest and stood straighter, leaning toward the man. Travis was thin, the kind of thin one gets from drinking more than they eat. Despite his scrappy appearance, he was still a large man.

"Get on outta here." The man didn't back down. "We don't have any rooms for you here."

Travis spit. "This is my town, boy. Don't you forget it. You seem to think that 'cause your daddy died, and gave you this place that makes you somethin'?" He spat again, and Hattie's stomach revolted. "I owned this place long before your mama spread her legs."

Hattie held her hand over her mouth. What kind of man spoke in such a way? Especially in front of ladies.

The boardinghouse keeper lunged for Travis, but his wife held him back.

"He's not worth it, Simon," she said with a shaking voice.

"Look Simon," Travis said his name like an insult, "I wouldn't be here if my lovely lady didn't want a place to stay while we get to know each other 'fore the weddin'." Hattie's face heated so fast that she was sure she'd catch flames.

Their heads snapped toward Hattie and both of their mouths hung open in surprise. A rush of relief washed over her as she found herself in the company of two decent-looking people.

Hattie stepped forward and pressed her palms together as if in prayer. In fact, she was praying for the new people to take her in and shield her from Travis. "I mean to cause you no distress," Hattie said. "If you would be so kind as to rent me a room, I assure you I can pay." She stepped forward, prepared to beg if she had to. "I can help around the house. I'm a decent cook and a hard worker. Please, I am here without friends or connections."

Travis didn't seem to register her words, as no protest came from him at the mention of no connections.

The couple eyed her with concern. The woman waved Hattie to come up onto the porch. "Please, come in. Are those your bags?" She pointed to the trunks on Travis's cart.

Hattie nodded and lifted her carpetbag from the wagon. Simon collected her trunks and walked them into the house like they weighed nothing at all. The woman rushed Hattie inside, and Simon turned and barred the door behind them.

Travis raged outside. "Let me in. You can't keep me from my woman." Hattie watched him through the window. He kicked the door and took his hat from his head. With his hat in his hand, he pointed it at the house and shouted, "Damn it, she's mine! We're going to be married in two weeks. I tell you, let me in!"

"You're not welcome." The man grabbed a shotgun from the pegs above the door and stood in the window where Travis could see him. "Don't make me call the sheriff!"

"You can't keep my woman from me." Travis still shouted, but the sight of the gun seemed to have made him back down a bit. Hattie hoped he would just go away and leave her alone, but she knew from experience it wouldn't be so easy.

"If the young lady wants your company, she is free to have it OUTSIDE and by her own accord."

Muffled curses came through the door and Travis kicked it one more time before taking off.

Hattie's heart lightened as the dust kicked up behind Travis's retreating wagon.

Hattie stuck her hand in her pocket and rubbed the buffalo Mark had carved. She took a deep breath and tried to sort out her jumbled emotions. Too much had happened in such a short time, and Hattie was ready to crumble. How could life turn upside down so quickly?

A cough behind her drew her out of her musings. Hattie turned to the couple, who looked as mystified as she felt.

"Miss? We do not mean to pry, but..." the woman spoke, looking to the man for support, "how are you acquainted with Travis Fletcher?"

"I am not acquainted with him." Hattie rubbed at the carving in her pocket and hoped these people would help her. "I am Hattie Thompson."

The woman wiped her hand on her apron, which must be out of habit because she hadn't touched anything. "Aren't we dull? I'm Edna Oakley, and this is my husband, Simon."

Hattie shook their hands in turn. "It's lovely to meet you, really." Hattie didn't have words to express her gratitude for them. "I arrived on the stage today, and Mr. Fletcher was there waiting for me. I have come from Boston to be a mail-order bride for Mr. Quinn Fletcher."

Edna gasped and pressed a hand to her chest. "You poor thing." She looked around and suddenly seemed to remember her manners. "Please sit down." Edna settled herself and Hattie in the living room and sent her husband to bring in more firewood and to make sure Travis had truly left. "Quinn was a good man. His death was quite sudden and the entire town is quite shaken up about it."

Hattie pressed a handkerchief to her eyes. Her emotions were overwhelming her and soon she would have no control over them at all.

Edna squeezed her hand. "If you were here to marry Quinn, why is Travis claiming to be your intended?"

"He seems to think he has some claim to marry me, though I do not wish to marry him. He seems to believe he inherited me, along with his brother's estate." Just saying the words was enough to release the dam and let the waterfall. Hattie sobbed into her handkerchief and Edna patiently waited for her to catch her breath.

When Hattie had settled down, Edna continued the conversation. "Travis inherited the Fletcher estate?" She shook her head and wrung her hands.

Simon returned and froze. He seemed unsure of how to proceed with Hattie in such a state, but when Edna patted the seat beside her, he took it.

"Travis told her that he inherited Quinn's estate and since she came as Quinn's mail-order bride, he believes he has inherited her as well."

"That's not right." Simon tipped his head. "I'm not even going to comment on the ridiculousness of a person thinking he inherited another person. But what about Harlan? Surely, Quinn left the place to his son," Simon said with certainty.

"I only know what Travis told me." Hattie straightened and cleared the last of the tears from her face. Simon's comment about the absurdity of Travis inheriting any sort of power over her was encouraging. She couldn't care less about the line of the Fletcher estate, she just wanted the freedom to travel back to Mark. "Travis really can't force me to marry him, then?"

"Don't trust a word that scoundrel says." Edna affected a warm smile ubiquitous to all kindly innkeepers. "Let's get you settled in and fed. You're safe with us." She stood and nodded decidedly. "Travis knows better than to come here, but Simon will keep an eye out."

Simon sent a sympathetic smile and nodded.

"We'll put you in the room right beside ours, so if you find yourself in any trouble, we should be able to hear you." Edna moved to the front desk and took a key from a hook.

Simon held up a hand and then scratched his head once he had his wife's attention. "Let's put her upstairs, above our room." He looked at Hattie and then at his wife. "We will still be able to hear any trouble, but it is better if she's not on the ground floor." He shoved his hands in his pockets. "Travis can't try to pry open a second-floor window."

Edna nodded and moved behind the L-shaped counter. She collected a key from beneath a red-painted carved number 5.

"We've got only one other guest at the moment, an elderly widow who keeps to herself, so I expect you'll find some quiet respite here." She rounded the desk and moved toward the stairs. "Just this way," Edna walked purposefully.

Something in her manner reminded Hattie of Mrs. Fritz. She imagined this is what it would have been like to have known Mrs. Fritz when she was young.

The stairs formed a T with the hallway, and three doors lined the walls on each side. "There are only five rooms. The outhouse is behind the kitchen. It has a good lock on it, so you needn't worry about being disturbed."

Hattie reflexively smiled. She'd never had to discuss such things. She couldn't imagine speaking of such personal needs to strangers every day.

"Your room is the last on the right." They shuffled down the narrow hall together.

The smell of fresh paint filled the air. The boarding-house was nicer than anything she'd expected to see in Montana. Her visions of mud huts and log shacks were maybe a little too inspired by the wild western dime novels she'd read. Fresh white walls and dark stained woodwork were a happy surprise. Paintings of people she didn't recognize lined the corridor. At the end of the hall stood a small table below a window. A vase overflowing with lilacs glowed in the afternoon sunlight.

The scent mingled with the paint odor and made Hattie's head ache.

Edna turned the key with ease and the door opened without a creak. She beamed as Hattie entered the small but beautiful room. The walls were painted a soft white, unlike the bright white of the hallway. A four-poster bed took up most of the room and was adorned with a delicate lace canopy and a vibrant star-patterned quilt. A rocking chair sat in one corner beside a small upright bureau. The only other furniture was a writing desk and chair below the window.

"I'm afraid we don't have gas here as they do in the big cities." She sighed and looked around as if judging herself, then she cleared her throat and smiled again. "But the lamp is full of oil and the window lets in a lot of light during the day." Edna motioned to the lamp on the night-stand. "If you need more oil, you just let Simon know and he'll come round and fill it."

Simon had stood waiting for his wife's direction the entire time they'd been in the room. Edna seemed to remember him then and pointed for him to leave her trunks at the end of her bed. As soon as he'd set them down, she shoved him out the door.

"I'll let you freshen up while I put together lunch. I'm sure you could do with something hearty and a strong cup of tea."

Hattie thanked her and stared at the door once it had

closed. The bed creaked beneath her as she flopped down. She closed her eyes and let the tears flow hot and heavy.

She pulled the buffalo from her pocket and prayed that Mark would once again burst through the door and rescue her. She sat up with Mark's words in her mind. *Please write to Opal or Angela with a word or two for me, so I know you're safe.* Clumsily, she wiped the tears from her eyes with the sleeves of her dress. She eyed the writing desk. She pulled up the chair and then retrieved stationery and ink.

My dearest Angela,

I write to you with tidings of sorrow from Silent Creek. I arrived today and learned my groom had passed away before my arrival. I now find myself in a place without friends and with little means to keep me. I was met at the coach by the man who would have been my brother-in-law, Travis Fletcher. Mr. Fletcher believes he has a claim on me because he inherited his brother's estate. But friends, I do not wish to marry him. He is a dreadful man.

I have secured a room at the boarding-house under the propriety of Mr. and Mrs. Simon Oakley. They seem to be kind people, but I do not wish to overstretch their generosity.

I am writing to ask for guidance. I will

send this in the evening post and pray it reaches you soon.

 With gratitude,
 Hattie Thompson.
 P.S.
 I will send a telegram to Mrs. Phillips seeking her direction as well.

Chapter Thirteen

Mark walked into his cabin and leaned his back against the door. As much as he had loved seeing his brothers and their families, he was wiped out. He pushed off the door and shrugged off his jacket with a sigh. He tossed it over a peg with his hat and then toed off his boots and kicked them toward the wall.

The cabin was too quiet after the noise of Hank's house. The family had come together for dinner and each of them welcomed him with hugs and expressions of love. Despite their warmth, he was drained. He'd anticipated intense feelings of belonging but found himself retreating and desiring isolation instead.

Mark went into the kitchen and splashed water on his face at the sink. It was late. He pressed a towel to his eyes and then tossed it onto the counter. Once he had the fire stoked, he flopped into his bed and said a prayer for the woman, who was never far from his mind.

He stared into the darkness and wondered if Hattie was asleep. There was no wall between them now to touch for comfort. There were only empty miles. He felt around his nightstand for her handkerchief and clutched it to his heart. He ran his thumb over her embroidery. I hope you're happy and safe.

Angela and Opal had asked after Hattie at dinner, indirectly telling Mark they had not heard from her. He imagined she would write as soon as she could. He wasn't sure how busy a new bride would be.

Thoughts of her as a bride hurt. Mark groaned and rolled to his side, and stared at the moon outside his window. The ache in his heart was worse than he'd ever imagined possible.

Iris's words came back to him, and she was right. He needed to move on now. Knowing it was one thing, doing it was another. He had never been in love before, and he didn't know how to make it go away. He fell into a bitter sleep plagued with dreams of women he couldn't save.

The rooster's crow stirred him into consciousness and the scent of coffee roused him. Mark swung his feet to the floor and sat on the side of his bed, scrubbing his eyes with the heels of his hands and trying to wake up.

Iris probably let herself in. She'd taken to mothering him like when he was a young man fresh on the farm. Mark smiled at the memories. She'd tried so hard to get him to live in the big house with the other boys, but he'd wanted to be a man so badly. Eventually, she'd left him in the bunkhouse with the other hired hands, but she'd always paid him special attention. Caine used to whine that Mark was Iris's favorite.

Mark was okay with that. He loved her dearly.

He was the only bachelor among them now, and Iris needed a place to put all of her love after the losses she'd faced. Mark got up and stretched. He made his bed, searching through the linens to find Hattie's handkerchief that he had fallen asleep holding. He folded it and stuffed it in his pocket as he dressed.

The air was cool around his bedroom, but a rush of warmth hit him as he entered the kitchen. Bacon sizzled and grits bubbled on the stove. Iris bustled along, humming to herself.

"Good morning," he said, clearing his throat after his words were garbled with sleep.

"Good morning!" Iris's cheerful eyes drooped a little when she took Mark in. "Didn't sleep well?"

"Is it obvious?"

She smiled and poured a cup of coffee. "This will help."

He nodded his thanks and sat at the table, picking up the Sun River Post.

"Your train made the front page," Iris said sadly. "Will brought the paper over last night, so I thought I'd bring it down here for you." She chuckled, "Don't tell Caine, though. I don't think he saw it before I left."

Mark laughed and sipped his coffee. He would absolutely tell Caine, and he would enjoy doing it.

Feeling a little brighter, he snapped the paper open and scanned the front page. The headline read, "TRAIN GOES OF THE RAILS KILLING 7 AND INJURING 11."

"Looks like one more of the injured died," Mark said. "It was only six when I left."

"It's such a shame." Iris sat across from him and sipped her own coffee. "I've been praying for them."

A hazy photograph sent shivers down Mark's spine. It was the train car that he had escaped and he knew that the victims were just out of the camera's range. He skimmed the article, which didn't tell him anything he didn't already know.

Iris set a plate in front of him. He thanked her, folded the paper, and set it aside.

"Caleb's building another barn. Thought I'd go over and help mind the children today." Iris sat down across the small kitchen table.

Mark wiped his mouth and said, "I was planning to go over and help too."

"Good. They'll be glad to have another hand." She added coffee to Mark's cup and then to her own. "There's always so much to be done and they've been short-handed lately. I swear, young men don't want to work anymore." Iris set the coffee pot sharply on the table.

"They've had a hard time keeping ranch hands?" Nobody had told him that the ranch was struggling for help. He could have left Boston much sooner if he'd known they needed him. Not that he was sorry for escorting Hattie on her journey. Those precious last days would stay with him forever.

Iris made a noncommittal noise as she methodically broke open her yolk and dipped her toast in it. "They come and go. Seems like they can't keep reliable men like we used to." She shrugged.

"There's been no trouble though? Not since Benson?" He had imagined if there was trouble, someone would have let them know.

"Oh no, nothing like that. The young men just seem to move on more quickly these days." She furrowed her brow and gave a slow shake of her head. "We could use a bunch of boys like y'all were." She smiled. "You boys worked so hard and built something beautiful."

"We had something to prove." Mark smiled and drained his coffee. "I have a few things to do around here, and then we can head over to Caleb's place."

Iris nodded and finished her breakfast in silence.

After breakfast, Mark donned his hat and left Iris inside to clean up. He checked the woodshed and barns to make a mental list of things that he would need to do, but his brothers had taken care of everything. He would talk to Caine and Sarah about getting a horse or two, and while he was at Caleb's, he would snatch up a few chickens and a rooster for his coop. It was a nice surprise that he wouldn't have to do a bunch of maintenance before he could settle in.

Iris had driven herself over in her little wagon, so he checked and watered her little mare before he went inside to see if she was ready to go.

Iris hung the dish towel neatly on a peg and then met Mark at the door. He held her coat so she could get into it. She picked up her hat and settled it on her head. They climbed into the little wagon and Mark drove them to Caleb's house.

He dropped Iris at the front door, where the women were gathered on the porch. Children scrambled around them, shrieking and giggling as their mothers tried to settle them.

A twinge of envy surprised Mark. He tried not to imagine looking up there and seeing Hattie talking with the women with a baby on her hip, catching his eye and smiling her bashful smile.

What is wrong with you? You need to stop.

Mark helped Iris up the steps and then climbed back onto the wagon and continued down to the stable, where the men were standing around with steaming cups of coffee.

"Alright, who do I need to talk to about getting some work done around here?" He asked as he jumped down and tied the wagon to the post.

Caleb laughed, "Oh, we've got work for you," he moved to the little mare and worked the harness while Mark moved up and worked the harness on the other side. In no time, they had the mare free and handed her off to a stable boy.

Mark leaned against the fence with his brothers. "Iris says young men don't wanna work anymore. Is that true?" He took his hat off and ran his fingers through his hair.

Caine shrugged. "Eh, we had a few bad seeds. Nothing too bad, though."

"So you haven't been shorthanded?" Mark wouldn't put it past his brothers to soften the truth for him.

"It's not like it used to be, but I think Iris just misses the way things were." Hank cocked a hip against the fence and then rested his massive boot on the bottom rail. "Since Rose died, she has been a bit nostalgic."

Caine jammed a hand in his pocket and nodded. "She's been talking a lot about getting you, Brian, and Dean home." He shrugged again. "She just misses the old days."

"I hear ya. I sometimes wish I could go back to those days. Before Boston."

Caleb patted his back. "You know what cures that? Building a barn."

Mark laughed despite himself. "So, what are we standing around like a bunch of old men for?"

"Old men! Please!" Daniel tossed the dregs of his coffee onto the ground. "Let's build a barn."

Will elbowed Daniel and then emptied his mug, too.

"And if that doesn't work, I got a bottle of whiskey. That will."

Mark poured his whole body into the building of the barn. His muscles burned, but he didn't care. He yearned to feel something other than all the anguish and loss he'd been feeling. By evening, the barn was up and the sweat on his back began to cool as he rocked in a chair on Caleb's porch.

The smell of roast and potatoes leaked onto the porch from inside. There was pleasure in the exhaustion.

The time he'd spent in Boston had dulled his muscles and he found satisfaction in the fatigue that came from building something. For too long, he had been breaking down doors. Now he looked upon his work and was glad. The men chattered around him, discussing the day's work and plans for the spring. Mark nursed a whiskey and enjoyed the moment. The whiskey and tiredness blurred his mind just enough to keep Hattie out of his reach.

HATTIE SAT ON THE PORCH AT THE BOARDINGHOUSE AND watched the postman come slowly down the dusty road. She had watched him every day, hoping he carried a letter for her. She knew the mail to Hope would take longer than a day or two each way, but she had at least expected a telegram from Mrs. Phillips by now. Three days had passed, though, and she'd had no response to her telegram.

Boston had turned its back on her. She shouldn't be surprised, but she was. She would never learn.

She accepted letters for the Oakleys and a newspaper.

The postman gave her a sad smile and wished her a good day before he left.

Hattie turned the newspaper over in her hands and scanned the headlines as she entered the house. Her eyes flew open when she saw the photo on the front page. She instantly recognized the train as the one she'd left Mark on. The letters in her hand scattered to the floor as she violently tore open the paper and searched for the date.

She covered her mouth, tears streamed down her cheek as she read about the causalities on the train she had ridden only a week earlier.

Edna walked into the room and stopped dead in her tracks. "What in the heavens is the matter?" She rushed to Hattie's side.

"Please forgive me." Hattie wiped away her tears and picked up the dropped letters.

"Here is the morning's mail, I, I just—" she struggled to form the words, "I was on this train, my friend was on it." Hattie sputtered out sentences between sobs. "Seven people died, and I don't know if he was one of them."

"Now, now," Edna said, enfolding Hattie in a hug. "Let's look again." She picked Hattie up from the floor and moved to the sofa with her. Edna opened the paper and scanned the contents of the article. "They usually print the names of the casualties in these sorts of situations." She shook her head and folded the paper. "I'm sorry, Hattie."

Edna turned the paper over so the photo was down on the table. "The way I see it, until you know he's dead, he's alive." Edna ran her hand in soothing circles over Hattie's back. "There were probably a lot of people on that train and going by numbers there is a good chance that your friend is okay." Edna patted her firmly, "Now, let's have some tea. Then, when you're calm, you can write a letter inquiring after him."

Edna's logic made sense to Hattie, but it didn't make her feel any better. She collected herself the best she could, not wanting to appear ungrateful, but inside she was falling apart. Her heart was already in so many pieces she had not thought it possible to break it into more. Life wanted nothing more than to grind her heart and soul down into dust until she was nothing left but debris carried away by the wind.

What if he's dead? Now you truly have nothing. You might as well marry Travis.

She was not sure why in her desperation this was her thought, but it came up nonetheless. Certainly, she could not marry the abhorrent man. As if her thinking of him conjured him into existence, a loud banging resounded at the front door.

"Get out here, you cheating whore!" Over and over, Travis shouted. Hattie's heart raced and her skin crawled. What if he got through the door?

Simon came with his shotgun in hand, yelling through the closed window at Travis, "Get out of here, using that kind of language. There are ladies present, haven't you any decency?"

"Since when do whores deserve decency?" Travis said in a slur.

Hattie worried the sleeve of her dress and panic flooded her mind. There was nowhere for her to hide, nowhere for her to run.

Simon wasn't having any of it, though. "A bit early to be hitting the bottle. Why don't you go dry out?"

"Get you some of her, did you?" Travis's sneer made Hattie shudder. "I read it in her letter. She's a used woman. More men have been by her than fought in the war, I reckon." When he laughed, his upper lip flopped over his missing and broken teeth.

Hattie was horrified to have her past thrown at her in such a way. She dropped to the couch and buried her head in her hands. Her mortification wasn't over though, because Travis wasn't done speaking.

"Well, you tell the whore I ain't gonna marry her, but she is coming with me." With this, Travis kicked the door and shouted, "I'll be back tomorrow," before he walked away.

Hattie fell to pieces then.

When Hattie pulled herself together, she sat up. Simon and Edna were shooting some sort of silent communication above her head.

Hattie stood shattered. She was sure if she looked on the floor, she would see pieces of herself scattered about like a broken mirror. Her lower lip trembled, and she began to mouth something, but no words came. She just puckered like a fish out of desperate for oxygen. Edna rushed over to her, and Hattie recoiled from her touch. It burned. Edna backed away; her arms raised as if to demonstrate innocence. Simon moved to Edna's side. His movements sent Hattie running up the stairs and into her room. She slammed the door, locking it, before crumbling to the floor. Violent sobs racked her body until she was unconscious.

A gentle tapping on the door roused Hattie. In the darkness, she was back in that room, tied to the bed, and they were coming for her.

"Hattie. Please, let us help you." Edna's voice brought her back to the present.

Hattie's breaths were ragged and her heart tried

desperately to break through her chest. She clutched her little carved buffalo in her hands. The tears came again. She held the figurine, each line so clear in her mind even in the darkness.

Hattie slowed her breathing and got to her feet. She took several deep breaths to work up her courage and unlocked the door.

Edna held up an old oil lamp. "Will you please come downstairs with me? Simon is waiting."

Hattie took a shaky breath but nodded. She followed Edna down the hallways to the smell of charred cotton and kerosene.

Simon smiled at Hattie when she entered the sitting room. His kind, round face reminded her of her sweet father.

"We just want to speak to you," Edna spoke in a slow measured voice.

Hattie was sure it was meant to be reassuring, though it only amplified her embarrassment and shame. She said nothing and took a seat in an armchair. "I suppose I owe you an explanation."

"We just want to help," Edna said, her sincere warmth giving Hattie the courage to continue.

"After I was orphaned, I was taken in by an old woman in my building. I thought her a blessing, but I was wrong. She sold me to human traffickers. The men were cr-cr-cruel," she stumbled over the words, wringing her hands together, digging her nails into her flesh. "I was rescued. They thought I was dead, and I nearly was."

Hattie stared into an empty corner, but her mind was back in that frigid room. Tears continued to fall as she told the story of her rescue and recovery, all of which led her to Silent Creek.

Nobody spoke, and Hattie felt their judgment all over her. She'd gotten too comfortable at The Rose Dunn House and she'd gotten some wrong ideas about the future she could have.

She should have known better.

Hattie dropped her face and said. "I am a fallen woman. Travis is right."

Simon angrily paced the far end of the room. Edna moved slowly to Hattie's side and kneeled next to her without touching her.

"It is not your shame. Do you hear me? It is their shame, those men. Brutal creatures, it is their shame, and you should never have to answer for it." Edna chanced a touch and held Hattie's hand. "No matter what men like Travis think or say, you are not a fallen woman."

Hattie held tight to Edna's hands. "Thank you for your kind words."

Edna pressed a handkerchief to Hattie's face. "I am not being kind. I am telling you the truth."

"But Travis isn't wrong. No man will marry me. Not as I am, not when they know the truth." She held her breath to try to stem the tears that threatened. She didn't want to sink into another fit.

"How did Travis learn? Did you tell anyone here?" Simon asked. His voice was sharp, but his expression was gentle.

"I told Mr. Fletcher, Quinn Fletcher, in a letter. I couldn't let him enter the marriage without knowing the truth." Hattie said.

"Quinn was glad to marry you and he knew the truth." Simon sat across from Hattie and caught her eye. "Quinn was a good man with a kind and noble heart. Surely, that must tell you something."

Hattie couldn't disagree. She did not know Quinn, but by all accounts, he was a decent man.

But what about Mark then? Why would he not marry me? A man who doesn't know you would take a chance, but a man who knows you well wouldn't.

This thought hit her with a painful certainty. I am damaged goods.

Chapter Fourteen

Mark stood and stretched, soaking in the heat of the summer sun on his back. Sore as he was, the manual labor restored his spirits in ways he hadn't expected. He wiped his brow and pushed the empty wheelbarrow back into the dark barn. Even now, mucking stalls, he smiled. His time in Boston had weakened him in so many ways. It was nice to get something back. After two weeks at home, he felt stronger, at least physically.

There was honor in a simple life. A man didn't have to be saving lives to do good in the world. Ranch life was hard work, but simple and meaningful. Each task was predictable and safe, and he appreciated that. So, he mucked; happy with the knowledge that he would discover no dead bodies in his hay. He simply pierced the soiled bedding, tossed it into the wheelbarrow, carted it away, and lay fresh. Each cleared stall was a small success. There was nothing more to it.

The days were kinder than the nights. During the day, he focused on one task at a time, the sensations of physical work, the smells of the barn, and conversations with the other guys. But at night, when he was alone, he would pick away the little details of his day and wallow in loneliness. The nighttime was cruel, and so Mark worked until he was too tired to stand and then dropped into bed, hopefully too tired to think.

Mark sighed and rested his pitchfork against the wall. He wiped his brow again and then headed for the pump in the yard. His problems would wait for the dark. He had other things to keep him busy while the sun was up. Mark pumped the handle and then dipped his head under the spigot. He ran his hands through his hair and let the water trail down his back and cool his warm muscles. Then he took a drink from the well and stretched his shoulders.

He looked around the peaceful yard and took a deep breath. The quiet soothed him, but the more he thought about it, the lonelier he was. It had been nagging at him since Boston and watching his brothers with their families needled him like a sliver gone sour. With no solution in sight, Mark returned to the barn to attack the next stall.

"You cleaned that barn like a bride with a new house." Caleb laughed and leaned against the stall.

It was nearly noon, but Mark had already put in a day's worth of work. "Where'd you come from?" Mark propped the pitchfork against the wall again and wheeled the barrow out into the sunlight. He sat on a stack of hay bales near the door and wiped the sweat from his face with his shirt. If only Caleb would understand that Mark's silence meant he didn't want to talk. There was no chance of that, though. His brothers were worse than women when they wanted information.

Caleb dropped to the bale beside Mark and took off his hat. "I was riding over to Caine's to sweet talk Iris into making me a sweet potato pie. I thought I'd stop by and see if you needed anything." He spun his hat a few times and then set it on his knee and ran his hands through his hair. "You've been walking around like somebody spit in your grits since you got home."

Mark was about to reply when Caleb held up a hand to stop him. "Don't bother denying it. What's going on? Is it Boston?"

Mark stood, wanting to walk away, but it was inevitable that the topic would come up. At least if he confided in Caleb, the news would spread to the others and he wouldn't have to explain his feelings over and over. Mark studied Caleb's concerned expression and then sighed. He sat back down on the bale and groaned. "Am I really that obvious?"

Caleb laughed. "You're one sigh away from Iris moving in with you."

Mark smiled and leaned back against the barn. "I thought I kept it to myself."

The sound Caleb made was more scoff than laugh, then he cleared his throat and asked, "Is it a girl or a ghost? We've all got 'em."

Mark stood and walked a few paces away, shoving his hands in his pocket unsure of what to do with himself. He rocked on his heels to buy time. Caleb's patience won and after an eternal silence, Mark spewed the one thing he'd tried so hard to keep to himself. "I've been thinking that it's time for me to get a wife."

Caleb jumped to his feet and punched Mark in his arm. "That's great!" He shoved his hat on his head and smiled.

"Is it?" Mark was surprised by Caleb's excitement.

Caleb punched him again and said, "Of course it is."

Mark shrank under Caleb's assessing stare.

Caleb grasped Mark's shoulder and squeezed. "You're still hung up on Hattie Thompson."

He shrugged. "It's too late for me and Hattie. She's married."

"I watched the love of my life marry another man once. I can feel it like it was yesterday." Caleb shook his head and crossed his arms. "I'd give anything to have Scott back, but losing Jeni that night is a pain that I didn't think I'd survive."

They stood silently in the middle of Scott's yard for a minute. Their eyes were drawn to the spot where their brother had died trying to protect his new wife.

After a few minutes, Caleb shook off his emotions and grinned. "Why not wire old Mrs. Phillips? She's tried and true. I'm sure she can rustle you up some fine young lady looking for a bit of that Western life." Caleb wriggled his eyebrows, and it was Mark's turn to punch his brother.

"I don't know how I feel about promising to marry someone I've never met."

Caleb shrugged. "It worked out for the rest of us." He took a few steps to the hitching post and untied his horse. He swung up into the saddle and then stared at Mark for a moment. "So, you know what you need to do, then?"

"No."

"Sure you do. Go to town now and send a wire to Mrs. Phillips. I'll go tell everyone the good news." Caleb took off like an overgrown boy on his first pony.

"Shut your damn mouth!" Mark shouted at his back.

Caleb was laughing as he rode away.

No amount of work would shake the idea from his mind and in the span of two hours, Mark had made up his mind. He doubted he would ever find love like he had for

Hattie, but he had love to give. If he wanted a family, he would have to go out and get himself one.

He washed and dressed and then pointed his wagon toward town. Before he could talk himself out of it, he was going to send a letter to Mrs. Phillips.

ANOTHER DAY HAD BURNED AWAY IN SILENCE FROM HER friends. Two full weeks had passed without reply. Hattie watched the postman trod down the road as she did every day and then greedily combed the morning post, restraining tears when she found no letter addressed to her. She was abandoned once again by people she'd allowed herself to trust. And worst of all, she didn't know if Mark had survived the train crash.

Edna found her as she placed the mail on the desk. The look of pity on Edna's face stung, but she tried to hide it behind a smile. "Would you help me with the laundry? My momma used to say, 'There is nothing quite like a good scrubbing in a laundry basin to cure what ails you.' But of course, that was just her way of getting me to do my chores." Her face pulled up in a genuine smile and again Hattie felt like she was meeting a young Mrs. Fritz.

Hattie nodded and followed Edna to the backyard. The wash tub was already filled with soapy water, and a pile of bedding and clothes dwarfed a chair beside it. Hattie rolled up her sleeves and set to work. Taking hold of a large wooden paddle, she stirred. She kept up the circular motion, listening to Edna hum hymns to herself. Both the labor and music were relaxing.

Edna stopped humming and her face assumed a thoughtful expression. "Help me out here." She nodded at the rinse pan and Hattie joined her. They each took one end of a water-logged sheet, rung it, and placed it into a basket to be taken to the line.

Hattie waited a few minutes for Edna to say whatever was twisting her face up, but her patience lost. "Is there something on your mind, Edna?"

Catching Hattie's eye, Edna nibbled on her lip. "You know, Quinn really was a good man. His death was quite a shock to the whole town."

Hattie simply nodded, unsure how to answer.

"How he and Travis are related, I will never understand. I suppose it's like Caine and Able. One was good and one evil." Edna lifted the sheet from the wash basin and set it into the rinse water.

Hattie let the activity distract her for a moment. She grabbed the next sheet from the pile and pushed it into the water with the plunger. When they had both settled back into their tasks, she asked, "He's really as bad as he seems?"

Edna arched her brow, her expression like an adult trying to be patient with a child. "If you ask me, he killed Quinn. I know they said it was an accident, but I don't think Quinn would have gone into that mine. He was the one who pulled the men out of it because he thought it was unsafe. He was a good man and always looked out for his miners, unlike some of the others who just work them to the bone. Quinn cared about this town, too. Invested in it, and wanted it to be a beautiful place, a home. Travis is just the exact opposite." She snapped a pillowcase.

They'd danced around this conversation for weeks, and now it seemed that they were both ready to have it. Travis's visits had become more and more unsettling because Hattie's hope for help from her friends had been dying with every passing day. "Did you know them well?"

"Quinn was a bit older than me, but I knew his wife Pauline very well. Shame she died so young. They were a lovely pair. Never thought he'd marry again. Pauline died more than ten years ago now, giving birth to their boy, Harlan. Never seen a sweeter boy. Pauline's mama Agatha moved to the ranch to help raise Harlan. They've both gone back East since Quinn passed. Quinn and Travis's parents died a while back. Scarlet Fever, I think. Travis had it bad too, but he lived. Maybe that's what's wrong with him. Fever boiled his brain." She laughed and Hattie returned a polite smile.

They were quiet for a moment, then Edna continued, "I think you would have been happy with Quinn." She sighed. "Shame, just a shame." Learning about Quinn made Hattie feel sad for something she never had, and probably never would. Her heart ached for Mark, and she hoped word of him would reach her soon.

The two women carried the heavy baskets to where clotheslines hung in neat rows. The early afternoon breeze and sun comforted her. She drew a deep breath and waddled to the clothesline, glad to set down the heavy basket. Helping Edna with the sheets, they pulled them taut and snapped them. Excess water misted the air and flashes of rainbows greeted them.

"This is so much easier with an extra pair of hands. I may keep you for myself." Edna laughed.

"I had a lot of practice at the rescue house," Hattie said, a bittersweet feeling twinging in her stomach.

"Well, your work won't go to waste—" Edna's words were cut off by Travis's voice.

"Hattie? Oh, Miss Haaa-ttie!" Hattie's eyes went wide

as he sang her name. Edna ushered her inside, the empty laundry baskets forgotten. "It's been two wee-eeks..." he sang.

Pushing the deadbolt into place, Edna pressed her back to the door.

Hattie's blood ran cold. "He said two weeks. It's been two weeks." Hattie babbled.

"What? What about two weeks?" Edna's face wrinkled with concern as she went to Hattie's side. Hattie recoiled from her touch, then remembered herself and accepted her hands.

"Travis said we would be married in two weeks' time. It's been two weeks now."

Edna's expression relaxed. "But that was before he found the letters. He said he wouldn't marry you. Besides, you don't have to do anything you don't want."

A banging on the front door made them jump.

"I've had enough of this." Edna straightened herself and marched out of the room. Hattie trailed behind her like a child. "Travis, go away! You have no claim here." She yelled into the closed door. Travis's silhouette loomed outside the draped window.

"I ain't here for trouble. I just came to apologize to the sweet and beautiful Miss Hattie. Let me talk to her. Please, I'll be real sweet, I promise. Look, I brought her flowers." Something rustled against the door and Edna shot Hattie a confused look. Hattie shrugged, her hands in the air unsure how to proceed.

"Do you want to talk to him?" Edna whispered, turning to face Hattie.

"No." The change in Travis was confusing. Regardless of his alleged change of heart, she found him offensive in every way.

Edna nodded and turned back to the door. "She doesn't want to see you, Travis. Now go away."

Hattie braced herself and prepared for Travis to fly into a rage, but he didn't.

"Oh, Mrs. Oakley, I'm so sorry. Please, I just haven't been right since Quinn died," he sounded on the verge of tears, "It's been a couple weeks since he passed. I'm still grieving and not thinking straight. Please, talk to Miss Hattie. Tell her I'm sorry."

Despite herself, Hattie felt for the man, knowing what it was like to grieve the only family you had. Maybe Travis wasn't as bad as he appeared. Moving to the door, Hattie gently nudged Edna aside and unlatched the bolt.

Travis came tumbling through the door, knocking Hattie to the ground. His body was atop hers. With more fumbling of her backside than Hattie felt was strictly necessary, he clambered back to his feet. His impropriety extended to assisting her to smooth the wrinkles from her dress. She batted his hands away, anger the only thing keeping her from shutting down from his unwanted touch.

"Here." He scooped the crumbled wildflowers from the floor, their wilted bodies drooping over his knuckles. He flashed his gapped smile and Hattie cringed.

"Thank you." Hattie took the flowers awkwardly and tossed them onto a table as if they were full of ants. "I think we need to talk. I do not wish to bend the Oakleys' rules by conversing with you in here, so let's sit on the porch." She motioned for Edna to go outside with them.

This was an opportunity, an experiment. Hattie had a sudden moment of courage, and with Travis's changed mood, this was her chance to change his mind about courting her.

As Hattie turned toward the door, Travis ran at her, offering his arm. Edna gave Hattie one last distressed look before they went outside.

Travis led Hattie to the porch swing. His boney arm felt insect-like joined with hers. She breathed deeply, trying and failing to repress the cold burning sensation brought on by his touch.

Instead of settling onto the swing beside him, Hattie lowered herself into a rocking chair. Travis bristled, but settled quite quickly. He sat on the swing and put it into motion. Edna sat in another rocking chair. Travis glared at her but seemed to accept her as chaperone and began his apology.

"I really am sorry about the grief I gave you when you first got here and everything else that happened after."

"I understand that you were grieving. Grief can lead us to make bad decisions." She fidgeted with the sleeve of her shirt and hoped he would accept no for an answer this time.

"Aw, ain't you so sweet? I could just eat you up." He lunged toward her, his hands snapping in a show of eating. He tickled her ribs as if playing with a child. If he sensed her recoil, he didn't show it.

"Please, stop," she whispered.

Edna half stood from her chair, but Hattie stopped her with a wave of her hand. Travis settled back onto the swing with a happy smile on his face.

"I'm just having fun. We'll have a lot of fun together." A devilish grin spread across his face as his tongue probed the spaces between his teeth. A wave of nausea forced Hattie to choke. Much to her horror, Travis mistook her disgust for pleasure.

"I bet a woman of your experience could teach me a

thing or two." Travis waggled his eyebrows at her and chuckled.

"Mr. Fletcher, you must understand that I was a prisoner, not a willing participant."

He shrugged.

She needed to get out of there. This experiment of hers was a mistake. What had she been thinking? He was never going to accept her disinterest.

"I seem to have misjudged my health and am not feeling well." She rose and turned from him, her hand covering her mouth.

Two steps from the door, his insectile arms were around her waist. He pressed his body against hers. "No kiss goodbye?" His breath reeked of decay as he forced his mouth on her cheek.

"Let her go." Edna grabbed Hattie's arm and pulled her free. They ran inside while he cackled behind them. Edna slammed and locked the door. "That man!" She stomped her foot and banged her fist on the door.

"I'll come by and see you tomorrow... lover." His words crept like bugs under the door, and Hattie wanted to stomp them out. As his footsteps trailed away, she slumped to the couch, hopeless and exhausted. She sat for several minutes, trying to figure out what she would do.

"Hattie?" Edna's voice came soft and gentle, like her mother had spoken when she was young.

Hattie looked up, and Edna stood, arms extended. Hattie walked with her to the kitchen. On the small circular table sat two tea cups on saucers and a plate of cookies. Travis's flowers peeked out the top of the compost bin.

Hattie took a seat as Edna poured the tea.

"I hope you'll forgive my forwardness, but I've been

thinking about your situation and I would like to ask my parents for help."

"Your parents?" Hattie's watery eyes glazed with confusion.

"Yes, Charles and Jennifer Coffey. My father is the reverend and I'm sure they can help you find your way." She moved to the counter to retrieve the butter bell and biscuits from the counter. "After church on Sunday, I invited them for dinner tonight. After that episode on the porch, I think we should discuss your future with them." She smiled, taking a seat and smoothing her skirt as though everything was settled.

"Thank you." Hattie picked up her teacup, but her hands trembled, sloshing tea on the table and burning her. "Oh dear, I'm so clumsy." She stood sopping up the spill with her napkin.

"Accidents happen." Edna handed her napkin to Hattie. "You are pressing yourself too hard. It's one thing to try to move on, it's another thing to put your numb hands in a fire; if you catch my meaning."

Hattie stopped mopping up the tea and stared at Edna. "I'm sorry, I don't understand."

"Well, if you got numb hands, you might think it's okay to touch fire because you won't feel it. But your skin will still burn. Do you see what I mean?"

"How am I doing that?" Hattie's brows pinched together.

"You've been through a lot. You may not always be making the best decisions." Edna dabbed the corners of her mouth and then refilled Hattie's teacup.

"What have I done wrong?" Hattie wracked her brain but couldn't think of anything she could have done to cause Edna to feel that way.

"Like entertaining Travis on the porch. What were you thinking?"

Hattie had enough of Edna's well-meaning forward-ness, and anger sparked within her. "I hoped that his changed mood would make him more reasonable. I was wrong, but I know what it's like to be misjudged."

Edna huffed. "Nobody is misjudging Travis Fletcher. We've known his character for decades." She stood from the table and carried the tea back to the counter. "You might try to trust our experience."

Hattie hung her head. She hadn't meant to hurt Edna's feelings. It was so hard for her to label anyone as bad. Why was it so hard to accept someone's goodness? Every day, she expected Edna to put her out of the house. She couldn't stop waiting for the other shoe to drop, for Edna and Simon to sell her to Travis and send her away. The abandonment of her friends reinforced that no matter how she tried, she couldn't trust anybody.

Eventually, everyone would let her down.

Hattie and Edna cleaned up in silence. Something had changed between them, and Hattie did not know how to fix it. With the dishes finished, Hattie retreated to her room to sort out her thoughts. She wanted to believe that there was good in people, but in her life, the people who had seemed to possess the most goodness had always turned on her. Why wouldn't these good people do the same?

Chapter Fifteen

Hattie awoke to a gentle tapping on her door.

She squeezed her eyes shut and pictured Mark. I can feel you. You must be alive. She caressed her buffalo and held it to her heart. Or is it just wishful thinking? She blinked to clear the cobwebs and adjust to the dim light. It killed her not to know Mark's fate. Why hadn't the Maxwell Group answered her letter?

The knock on the door came a little louder this time. "Hattie, it's Edna. My parents are here, and we would love for you to join us for dinner."

Hattie wanted so badly to believe in Edna, to trust in her goodness, but she'd learned the same painful lesson over and over in her life. She stared into the white eyes of her carved friend. Wasn't he just another example of how people could let her down?

Regardless, she cherished the gift.

"I'm sorry if I was out of line. I'm just trying to help. I would never hurt you." Edna's words flowed sincerely through the cracks in the door.

"One minute, please." Hattie called, sitting up and fumbling for matches to light the lamp. The room was dark, but she found it comforting. The match struck and lit with a hiss and amber light flooded the room.

Hattie tucked her carving into her nightstand and then smoothed her skirt. A few small steps brought her to the door. Hattie swallowed frustration and shame and unbolted the lock. She opened the door to Edna's apologetic face, illuminated by the lamp.

"Hattie, I'm sorry," she began immediately.

"It's fine. I didn't mean to fall asleep," Hattie replied with the coolness she felt inside. "The interview with Travis exhausted me today." Hattie closed the door and tried to smile.

Edna frowned but said nothing. They walked in silence down the hall. The clean and neat boardinghouse seemed less welcoming now that Hattie and Edna weren't quite on the same page.

The dining room held a long table, draped in navy blue cloth. A candelabra chandelier hung above the table, providing ample illumination. Simon sat at the head of the table talking with a dog collared man dressed in black. Beside him sat a short gray-haired woman with a kind, round face. The widow, who was also staying at the boardinghouse, sat across from them. Her name was Camile Johnson, but Hattie knew nothing else of her. She kept to herself and spoke little during their previously shared meals.

The air smelled of roast chicken and potatoes, mingled with something sweet and yeasty. A carved chicken sat in the center with several bowls dotted around the table.

Edna cleared her throat, and everyone looked her way.

The men stood politely and waited for Edna to make the introductions.

"Hattie, you know Simon and Mrs. Johnson. I would like to introduce you to my parents, Reverend Charles and Jennifer Coffey." Then she turned to the group. "This is Hattie Thompson."

"It's a pleasure," Hattie said with a bow of her head, "I hope I have not kept you all."

"Not at all!" Jennifer said warmly.

Hattie returned a genuine smile as Edna ushered her to the seat beside Mrs. Johnson. Edna moved to the corner of the table and began serving, beginning with her husband and working her way clockwise around the table before taking her own seat.

"Oh, Edna, you've outdone yourself. This chicken is marvelous." Charles said with pride.

Others around the table were prompted to complement the meal and the main course passed with polite chatter. They spoke mostly of town news—the new church bell, the fire that took down a barn, rumors of a storm coming, and trivial bits of information about people Hattie didn't know.

Hattie was wiping away the last bits of her meal from the corner of her mouth when Edna spoke up. "Simon, why don't you share with Hattie what you learned today?" Edna gave him an encouraging nod.

Hattie sat up straighter and turned her attention to Simon. What could he have learned that might interest her?

"Edna asked me to head out to Quinn's place today." He said in with a sigh, his tone tight and hesitant. "His boy, Harlan, was there with Agatha, his mother-in-law." He pushed his plate forward and rested his elbows on the table. "They informed me that Travis did not inherit the estate, like he said," he drank a sip of water, "Everything was bequeathed to Harlan, under the care of Agatha until he comes of age."

"I see." Hattie dropped her gaze to her plate, pushing food around with her fork. Her appetite gone. Simon's words only further confirmed her suspicions that no one was trustworthy. "I suppose we all suspected that to be the case."

"Agatha mentioned that Travis had broken into the house shortly after Quinn's untimely death. From what she says he didn't make off with much of anything, but she caught him in Quinn's study. I think that's how he got hold of your letters."

Charles cleared his throat and straightened his collar. "Miss Thompson, if we may speak on this matter." He waited for her to nod before he went on. "Simon and Edna have shared some of the details of your situation with us." Charles spoke gently, like a person trying to gain favor with a stray dog.

Hattie's face heated with embarrassment and betrayal. She had expected to share her story in her own time, not have it carelessly passed along. She shot a terse look at Edna and then glanced at Mrs. Johnson, who seemed uninterested in her surroundings as she took tiny bites of food. Hattie breathed deeply, trying to calm down. She was sick of being betrayed.

No one wanted to help, they just wanted to pass her around, take what they can and then leave her. Come to think of it, wasn't that why she was here? She was a burden, passed from the woman who took her in after her parents died to Benson's men and again with the Maxwell's. No one wanted her. They were all too happy to send her out West to become a stranger's burden and then Quinn died, which was just her luck. Her thoughts spiraled out of control; she couldn't stop. If her thoughts were unfair, it was lost on her. She was too far gone. She didn't want to be here anymore; she didn't want to be anywhere.

Life was too hard and too unfair.

"Hattie?" Jennifer's soft voice drew her out of her downward spiral. "May we speak privately after dinner? This really is a matter best sorted by women with full bellies and a nip of brandy. Wouldn't you agree?"

Hattie grinned despite herself. Jennifer's cadence and phrasing were so much like her mother's. Had she blindly heard her speak, she would have thought her a ghost.

"Yes, I think so." She said, grateful for Jenifer's tact. The rest of dinner crawled by with idle conversation amongst the men, trying to make everything seem normal. Hattie didn't begrudge them their efforts, but their chatter was tiresome and she just wanted quiet. When the meal finished, Hattie offered to help clear up while Mrs. Johnson excused herself.

"Thank you, Hattie. Why don't you go through to the sitting room with my mother?" Edna took the plates from Hattie and nodded toward the door. "Simon lit a fire in there, and it should be quite cozy by this time." Edna smiled, but it didn't quite reach her eyes. Hattie tried to decipher the meaning in her darkened stare, but failed.

Hattie followed Jennifer while the men went to sit on the porch. The sitting room was cozy, and Hattie felt a bit lighter. It was laid out like a combination between a parlor and a study. A paned window with a cushioned bench seat on the far wall overlooked the front yard. Gold and maroon patterned drapes were still open despite the later hour. A nook adjacent to the window held a maroon backed chair tucked into a black walnut writing desk. Built in shelving flanked a fireplace, which danced lazy shadows on the ceiling as it crackled.

Hattie went to survey the books lining the shelves, fingering each title as Jennifer took a seat on the edge of the chaise. Hattie had a well-worn copy of Jane Eyre gifted to her by Elizabeth, but she was growing tired of the quarrelsome Mr. Rochester and the stubborn Jane. If anything, they reminded her of Dean and Elizabeth, one cynical, the other hell bent on independence. She preferred gentler love stories, like that of Marianne and Colonel Brandon. She had imagined herself and Mark having a love like that. Brought about through patience and healing, but she'd missed her chance.

"Do you like to read?" Jennifer broke the silence and Hattie jumped, her companion nearly forgotten until that moment.

"Oh my," she said with a hand on her frantic heart, "forgive me. I can be a bit skittish. I do enjoy a good book. Helps keep my thoughts away from the darker corners of my mind. My friend Elizabeth gave me a book for the journey out here and I've finished it twice."

"It must be hard being so far from home. I'm sure you must miss your friends." Jennifer motioned with her hand to the seat across the table from her. Edna entered, wordlessly placed a tray with two brandy snifters and a small glass decanter on the table in front of her mother, and then left again. Hattie crossed in front of the fire, enjoying the warmth on her body before taking a seat across from Jennifer. Jennifer handed her one of the snifters and they both sipped.

"I miss my friends. It was strange the way we all came

together. You see, there was an understanding between us that outsiders could never comprehend." Hattie nervously sipped the brandy, the plum flavor sticky on her tongue.

"You're blessed to have found each other." Jennifer's motherly demeanor mixed with the brandy to settle Hattie's nerves.

Hattie shrugged. "It sure seemed so." Hattie sipped. "Right up till they sent me away and then forgot about me."

Jennifer didn't react to Hattie's words. She calmly regarded Hattie for a few minutes and then spoke as if the last comment hadn't been made. "Would you tell me your story? I'd like to hear it from you, if you're willing."

A feeling of guilt welled in her belly over her thoughts at dinner. She hadn't been fair, especially to those offering kindness. If only trusting was easier and came with guarantees.

Hattie studied Jennifer's face. "I thought Edna had told you everything."

Jennifer sighed. "Edna told us you had come to marry Quinn Fletcher, but since his death, his brother Travis is trying to force you to marry him. If she knows more of your situation, she has said nothing to us about it."

Hattie nodded. She believed Jennifer's ignorance. That meant she owed Edna an apology.

Something about Jennifer made Hattie want to share. She cherished memories of her dear parents and held them close to her heart. She rarely spoke of them, but Jennifer made her want to talk. "I had such a nice life. My childhood was so warm that my memories glow." Hattie sat back in her seat and relaxed. "The sweet years before my parents died were all that kept me sane during my time in captivity."

Hattie watched Jennifer, trying to gauge how much Edna had actually shared with her mother. When she mentioned that she'd been in captivity, Jennifer's eyes had widened and she was sure it was the first she'd heard of it.

"My parents were sweet, quiet people. Our home was full of love and kindness when I was little. I had no idea that there was bad in the world, because our world was beautiful and loving." Hattie smiled and let another sip of brandy warm her.

Her heart sank as she pushed on. "My parents died when cholera passed through our building three years ago. When they fell ill, they sent me to live downstairs with an elderly widow, Mrs. Chadwick. She was so sweet to me throughout their illness. I'd known her my whole life, so I wasn't uncomfortable there. I thought of her as a grandmother, really." Anger welled up and tears sprang to her eyes as she remembered the time when her sweet childhood turned into a nightmare.

Jennifer listened and sipped. Every time Jennifer sipped, Hattie sipped, and the story became easier and easier to tell.

"My parents never recovered. They died within days of each other and Mrs. Chadwick said I could stay with her as long as I needed. I was heartbroken, but grateful that I wasn't alone in the world. I was so wrong."

A cold tear streaked down her cheek, but she didn't bother to wipe it away. She took another sip of brandy and went on, "There was a man, I don't know his name. I used to see him around. He would leave packages and envelopes for Mrs. Chadwick sometimes. I thought he was a courier or something. A couple of weeks after my parents passed, he came to the apartment. We had just finished supper, and it all happened so fast."

Hattie had to stop in her tale. She'd never really told the story in such detail, and the betrayal was still a knife in her chest. "I was washing up the dishes when there was a knock on the door. I listened to an exchange of pleasantries, and didn't think anything of it. Then suddenly the man was right behind me. He grabbed me and put a rag over my face." Hattie's pulse raced and her hand shook. Tears streamed down her face as she rushed through her story. "I just remember this fat hairy arm wrapped around me. I was fighting as hard as I could. And as everything went black, I saw Mrs. Chadwick, smiling." Tears flowed freely and Jennifer was crying, too.

Jennifer pulled a handkerchief from her sleeve and dabbed at her cheeks. "You poor child. What a horrid thing to have happen. I am truly sorry you had to go through that." She looked like she wanted to embrace Hattie, but didn't. Hattie finished the brandy in her glass and placed it on the tray. Jennifer reached forward, grabbed the decanter, and poured more brown liquid into each glass.

Hattie burped. She slapped her hand over her mouth and cringed. Jennifer chuckled as she dabbed more tears. Hattie picked up the glass and sipped, then she wiped the last of her tears and prepared to tell the rest of her story.

"When I awoke, I was in a nightmare. I was in a room with other women. Some dressed and others…," she trailed off, not wanting to go into detail. "Well—"

Jennifer pressed her handkerchief to her chest and sipped her brandy. "Oh, dear. This is worse than I had imagined. You poor thing."

"Do you really want to hear the rest?" Hattie asked. "The story doesn't get better from here."

Jennifer nodded. "I do, but don't you think we should

bring Edna in? I think I probably know as much at this point as she does."

Hattie paused. Jennifer was right, she really hadn't shared more with Edna than that, and she had lived with her for weeks. She nodded, and Jennifer rose from the chaise and tottered into the kitchen. Hattie took a sip of brandy and wondered if she would walk straight after two snifters.

The ladies returned, and Edna filled her own little glass with brandy. After a few sips, Jennifer had filled her in on the parts of Hattie's history that had been shared. Edna nodded and gazed sadly at Hattie as her mother related the terrible facts.

Jennifer stopped and once again refilled their glasses. Hattie wondered at a minister's wife taking quite so much drink, but she needed liquid assistance to get her through the telling of her story. Jennifer settled the top on the decanter and returned it to the tray. "Go on, dear, tell us about your captivity."

Hattie cleared her throat and drank a bigger sip than she should. She choked and coughed and after sputtering for a minute, she settled down again. "I won't go into detail. I can't. I'll just say the conditions were atrocious."

She couldn't look at their sad faces, so she stared into her glass. "I survived eleven months in Hell. My memory is gone for much of that time. I'm sure that is a blessing."

The brandy dulled the edges of her pain, and she grabbed the snifter again, hoping to increase the effect. Taking her largest mouthful yet, she swallowed and continued with Jennifer's eyes, patiently watching.

"Mark found me. Well, The Maxwell Group found me." Hattie smiled when Mark's handsome face flashed in front of her eyes. She remembered his strong arms, his scent, the beat of his heart against her ear. Her body grew warm, and she relaxed.

Jennifer brought her attention back with a gasp. "The Maxwells from Hope?" she asked.

Hattie straightened, sure that her face must mimic the surprise on Edna's. "You know them?"

"Everybody knows The Maxwell Group. I grew up with Rosie and Iris Dunn." My dear Charles moved us here from Hope after we were married." She smiled. "I don't really remember one named Mark, but I remember the Maxwell twins pretty well. They were good boys, and Rosie and Iris took good care of them."

"They are the ones responsible for taking down the gang that kept us prisoner. Mark found me moments from death, and it was already too late for the other girls. They brought me back to the rescue house, and back to life, really."

Hattie looked at Jennifer, feeling closer to her with their new connection. "The rescue house is named The Rose Dunn House. A plaque on the wall in the Mansion tells the story of Rose Dunn's tragic death.

Jennifer wiped frantically at her leaking eyes. "Rosie was a handful." She smiled. "When we were girls, she was the one with all the ideas that would get us in trouble. But there was Iris right beside her to stop us from doing most of them."

Hattie and Edna laughed. Hattie was more at ease than she'd been in a while. She'd really needed to get the story off her chest. "I'd love to hear some of those stories one day."

Jennifer nodded. "You will, dear. But for tonight, let's hear the rest of your story so we can pray for a solution."

"There's not a lot to tell after they brought me to the

Rose Dunn House. They let me heal as slowly as I needed. I don't just mean physically. That was a lot faster than the emotional and mental healing. I still struggle, but I'm a lot better than I was a few months ago." She finished with a sad smile.

Her memories swirled in her mind, some happy and some sad. Jennifer extended a hand, bridging half the distance between them, and Hattie took it. Her soft wrinkled hand was a welcome touch and again she thought of her mother.

"Thank you for telling us, Hattie. It can't be easy to recall all of that. And how did you end up out here as a mail-order bride?" Her voice was without judgment.

"It all happened so fast. My mother used to say, 'You always try to run before you can walk.'" Hattie laughed, "The well-meaning housekeeper thought the local matchmaker was our best chance at new lives. It seemed like the right answer at the time, but once I got here, I felt like I had been tricked again."

"It is tragic what happened to Quinn. How unfortunate for you to take this leap of faith and be met with such circumstances. I think we should pray. Would you like that?" She waited for Hattie to nod, just as her husband had earlier in the evening. "The Good Book says, 'For where two or three are gathered together in my name, there am I in the midst of them.'" Jennifer smiled and squeezed Hattie's hand. They each reached for one of Edna's hands and prayed.

What kind of solution would they get from God? He'd abandoned her just like everyone else in her life. Perhaps he would help her if Jennifer and Edna asked. He certainly hadn't bothered with any of Hattie's prayers.

Chapter Sixteen

A week passed on the ranch with several telegrams crossing the country between Mark and Mrs. Phillips. As she'd met him several times, she waved most of her requirements for personal references. She asked him several questions about his temperament and preferences and then promised to do her best.

Their correspondence concluded and Mark was satisfied to wait for the good woman to find a suitable match for him. Mark focused on his work, expecting months to pass without news.

He was wrong.

A letter from Mrs. Florence Campbell arrived within two weeks from his first contact with Mrs. Phillips. With the speed of the post, the letter must have been sent before he'd even answered all of her questions.

Mark sat at his kitchen table, sipping coffee that had long lost its heat. The bitter brew was sour on his tongue, and he grimaced but absentmindedly took another sip. He stared at the letter, unprepared for what it contained. He didn't have the heart to open it right away, because opening the letter meant that he had to truly let Hattie go and he just couldn't bring himself to do it.

He dropped the letter on the table and stomped into the kitchen. He turned his mug over into the sink and then pulled a bottle of whisky from the shelf. After tossing back a gulp, he left his mug on the counter and returned to the letter.

With no more reason to delay, he slid his finger under the seal.

Dear Mr. Webb,

May this letter find you joyfully.

I was unable to provide a photograph, but you may recall that we met briefly the day your journey at The Rose Dunn House ended and mine began.

Mrs. Phillips and Mrs. Fritz have assured me of your character. In fact, you received glowing support from all the occupants of the house.

I, myself, am a widow with little to tell. I have had a blessed life, but I am still grieving for my late husband, Troy. I could not enter into another union without first confessing that my heart still belongs to him.

I have prayed on the matter and believe I am being called Westward to serve God. I am a fine cook and an excellent worker.

I believe, given time, we should find great comfort and companionship in one another's company. Should you find me satisfactory to your situation and mind, I am prepared to travel to you.

I eagerly await your response.

Sincerely,

Florence Campbell

The image of the beautiful woman standing in the doorway of The Rose Dunn House flashed in his mind. Any man would be lucky to marry such a woman, though the prospect still made him sad. She wasn't Hattie.

Sophia had sent letters with news from Boston. The letters passed around the ranch and were eventually responded to by one of the women. Most often Abigail or Maggie wrote back, but everyone added questions or bits of information to share with their friends in the East. Sophia had described Florence as a sweet-tempered woman. Sophia found her a bit boring and peaceful, but Mark liked those qualities. Her claim to be a good cook had been confirmed by Sophia, as was her religious nature.

While these traits mattered, the most prominent detail came from her letter. She, too, was full of love for someone else. He could enter into the marriage with a clear conscience. She would understand that he was grieving the loss of his own love. Given time, perhaps they might transfer that love to each other.

He folded and tucked the letter in his shirt pocket. His chair scuffed on the floor in his haste. Donning his hat, he left. The door slammed behind him, sending crows flying off the rooftop. His long legs ate up the ground as he crossed to where his mare was lazily grazing. When he whistled a few notes, she moseyed his way, still tacked from his morning ride.

"Atta girl," he said, stroking between her eyes when she reached him.

He'd never experienced a longer ride into town than that one. It was the ride that would change his life forever. He didn't rush, he didn't want to arrive. Because when he arrived at the General Store, he would send a life altering telegram and all of his dreams of a life with Hattie would evaporate forever.

THE DAWN CREPT THROUGH THE TREES, CASTING LONG-fingered shadows on the bedroom floor. Hattie laid on her side, thumb stroking the bison gently in its cloth. She'd already smoothed some of the curves and didn't want to lose more of the detail Mark had put into it. A numbness settled inside her and she couldn't decide if it was peace or apathy. Which would be better?

She was out of money and prospects. The Oakleys hadn't asked her for payment, but she couldn't stay with them forever. Edna had promised that she could stay as long as she needed, but she couldn't do that. She'd done that at The Rose Dunn House and look at how that had turned out for her.

But what was the alternative?

She'd prayed with Jennifer and Edna more than a week ago, and each night, she had repeated her prayers until she drifted into a fitful sleep. Still, God and her friends remained silent.

Why had no one written to her?

She had sent several letters to Hope, pleading with Opal and Angela for help with no reply. And Boston may as well have been another continent. The only constant she had was daily visits from Travis and the pitying looks from Edna and Simon.

The encounters with Travis were by no means pleasurable experiences. He seemed to be making an effort to be kind, though his behavior was fairly lascivious at times. He was like a child, never schooled in anything resembling manners. Hattie sighed. He had no duplicity, at least. He was the only person around her who she knew was exactly who he seemed to be.

Hattie dressed, donning the fine navy frock she had worn the day she left Boston. As she exited her room, she caught sight of three men at the far end of the hall and stumbled backward into a table. A glass vase clattered to the floor and shattered in a thousand tiny pieces. The explosion caught the attention of the men and they all turned to her.

Her heart stopped, then raced.

"Are you alright, sweetheart?" One of the men called, his voice light, but it was a trick. It had to be a trick—they were there to get her, to take her away. She ran into her room and locked the door. She pressed her back to the door and squeezed her eyes shut.

Male laughter was all around her and she couldn't breathe. She clutched her ears—she didn't want to hear it, but it didn't matter, the sounds were in her mind. Hattie took a rapid breath as footsteps trickled down the hall toward her.

"Hattie? Is everything alright?" Edna's soft voice came slightly muffled, like she was speaking too closely to the door. Hattie gasped for air, but her lungs couldn't get enough.

"Don't worry about the vase. I promise it wasn't expensive. Please don't fret, Hattie, it's only a thing. Things can be replaced."

Still, Hattie kept silent, a war raging in her chest.

"Please, open the door? I just want to make sure you're alright. You didn't cut yourself, did you?"

Finally, her breath caught and her heart rate slowed. The panic slipped back to the dark corners of her mind.

Hattie's voice sounded strangled when she finally managed to speak. She pressed her hand to her throat and forced herself to ask, "Who are those men?"

"They're guests, Hattie. They came early this morning from West Branch."

Hattie wouldn't be tricked again. "Why did you bring them here?" She couldn't believe it was happening again.

Who was she kidding? Of course, it was happening again. This is what happened in her life. People made her comfortable and then they stomped on her.

Edna's soft voice sounded teary. "They are miners of some sort or other. I don't really understand much about it."

"Does Travis know?"

Edna laughed bitterly, "What does that fool know?" After a moment, she said, "I'm worried about you. Please open up so I know you're okay?"

"I'm fine." Hattie couldn't bring herself to open the door when she still heard the terrible echo of male laughter in the back of her mind. "I'm not feeling well and I need to change my dress."

"Okay. I'll clean this mess and get these men on their

way to work." Edna tapped the door softly. "I'll let you know when they have gone."

Tears fell silently and Hattie slid her back down the door until she sat on the floor. She wanted nothing more than to open her eyes and be back at The Rose Dunn House. Better yet, back in the home she grew up in before her parents had died.

She cried until her adrenaline ebbed and she got up. Picking through her dresses, she changed into a simple gray house dress, speckled with grease stains from her days under Mrs. Fritz's instruction.

Hattie hung her dress to dry on a peg beside the door and then sat on her bed for news that the miners had gone from the house, but when Edna tapped on the door, Hattie struggled to believe her.

Eventually, Hattie opened the door to find only Edna waiting on the other side. Hattie's eyes scanned, but she could not see or hear the men. "Where are they?"

"I expect they're halfway to town by now." She smiled. "I waited until I was sure they wouldn't be back to come and find you. Simon is gone for the day as well, so it's just us women today. Why don't you grab a cup of tea and sit on the porch for a while?"

The ease of the late June morning sun was calming and after a while, her scattered thoughts eased. A raspy singing accompanied by the clip clop of hooves ruined her delicate peace.

> *"Ding dong, ding dong, ding dong, I love the song,*
> *For it is my wedding morning,*
> *And the bride's so gay in fine array,*
> *For the day will be now adornin'."*

Travis pulled Jeremiah to a stop in front of the boardinghouse. The tired donkey's eyes pleaded to be free of its owner. Travis hopped off the rickety wagon, grunting as he landed on his feet and slapped his knee.

"Good morning, Miss Hattie! Isn't it a fine day for a wedding?" He removed his hat to greet her, and she was shocked to see his hair had been slicked back and beard somewhat groomed. There were no holes or stains in his wrinkled shirt and slacks, which were a drastic improvement from his regular ware. He beamed with delight, thumbing his suspenders.

Her pulse flickered, and she felt faint. Hopelessness overwhelmed her.

Where were her friends when she needed help? Simon was away, and she couldn't see Edna anywhere. She should have known not to be alone on the front porch. "Mr. Fletcher, how can I help you?"

"Why, Ms. Hattie, I think it's about time you and I tied the knot, so we can get down to..." He winked and wriggled his eyebrows as he liked to do. It took every ounce of her resolve not to recoil.

"I never promised to marry you."

Travis climbed the stairs and stood too close. Hattie kicked herself for not standing as soon as she'd seen him. Now he hovered over the rocking chair and she had no escape. To stand up would mean bumping right into him.

Travis squinted his right eye and bulged the other, searching her face before arching his back and releasing a knee slapping laugh. "Miss Hattie, you playin' hard to get? Looks like you were ready for me, wearing that pretty white gown."

Hattie looked down at her worn attire. "My dress is gray?"

"Well, you ain't no pure blushing bride now, are ya? Probably started out white as Moses's beard and you turned it to gray." He guffawed again, seeming amused with himself.

Hattie searched for an escape, for anyone to help her, but she knew Edna had taken laundry to the backyard. She was alone and out of fight.

"Please let me be." She looked toward the door, wanting to run inside. But he followed her gaze and rushed to put himself between her and the entrance.

"I've waited long enough. It ain't right. I played your courtin' game." He thumbed his suspenders again and leaned against the wall. "I come by here e'ry day and talked real sweet to ya. I ain't even touch you that much or ask for no kissin'. Enough is enough."

He grabbed her by the arm and dragged her out of her chair and over to the wagon. Whatever flicker of fight she had in her was gone the moment he put his hands on her. Numbness set in. She'd tried everything to get help, and she'd been abandoned by friends and God. There was nothing left but to accept her fate.

Hattie didn't even try to collect her things. The carving bumped her leg as she climbed onto the wagon. It was the only thing she was bringing with her.

She didn't expect to live long enough to miss her belongings, anyway.

As Jeremiah jolted forward, she gave up all hope.

Chapter Seventeen

Horses beating up the drive, pulled Mark from his lunch. Daniel and Paul thundered toward the cabin with matching looks of determination on their faces. Mark abandoned his meal and bolted to the door. Fumbling with his gun belt, he fastened it on, donning his hat as he pealed out of the house.

Nobody rode into the dooryard like that unless there was an emergency.

As soon as the two bay mares stopped, the men hit the ground in unison.

"What's going on?" Mark asked, not wanting to waste time.

"It's Hattie." Daniel said. He handed his reins to Paul, who walked both horses over to the hitching rail. "She made it to Silent Creek safely, but her groom died before she arrived."

Mark's heart was fit to beat out of his chest. Hattie's groom was dead? So, what had she been doing for the last five weeks?

"She telegrammed Boston, but they haven't been able

to reach her back and none of our ladies have received any letters from her." Daniel said calm and quickly.

Mark pulled his hat from his head and ran his hand through his hair. "Shit."

"And there's something else," Paul said, looking at Daniel, then Mark. "There was a man, the dead groom's brother. He claims he inherited her as part of his brother's estate." Paul pumped water into a bucket and then dumped it into the trough.

Mark froze. "What the hell? How do you know this?"

Paul dropped a heavy hand on Mark's shoulder. "The owner of the boardinghouse, Simon Oakley, rode in this morning looking for us." Daniel and Paul exchanged glances. "He came here mad, wanting to know why we ignored all her letters for help."

Daniel slammed his fist on the rail, startling the horses. "This would-be groom sounds like a real piece of work. Oakley says she's been living with him and his wife since she arrived, but they can't seem to drive away this suitor, Travis, something."

"Fletcher?" Mark knew the name well enough. He'd hated that name since the day Hattie opened the letter.

Daniel nodded. "That's it. Travis Fletcher. Seems he just won't leave her alone."

Mark charged toward the barn. "What are we waiting for? She could be in danger or—" He didn't want to say it and he didn't need to.

Paul stopped Mark with a hand on his arm. "Mark, there's more."

"What else?" Mark searched his brother's faces but only read more dread on them. "What the hell else could have happened?"

Paul squared off with Mark and said, "She's missing."

Mark pulled his hat off his head again and ran his hand through his hair. "What do you mean?"

"When Oakley returned home from running errands this morning, his wife was frantic that Hattie had gone missing. He let the sheriff know, then rode straight to us." Paul crossed his arms over his chest. "He said her belongings are still in her room and she was out of money. There's a chance she just went out and didn't come back yet, but nobody believes it." Daniel's voice was level, but his face showed a lot of anxiety.

"We're going, now. I'll go alone or you guys can come, but I'm leaving right now."

"Woah," Paul said, patting his hands in the air like he was trying to calm a wild animal. "The group is assembling at Caine's. Oakley is already there. We sent him with Will to round up the guys."

Mark filled his lungs with air and pushed it back out. He nodded his head.

"Silent Creek is a four—five-hour ride from here. We need fresh mounts and then we go." Daniel tipped the last of the water from the trough so it wouldn't mildew and untied his reins. "Caine will have horses ready when we get there."

Mark nodded, well aware of just what kind of damage could be done during every wasted minute. "I'll grab my gear and meet you at Caine's."

Mark nearly ripped the door from its hinges in his haste to get on his way. His brothers left a trail of dust behind them as Mark pulled his saddlebag from the peg beside the door. He stuffed some ammo, jerky, and canteen inside and then slammed the door on his way to the barn.

He should have never let her go.

He promised to protect her and he failed.

~

"Ding dong, ding dong, we'll gallop along,
All fears and doubting scorning.
Through the valley, we'll haste, for we've no time
*   to waste,*
As this is my wedding morning."

TRAVIS'S CROAKY SINGING CARRIED THEM OUT OF TOWN. PART of her brain was waking up, while the other shushed it back to sleep. She stared blankly as the dirt road gave way to a rolling rocky terrain. The grass was sparser here, with short scraggly trees cropping up every few feet.

"We're going to have such fun when we get home." His eyebrows wiggled like two fat caterpillars beneath the brim of his hat.

She swallowed loudly.

"Oh no need to me nervous. I know you've done it before." He freed one of his hands from the reins and pinched her bottom.

"Ouch."

"Ooo, you liked it, want another?" He pinched her again, and she nearly toppled off the wagon. "I'm gonna have a real good time with you. Yessiree!"

"Please, where are we going?" Hattie had very little fight left in her, but she had plenty of fear. "I can't go to your house. We're not married, and it is terribly inappropriate."

"You had a whole," He seamed to be counting days on his fingers. "You had a whole lot o' time. We'll be married in every way that counts and I'm ready for some weddin' cake."

This time, he reached between her legs and tickled the inner part of her thigh.

Hattie deflated as his brazen touch broke whatever strength she had mustered. The part of her brain that was waking went silent as the last of her hope dissolved.

Hattie prayed for a swift end this time before everything went black.

～

WILL, CAINE, SARAH, HANK, AND DANIEL WERE MOUNTED up and ready to fly when Mark arrived at Caine's house. The sight lifted his spirits. They were family and a damn good one.

There was one stranger among the group, and he was quickly introduced as Simon Oakley. Oakley mounted as Maggie, Jeni, and Abigail loaded the food into saddlebags. Iris stood on the farmhouse porch with children all around her and a worried look in her eye. She caught Mark's attention and held it. No words passed between them, but warmth rushed through Mark. Then she nodded, and he turned back to the group.

Caine—always the leader—spoke above the din of voices and hooves in the yard. He addressed the group, but he looked at Mark as he spoke. Though Mark had no claim over Hattie, it was clear that they all regarded her as his woman. "Caleb and Paul are staying behind to take care of the ranch. We've got a long ride ahead of us, so let's not waste any time."

The Maxwell Group kicked up a sandstorm in their wake. Their horses galloped like beasts ready for battle. Mark found the thunderous storm of hooves calming and he forced himself to empty his mind.

The ride to Silent Creek was by no means the longest ride he'd been on, but each mile seemed to stretch on longer and longer. They took the most direct route, riding through thicker swaths of forest and crossing the Madison River.

Every stop to rest the horses was a delay that Mark detested. Every pause was a holdup he couldn't stand. But he knew the dangers of not stopping. Thank God it wasn't up to him, because the horses would drop from exhaustion and they would never get to Hattie. So, when Caine said they needed to stop, Mark stopped.

The horses moved steadily and sure-footed through the forest, their hooves thudded against the soft layers of moss and fallen leaves. The tall trees towered overhead, their thick branches formed a canopy and dampened much of the afternoon sunlight. The woods were alive with birdsong, leaves rustling in the wind, and the distant calls of animals.

The breeze carried the sweet scents of pine and cedar, with the occasional hint of wildflowers and berries. As they moved deeper into the woods, the trees became larger and more imposing, and the underbrush thicker, making it harder to ride side by side. Mark knew little about this part of the territory, but trusted Hank to lead them through. He was an excellent tracker and navigator. The horses plowed on until they trotted down the Main Street of the freshly painted little town.

Simon led the exhausted group down the lane toward his house.

A puffy eyed brunette stepped onto the porch and straight into Simon's embrace. "This is my wife, Edna," he said over her head.

"Is she back? Have you heard anything?" Simon asked his wife.

Edna shook her head. "Sheriff Page has been looking for her. The ground is so hard they don't have any tracks to follow." She wiped her eyes on her apron and turned.

"I'm Mark Webb."

Edna studied him. "There was some question about whether you'd survived the train crash."

Caine stepped forward and politely interrupted. "Pardon me. We need to rest our horses and feed them."

Edna nodded. "Go and settle the animals and I'll get supper on the table." She patted her husband's chest and then stepped back.

"Of course." Simon pulled his reins from the rail and walked toward the barn.

Mark shook his head and crossed his arms over his chest. "We don't have time to stop. Every moment matters."

Sarah handed her reins to Caine and linked her arm with Mark's. "You know the horses need to rest and eat. And what good are we to, Hattie, if we don't keep our strength up?" She gave his arm a shake. "You know better, Mark." She gently pulled his reins from his hand and passed them to Hank.

He couldn't argue because she was right. No matter how badly he wanted to keep going, the horses couldn't do it. Mark let the others mind the horses as he stepped away to wrangle his emotions. Now that they were so close, it killed him to stop moving.

The table was laid for a feast, and Edna bustled about to accommodate everyone. "There's plenty to eat. Please help yourselves." Something about her reminded Mark of

Mrs. Fritz and it gave him the slightest bit of comfort to imagine Hattie thinking the same.

"Do you know anything we don't?" Mark asked.

Edna froze with a plate in hand and sighed, then she started moving and talking at the same time. "That Travis is a right old piece of you-know-what." She stamped her foot and huffed. "He's a dirty man, with dirtier friends. How he and Quinn were from the same womb, I will never know. Caine and Abel, I tell you, I told Hattie the same thing."

The group fell silent as Edna filled plates and then passed them around the table. "I don't know why he wouldn't take no for an answer, but once he had it in his mind that she was his, he was like a dog with a bone."

Three men scooted behind Hank and Caine to sit at the far end of the table. Mark eyed them. "Hey." The men looked at Mark and so did everyone else. "Did any of you see what happened to the young woman who was staying here?"

The largest of the three spoke. His broad forehead and jawline made him look like something carved from rocks to ward off evil spirits. "We saw her when we first arrived." The other two nodded in agreement. "Think we spooked her. She came out of her room, saw us, and bucked like a scared horse. We'd left for the mine when she disappeared, though."

Could Hattie have panicked and taken off on her own?

"What else?" Mark was desperate for any information.

Edna pushed her plate forward and propped her elbows on the table. "She was not well lately. She seemed to withdraw into herself and became mistrusting of everyone. Even us."

"Was Travis here today?" Mark shoveled food into his

mouth. The sooner they finished eating, the sooner they could get back on the trail.

She shrugged. "I didn't see him. She wanted some air after her fright this morning. I was in the back with the wash."

"Do you think she left?" Sarah asked.

"No." Edna's mouth pressed into a straight line.

"She went with 'im." The widow said blankly.

"What?" Edna looked as shocked as Mark felt.

"I saw 'em, out my window. She didn't look happy, either. Just like," She let her face hang flat, her wrinkled skin dangling like a bloodhound before her face relaxed back into a withdrawn glare.

"Why didn't you say anything? We've been in a state all day!" Edna half-shouted at her elderly boarder.

"Not my business. But I can't stand seeing this man so heartbroken." She pointed her crooked old finger at Mark.

Every head in the room snapped to look at Mark as if a big secret had been revealed, but he brushed it off. Looking at the Maxwell Group, he said, "Why would she leave without her clothes?"

"That doesn't make sense to me either," Hank said thoughtfully.

"Hattie wouldn't have gone off with a man she barely knew." Paul said. "The last time I saw her, she couldn't even be in a room with an unfamiliar man."

Mark agreed. "She is too delicate to be running away with a stranger."

"She traveled across the country to marry a man she didn't even know." Sarah said with a raised brow. "She obviously gained some strength since the last time you saw her."

"You don't know her, Sarah." Mark said. "She isn't like you. She's sweet and gentle."

Sarah laughed, "Well, I suppose that's not like me. I'm just saying, none of you are giving her enough credit. It takes gumption to be a mail-order bride."

"That's different." Mark's anger flared.

Sarah glared at him. "I was a mail-order bride." She half-stood with her hands braced on the table and leaned toward Mark. "You can't imagine the courage it takes to step off a stage prepared to marry whoever is standing there waiting for you. At least I was wearing a gun." She swatted at Caine when he rubbed her back. "She might be struggling now, but if she made the trip, then the girl has more grit than you're giving her credit for."

"Look," Caine cleared his throat, "emotions are high. Let's just find her and once she's safe, we can go from there."

"Alright, I'm sorry." Mark sulked back in his chair.

A sweaty Simon barged into the dining room reeking of horse, gasping for air. "Travis was spotted heading for Red's Bluff." He wheezed and sputtered.

"Who told you?" Edna demanded.

"Ollie. He said there was a body in the back of Travis's old cart. A woman, whiter than a sheet with sun colored hair. It has to be Hattie."

"She can't be dead." Mark stood and pulled her handkerchief from his pocket and ran his thumb over the letters. "Maybe she was knocked out or fainted?"

Sarah jumped to her feet and raced out the door with Caine hot on her heels.

"Where does Travis live?" Mark and Hank stood beside the table while the others all headed toward the barn.

Simon shook his head, but then reconsidered, "No one

really knows where he lives, but there's are miners' shacks out by one of the dead mines. I've heard folks say they'd seen him skulking about out there. It's a rough journey for someone who knows the way, let alone someone who doesn't."

"We'll manage." Hank shoved his hands in his pockets. "Give us the directions and we'll make do."

Simon nodded and dashed over to a writing desk tucked into an alcove in the living room.

Mark's heart raced out of control.

He found her dead once before, and she lived.

Please, God, let her live again.

Chapter Eighteen

Bony fingers dug into her forearms, violently tugging her off the wagon. Hattie came to just in time to land her feet. She stumbled back into the wagon bed and hung on for dear life. Travis seemed unconcerned with her renewed consciousness or loss of balance.

Consciousness and control were two very different things. Hattie had drifted away in the wake of Travis's tide and there was nothing she could do. With her current situation staring her in the face, Hattie wished for the oblivion of sleep.

Her body shook as she gazed into the distance. A painting of pine and rock laid out before her, but the beauty was lost in the maze-like wilderness.

So, this was her new prison.

The woods were dark and foreboding. Her isolation was palpable amid the vast landscape. She spun, searching for any sign of hope to cling to, but there wasn't another house or person for as far as she could see.

Hattie's heart dropped into her stomach, and she swallowed a lump. Now what?

An incessant droning came into focus. It was Travis singing that wretched wedding song under his breath. He caught her looking at him and smiled his grotesque smile. Then he grabbed her arm and pulled her along toward the rickety cabin. Hattie tripped over a large rock in the path, and he dragged her, feet thumping along as he rambled on.

She struggled to get her feet back under her and stand up, but he was too fast and too rough, and she couldn't gain any footing. Travis was no longer singing, but instead he described in horrid detail the things he planned to do once inside. Her muscles tensed, and she wanted to fight, but there was no fire in her.

"Goin' like it too," he said, pulling Hattie to her feet in front of the cabin. He turned her around like the rag doll she was and pointed her at the front door of the shelter. "Home sweet, home." Hattie couldn't bring herself to look up. Her eyes were trained on the rotting floorboards of the porch. It didn't even look like it would hold their weight, and she expected it to collapse at any moment.

Travis, on the other hand, hummed happily behind her. "Welcome home, darlin'." He smacked her bottom and returned down the walkway to lead Jeremiah to a three walled lean-to of sorts. The shed was cobbled together with mismatched scraps of wood, branches, and metal. He tied the poor creature up in front of an empty pail. Jeremiah protested loudly and kicked it over. "I'll tend to you later." Travis waved the donkey off and went to the door of the shack.

Home, if it could be called a home, could scarcely be regarded as a shack. It was the carcass of a house, picked clean by time and buzzards. The walls were thin slat boards with more gaps than Travis's smile. The mossy roof smelled of rot and was partially caved in. When Travis opened the door, two birds flew out of a hole near the corner.

"Come on now," he shoved her with one hand on the small of her back.

Hattie's feet wouldn't go, but when he gave a second, harder shove, she stumbled. Once her feet were moving, she stepped up onto the porch. Running away passed through her mind like a fantasy, but where would she go?

Hattie swallowed tightly and accepted her fate.

Some people just weren't meant to have safety and happiness.

Finding her feet, she took timid steps. Each creak and groan of the floorboards was a warning she couldn't heed. If this was God's plan, she wished she knew what she'd done to deserve it. She clung to the railing as she took another terrified step up onto the porch.

But she wasn't moving fast enough. Travis's lanky arms scooped her up and carried her across the threshold. He crushed Hattie's body to his, and she wriggled to get as far away from him as possible. He was too close, and his rancid breath was on her face.

He huffed as he set her down. Hattie stepped away from him and scanned the little house for exits. Travis resumed his singing as he barred the door with a heavy plank and then pulled the hat from his head and plunked it down on a broken little table.

The damp and musty air inside mixed with something fetid and turned Hattie's stomach. The squalid room was littered with tin cans and crumpled wads of butcher paper. It was worse inside than she could have imagined. Oiled papers clung to the walls with maps and other stay paper, poor man's insulation. To the right, a rusty potbelly stove was pushed against the wall with one cook top and a store cupboard beside it. There was a small wash basin atop it, but it didn't look as if it had been used in a while. A few pots and pans scattered about the floor alongside a collection of tools, including a pickaxe, a shovel, and a sieve.

Hattie inventoried the items, cataloguing each possible weapon for future need. Everything was filmed with dirt and greasy grime. She could feel the nastiness with her eyes and had to wipe her hands on her skirt. A crooked table slumped in the middle of the room, burdened with miscellaneous bits of food and trash. Flies buzzed, interested in the new inhabitant. Hattie swatted them away and continued her quick study of the room as Travis finished securing the door.

On the left was a water-stained corn husk mattress on the floor with a tattered blanket and one pillow. Hattie couldn't tear her eyes away from the make-shift bed and her heart raced. How would she endure what was coming for her? A small chest beside the bed must comprise his wardrobe, but it was the mattress that had her frozen to the spot.

"Fix us up some grub. It's our weddin' night, after all." He winked, cackling, and her stomach turned.

"I don't know where anything is." She murmured, trying not to think of wedding nights. Feeling a bit of boldness, she added, "And we're not married."

Travis squinted threateningly, then smiled and ignored her statement. "I'll show you." He stepped too close until his body was pressed against hers and both of his hands were on her shoulders. He turned her toward the kitchen. "You build a fire in this." He pointed to the stove, then placed his right hand on her hip. "There's wood there," he pointed to a misshapen metal ring with thin pieces of kindling in it and then dropped his left hand to her hip, "and there's more wood out back." He pulled her against himself and nuzzled her neck. "Matches are on the table." Hattie was paralyzed, frozen to the spot. He flicked her earlobe with his tongue and Hattie's skin crawled. Travis whispered in her ear, "Foods on the table or in that there cupboard."

He stepped back so fast Hattie lost her balance and had to catch herself on the table.

"That's simple enough. Even you should be able to figure it out." He slapped her on the bottom again and she cringed, but he didn't seem to notice or care about her disgust.

"I'll get water from the creek this time, but it'll be your job after today. I'll be back." He crossed the room, grabbed a bucket and began singing his wedding day song in earnest.

Hattie wanted to vomit, but she had nothing in her after skipping breakfast.

When the door closed behind Travis, she made the mistake of taking a deep breath. The retched odors filled her lungs, and she gagged. She touched the buffalo in her pocket and drifted like a ghost to the table. A half black head of cabbage sat beside wilted carrots, wild celery, and the carcass of some sort of fowl. She gagged again and watched maggots wiggle around in what was to be their dinner.

She couldn't do this.

"When heart joins hand, there's none in the land

Can be richer in joys than we." Travis's voice faded.

The matches were pushed into the compost heap that

was his pantry. She removed them and set her sights on keeping busy. Shaking hands on wobbly legs carried her to the stove. She squatted and grabbed the corkscrew shaped handle, tugging open the door. She screamed and bolted upright when a mouse jumped out and scurried across the floor.

Peeking nervously into the stove, she was relieved no other creatures were lying in wait.

Hattie tented bits of wood in the belly of the stove and used some of the stray butcher paper to light it. Starting the fire was simple enough, but making the food edible was another matter.

She opened the cupboard, hoping to find something she could work with. Instead, she was disappointed to be greeted with a cornmeal sack riddled with worms and mouse droppings. The potatoes were so shriveled with eyes so long they may be in luck and have new potatoes by morning. What would she make for breakfast? She hadn't noticed any chickens in the yard when they'd driven up.

How did he plan to survive the winter? Summer would end before they knew it, and he didn't have proper fixings for a single meal. If the spoiled meat didn't kill them, starvation would.

Hattie was desperate for fresh air, so she took the wood ring and walked briskly to the front door. Once again, she scanned the area for any sign of help, but restrained the instinct to run away because all she saw was a desolate forest. Her foot slipped on the punky wood of the doorstep and her determination slipped with it.

This was her life now.

~

HANK AND MARK TOOK THE LEAD RACING NORTH OF TOWN. They departed from the dirt fairway to the rocky trails leading toward the mines when they passed two gigantic boulders, as indicated on Simon's map.

The rockier path slowed them down and Hank seemed to grow more chatty with each mile. "Why didn't you say you were still in love with the girl?"

Mark shrugged.

Hank shook his head. "We all thought you'd moved on."

Moved on. Like a man could just move on. Mark shook his head and avoided Hank's eyes. "She was married."

Hank nodded. That's the thing Mark liked most about Hank. He accepted things the way they were. Mark glanced behind them to check on the others. Caine and Sarah were bickering about something or other, and Daniel and Will were scanning for threats. Thank God it was Hank up front with him. Every one of the others would have drilled for more information.

Simon's rough map barely made sense, but as they passed landmarks, the map became more and more clear. The ink blotted paper showed two Xs. One marked the boardinghouse, and the other indicated the location of Simon's house. A dashed line winded its way between the two points, through several blobs which were mountainous areas and hatch marks for woods. It reminded Mark of treasure maps he'd drawn in the dirt as a boy after his father had filled his head with tales of explorers seeking their fortune in the wild.

The rocky path wound up a hillock, which gave a glorious view of the mountain dotted with timber supports for the mines. As they descended on the other side, they veered onto a wide trail through the woods. The ground was padded with pine needles and the horses sprang along, welcoming the softer earth. Thin pines and white birches stretched finger like to the sky, their roots creeping as snakes along the trail. The group staggered, aiming to guide the horses safely through. One trip on a root could mean the end for a horse and its rider.

Travis reportedly had a donkey and a small wagon. Mark couldn't believe anyone would drag a cart over such terrain. It was ridiculous with the roots and ruts and rocks. What sort of idiot was this, Travis Fletcher?

The ride to the shack wouldn't be too long if they got it right, but getting it wrong could see them camping in unknown territory.

And who knows what that would mean for Hattie?

Hank stopped suddenly and pointed to a rivulet crossing the trail. Wagon wheel ruts appeared on both sides, with the unmistakable oblong cupped hoofprints of a donkey.

The tracks disappeared quickly, but it was enough to give Mark hope. "We're on the right trail."

Hank nudged his horse into motion with a little more energy than before, and Mark gladly matched his pace.

Less than five minutes later, the trail began to narrow before abruptly splitting. One path led along a thin creek, riddled with brush. The other led down the side of the hill they had been climbing. It was clear, but steep and rocky.

They stopped and considered Simon's map, which was useless. There were no landmarks close enough to figure out where they were, and the creek wasn't even on the map.

"Damn it!" Mark crumpled the paper and threw it to the ground. He sat up in his saddle and scanned both trails.

Hank dismounted and picked it up. He folded the map and tucked it in his pocket before he kneeled down with his face inches from the ground. He studied both trails before he stood and indicated the path along the creek. "They went this way."

"You're sure?" Mark asked, but he felt the truth in his gut. Hank was right. Hank was always right.

"You really doubting him?" Will asked, sidling up next to him.

Mark started down the creek trail. "No."

They needed to find her soon. Nothing good would come of sundown.

Chapter Nineteen

Biding her time, Hattie set to cleaning the shack and preparing dinner. The task was impossible. No amount of scrubbing would make the hut livable, and she didn't have any proper cleaning supplies anyway. She searched inside every nook but couldn't find a sliver of soap, and it would break her heart to sacrifice her buffalo to the task. She found several rags, but they were black with filth and soiled with droppings of bugs and rodents. She kept her eyes from wandering to the bed against the wall and determined to do whatever she could.

It seemed the most impact could be made by collecting trash from the floor. She started at the base of the stove and worked outward from there. As she picked up papers, leaves and sticks, she tossed them into the fire to dispose of them. She picked up a packet of butcher paper containing a dead mouse and screamed when the thing tumbled to the floor at her feet. She tried breathing deeply to steady herself, but the stench in the cabin only made her nausea worse.

She pressed on, using the trash to fuel the fire and

stacking tin cans in one corner. As she worked, Hattie hid several items around the cabin to be used in case she needed to defend herself. She broke her vow not to touch the mattress when she slid a rusty knife under the top corner. She gave the stained cot a shake to clear the debris and discovered more trash beneath it. Hattie collected the papers to toss in the fire, but stopped when she saw her name.

In her hands she held several telegrams addressed to herself per care of the Oakley's Boardinghouse. Mrs. Phillips had wired five times in her attempt to help her travel back to Boston. She also found two telegrams from Mrs. Fritz, asking after her health and for some news of her new life.

Hattie peeked outside through a gap in the boards and spotted Travis leaning against a tree. He seemed to be talking to Jeremiah, so she turned back to the mail in her hands. She found several letters from Hope, along with all the letters she'd sent since arriving.

Her heart beat so loud in her chest, she swore Travis would hear it and know what she was doing. Travis had obviously intercepted all of her correspondence in order to make her feel abandoned.

Fear and relief washed over her at once.

Then utter dread took over. She'd truly put her numb hands in the fire this time. Hattie double checked that she had all the letters, tucked them carefully into her pocket and then put the ratty old mattress back in place. She, once again, slid the rusty knife into place and prayed that she could get away without needing it.

She peeked out at Travis again and tried to think of a plan, but nothing came to her.

The sun was setting quickly, and Hattie didn't know

what to do. She struggled not to gag as she sliced the meat into tiny pieces and tossed it into a pot with the best parts of the disgusting vegetables. The cabin was sweltering with the stove going, but she added another pile of papers and set the pot on top.

She removed the last of the refuse from the counters, table and floor, and fed it to the flames. She imagined all the ways that she could escape Travis's clutches when she heard his boots on the creaky old steps.

Hattie held her breath and stirred the pot as the rusty hinges complained. Travis entered and then barred the door again. After a second, he cussed the heat inside the cabin and propped the door open. It wasn't enough circulation to air the place out, but it was a million times better than being shut in with Travis.

Hattie avoided making eye contact as she stirred the disgusting food. Travis sauntered to the corner and pulled a bottle from inside a saddlebag. Hattie kicked herself for not searching his bags when she had a chance. After finding the intercepted mail and learning her friends hadn't abandoned her, she'd became too engrossed to search anything else.

Travis took a long draught of amber liquid and then sighed loudly. He slouched in his chair and leered at her, but aside from occasionally singing his wedding song, he didn't speak. Hattie was content to let the stew cook all night if he sat quietly in the corner waiting.

With every trip of the bottle to his mouth, she hoped he would get his fill and pass out. She'd determined to take her chances in the forest. If she was going to die, she'd rather do it without Travis nearby. So, she stirred and counted the seconds. but he just didn't pass out.

"You gunna cook that all night?" Travis pulled himself

to his feet and stumbled to the table. He dropped into the only chair and plopped the bottle on the table with a bang.

Hattie jumped, but regained her composure quickly. "I'm sorry." She grabbed the bowl she'd wiped out for him and filled it with stew. Her stomach turned again, and she heaved before she could stop herself. Travis didn't care, he received the bowl and tucked into it.

In a bit of luck, he had no interest in Hattie's comfort. He didn't seem to care when she chose not to join him in the meal. Instead, he slurped at his broth and in between bites, he sucked on the bottle. He swayed in his chair, but still wouldn't pass out.

"I ain't tasted food this good since my mama was alive." He scraped his bowl clean and handed it to Hattie. "Give me seconds, wife."

She handed him the bowl and then took a chance. "I'd like to clean up. Where can I get water?"

Travis eyed her and then shrugged. "Don't see the sense in it, but the creek's just down the path."

Hattie wrestled the hip tub beside the fire and grabbed the handle of a pail. She slipped out the door and breathed the fresh air. With any luck, Travis would finish his bottle and pass out before she returned. Or die from eating that rotten food.

She took her time walking down the hill. The best plan she could come up with was to wait him out. He would eventually finish his bottle and then it seemed that he must fall unconscious. That was her only hope. So, she'd decided to prepare a bath as that would take a long time to accomplish.

Trip after trip, she carried the pail to the stove. The hot plate steamed and hissed as she set the pail on top. There was no other pot to heat the water in, so she was able to stretch each trip out longer. Earth smells filled the air as dust and debris burned from the exterior of the pail.

Hattie watched the flames flicker and listened to the crackling of the wood. She startled when the heart wrenching cry of an animal screamed somewhere in the woods. Could it have been a horse? Resisting the urge to look outside before her next trip, she instead kept adding bits of wood to the fire and slowly craned her neck to eye Travis in her periphery.

He didn't react. His eyes remained focused on his food.

Her skin prickled, flushing with the quickening of her heart.

Could they be coming for her? The letters in her pocket took away her hopelessness.

Mark was coming. She could feel it. He was alive, and he was coming for her. Hattie was through with helplessness. She was through with hopelessness. From now on, she would assume the best, and deal with whatever happened. She wanted her childish trust back. Her determination doubled.

She just had to keep Travis busy until they arrived. "I just need one more pail," she said as she tipped the warm water into the tub. "Would you like more stew while I fetch it?"

Travis ogled Hattie and hiccupped. He chuckled and then waggled his eyebrows at her in the way she hated. "I was thinkin' 'bout dessert." his hand left his beard and snaked down the waist of his pants.

"I think the bath first, don't you?" Hattie stepped toward the door.

"Fine. But you have to wash me and then I get to wash you." He clapped his hands together like a little boy at Christmas.

Hattie fled. Once down the hill and out of sight, she fell to her knees. She rocked and prayed and held herself tightly. She scanned the woods, but when she looked back at the house, Travis' body was silhouetted in the open doorway. She'd never get away with him watching.

The deep blue of the sky was going navy. There wasn't enough time. Travis had drank so much that he shouldn't be able to walk.

Too late, her plan was flawed.

Travis would never pass out from drinking.

THE WOODS WERE GETTING THICKER ALONG THE CREEK BANK and the group filed into a line. Mark's heart and head warred with each other. He still felt that they were on the right trail, but how could anyone have pulled a donkey cart through there? He trusted his brother, but as the evening came on, he became more and more desperate.

Spooked by a snake, Sarah's horse screamed and bucked. "Goddamnit," she cussed and wrestled him into submission, but Mark thought he heard something over the commotion.

"Shhh." He waved his hand to stop Caine from an inevitable rant. "Did you hear something?"

Everyone stopped moving, and even the horses seemed to be listening.

"What did you hear?" Will moved up beside Mark.

"I thought I heard singing." Mark shrugged in response to the stupid expressions on his brothers' faces. "I don't know." He nudged his horse. "Let's keep going."

The creek wound upward and his horse grunted with the incline. The trail was smoother rock now. While less treacherous, the unforgiving stone was harsher on the animals. The sun dipped out of sight and twilight was upon them. They would have to quit soon. They wouldn't be able to see much longer. Coming around a bend, they merged with a dirt and stone path.

Mark strained his eyes into the darkness. He hated to do it, but there was no choice. "We need to leave the horses here and go on, on foot," he said.

"I think we should camp and continue tomorrow." Daniel sounded defeated. "It's too dangerous to go on in the dark."

Will nodded, but Hank shook his head.

"We can't stop, not yet. We've got to be close." Mark dropped to the ground and looped his reins over a tree branch. "I feel it."

Sarah slid to the ground and tied her horse beside Mark's. "I agree. I'm not ready to stop."

As soon as Sarah spoke, there was no debate. If Sarah was going, Caine was going. And if Caine wasn't stopping, then nobody was. Mark nodded a thanks to Sarah and pulled his rifle from his saddle. It only took a moment for the others to gear up and they were on their way again. Will stayed behind to protect the horses, and the others made their way up the side of a steep slope.

The hilltop was grassier, with fewer trees. The wind carried the slightest smell of wood smoke.

"This way," Hank sniffed the air like a hound and led them away from the creek, which sharply turned and ran along the hill. They followed the edge of the forest as they made their way towards the smokey smell.

"Look, there!" Mark whispered. Everyone seemed to take a sharp inhale at the same time. Up the hill, a shanty could be seen. The smallest light flickered inside.

It had to be Hattie.

THE WATER STEAMED. HATTIE WATCHED FINE BUBBLES LINE the inside of the pail. She'd run out of time. The wash tub wouldn't hold another bucket of water, and Travis had emptied the bottle.

He was no closer to passing out than when he'd started.

With the help of the wash rag, Hattie lifted the handle of the pail. She hesitated, looking from Travis to the tub. He'd gone silent. Something tense and ominous filled the air. She was afraid to turn her back on him.

Her slow, measured steps creaked across the dingy room. And her nightmare unfolded, as she had feared. His chair scuffed on the floor. Hattie didn't turn. She continued her slow walk to the tub. But his urgent steps boomed, and in an instant his hands were on her waist.

"I think I'll have dessert now," he crooned in her ear. His fingers dug into her hip bones and she spun. She scalded him with the water and smashed him in the face with the pail. She didn't wait a second for him to respond, but dashed for the open door.

Surprise and rage twisted his face as he screamed. He hissed, "You bitch, you goddamn whore."

Travis tackled Hattie from behind.

She screamed as her knees smashed on the hardwood. He came down on top of her so fast she didn't make it halfway to the door. His lanky arms wrapped around her waist as she landed on her stomach. He straddled her legs and clutched at her dress, ripping the waistline seam, and exposing her petticoat.

All the time she wrestled for her life; he cursed her.

Dragging herself forward beneath his heavy weight, she clawed the wood floor. She stretched as hard as she could, desperate to clutch the bottle. In his drunkenness, he fumbled with the layers of her dress.

"I'll skin it off you." He said, and she didn't know what he meant.

She looked back at him as he shifted his weight. He pulled the giant knife from his belt, and it gleamed in the lantern light.

With her heart beating out of her chest, Hattie propelled herself forward with her toes, bridging the gap and grasping the whiskey bottle. He sliced her dress as the bottle came down on his head with a hollow thump.

The bottle clattered to the floor.

Travis gurgled and fell forward across her legs. He stabbed at her as he dropped. The knife pinned her dress to the floor. Hattie kicked her legs free of his body. She reached down and grabbed her skirt with both hands and yanked. She stumbled to her feet and bolted once again toward the open door.

Chapter Twenty

D arkness came quickly as they crept around the hill. Mark's pulse quickened and his breath was shallow. He could feel her. He stood in the tree line with the others and they watched the cabin. Smoke poured steadily from the chimney and the door was propped open. Hank's big hand on his shoulder kept Mark from flying up the rise as they all strained to see or hear anything to hint at the situation.

Caine leaned forward and whispered. "We still don't know that this is the cabin we're looking for."

Sarah nodded and added, "And we don't know that they're alone if it is."

"They're in there." Mark said. "I thought it was stupid when Paul said he could feel where Angela was." He looked at Daniel. "When her father had her... It just didn't make sense. Even when he was right, I thought it was just a coincidence." He shrugged and turned his eyes up the hill. "But I know Hattie is in that cabin." He stepped forward and stared at the silhouette of a little house. "I can feel her."

It was impossible to know what, or who, could lie in wait for them. Travis was—by all accounts—a dangerous man. Alone or not, the worst thing they could do was burst in and spook him into doing Hattie more danger than he already had. Travis was known to cavort with a gang of miners who weren't opposed to murder when it suited them. The Oakleys believed Travis and his goons were responsible for the death of his brother. If those men were lurking about, there's no knowing what kind of ambush the Maxwells would be sneaking into.

Hattie had been isolated all day with that man or his men. Every muscle tensed in Mark's body. He wanted to kill them. One man, or ten, he didn't care.

The Maxwell group continued their ascent, keeping close to the shadows in the forest. Their movements were patient and calculated. They'd stalked villains together long enough to know what to do. Caine and Sarah broke off from the group and made their way around the clearing to come at the house from the other side. Will and Daniel moved to the back of the cabin, so they had it surrounded. Mark waited with Hank for them to all come into position.

As they crested the rise, the dim light grew brighter. The miner's shack was tucked away in a cluster of scrawny pines and birches. A ramshackle building made of rough-hewn logs and flimsy slat boards. The wide-open front door was a promising sign. At least it wouldn't be difficult to get inside.

Mark circled the cabin, surprised when they received no response to the sound of a snapping twig. Muffled voices came through the wide gaps in the walls. Mark couldn't make anything out, but Travis seemed to be singing. Mark stepped to the side of the cabin and peeked through a hole.

Hattie stood at a stove near the back of the cabin, staring into a metal pan. Travis slumped in a chair at a rickety table with an empty bottle of whiskey in front of him. After a glance at Travis to assess the situation, Mark's gaze was drawn back to Hattie.

She'd lost weight, and she seemed jumpy. She kept peeking over her shoulder and toward the open door, but then always settled her sight back on the bucket in front of her. Mark watched her rub her pocket a third time and wondered if she had found a weapon and stashed it in there.

Hank whistled a birdsong and Mark stepped back. The others started to retreat, and Mark followed, knowing they would need to make a plan to get Hattie out safely now that they knew what they were facing. Mark's heart drummed. He was so close; putting off her rescue even minutes was like trying to breathe under water.

As he reached the tree line again, all hell broke loose. Travis screamed in pain and then Hattie's cry shattered all of Mark's reserve. He freed his pistol from his holster and ran with abandon straight at the open front door. His brothers' boots pounded behind him, and he had no doubt that Sarah was hot on their heels.

Mark burst through the door with his lungs screaming and stopped to take in the sight. The room was dimly lit by the flickering light of a single lantern. The air was thick with the smell of smoke and the tang of rot and mildew. The water pail was overturned on the floor and Travis was soaking wet and squatting in front of Hattie.

Hattie was crumpled in the corner, holding herself and sobbing. Relief and rage swirled inside him, but Mark backed up and held his hands in the air. He didn't holster his gun, but he aimed it away from Hattie and her subduer.

Travis was wilder looking than Mark had imagined. He resembled the homeless men milling about the streets of Boston. But what caught Mark's attention most was the blade of a bowie knife pricking the skin of Hattie's arm.

"Who the hell are you?" Travis spat on the floor and sneered at Mark.

Mark stared Travis in the eye. "Drop the knife and let her go."

"This is a matter between a man and his wife. If you know what's good for you, you'll get on outta here." Travis hissed.

Hank stepped through the door and a little starch came out of Travis's spine. It helped that Hank was as big as a barn. Mark was a decent shooter, but not as good as Hank.

Neither had a clear shot without hitting Hattie, and they'd never take that chance. In a move they'd choreographed over years of hunting together, Mark stepped left, and Hank stepped right. Sarah appeared in the doorway to fill the gap with Caine at her back. Sarah was a crack shot and with Caine beside her, Travis wasn't going anywhere.

Hattie lifted her face in surprise and mouthed Mark's name as she rubbed her pocket again. Mark barked at Travis, "Stand up and step away from the woman!"

Travis rocked on his heels but continued to hover over Hattie. "A man has a right to deal with his wife, however he sees fit. Y'all just git on out of here."

With more spunk than Mark expected, Hattie glared at Travis. "I am not your wife."

Travis raised his hand to strike her, but the cocking of a gun echoed off the walls and stopped Travis in mid-action.

"Step away or I'll shoot," Mark barked, pistol trained on Travis' heart.

Travis swayed again and then stood. He stepped in front of Hattie, the Bowie knife still clutched in his hand. "I told you; this is a matter between me and my wife."

Mark didn't lower his revolver. "She's not your wife." He stepped forward, satisfied when Travis cowered slightly. "She was never meant to be your wife."

Travis turned his back on Mark. "You wouldn't shoot a man in the back, would you? Or are you a coward?"

"Get away from her or you'll find out." Mark stepped closer and as he did, Travis lunged and grabbed Hattie by the hair. He spun around to face Mark with Hattie in front of him and the knife to her neck.

Hattie's eyes were big as saucers as she stared into Mark's helpless face. What could he do? Travis would never get out of there, but he couldn't stand to lose Hattie in the process. Hattie mouthed something that Mark didn't understand and then turned her gaze to Sarah.

Travis turned quickly toward Hank. He'd been sneaking closer, but stopped as soon as Travis moved. Hattie nodded at Sarah, then stomped on Travis's foot when he was distracted. Travis howled and dropped the knife. Sarah and Caine jumped forward and clobbered Travis.

And in an instant, Hattie was in Mark's arms.

"Stay down, you piece of horse shit." Sarah kicked the Bowie knife across the room.

Mark holstered his pistol and scooped Hattie into his arms. He left Travis shouting and complaining behind him and carried Hattie down the Hill.

"Mark, oh Mark." She sobbed into his shoulder. "I thought you were dead."

He wrapped his arms around her and vowed he would never let her go again. "I've got you now. You're safe." He whispered over and over in her ear, stroking her hair, images of the first time he held her flashing in his mind. Tears pricked as he wrestled with the relief, regret and anger. "I'll never let you go again."

Mark couldn't bring himself to put her down, though she didn't seem to be injured. When they reached Will and the horses, he sent Will up the hill to help the others. Mark found a dry stump for Hattie to sit on and kneeled in front of her. "Did he hurt you?" He asked.

"No." Hattie wiped a tear from her face. "He was about to." Hattie shook herself and sat up straighter. "I scalded him and hit him with the bucket."

Mark pulled her close and kissed the top of her head. "Good job."

Mark returned his shotgun to his saddle and set to work. He tightened their girths and checked the horses' hooves for stones. After a few minutes, the others came into sight. Daniel and Caine led Travis between them, stumbling and complaining the whole time.

"Stay still, or I'll shoot." Sarah threatened, and Travis balked and pulled away.

Daniel and Caine grabbed Travis by the arms. He thrashed and flailed like a child in a temper tantrum.

Travis bucked and kicked, and Daniel lost his grip. With his left arm free, Travis pulled another knife from the small of his back.

Mark moved without thinking. His arm hooked around Hattie's waist and pushed her behind him. She pressed her face into the space between his shoulder blades and clung to him.

Sarah fired a warning shot, but in the confusion, Travis slipped into the forest and Sarah took off after him.

"I'm sorry," Daniel said, guiltily. "We should have checked him for another weapon."

Caine flapped his fingers at him, "At least nobody is hurt. Let's just go make sure Sarah gets back in one piece."

Mark stood torn. His friends needed him, but he couldn't leave Hattie.

Luckily, Sarah saved him from making a choice. "I'm here," she said, panting. She took off her hat and slapped it against her thigh. "Bastard got away. It's too dark. I couldn't see shit." Her eyes were locked on Caine.

"Don't run out alone like that again." He pressed his cheek into her hand when she rose up on her toes to kiss him.

"I'll try not to."

Mark pulled Hattie back into his arms and rocked. "He's going to come back."

The others nodded. "It's too dark to get out of here tonight." Will said.

"We'll make camp here then." Daniel motioned to the cabin up the hill.

"No." Hattie's voice was firm. Mark peered down into her face, surprised to see more strength than she'd ever displayed. "I'm not staying in that cabin even for one night."

Mark nodded. He couldn't stay there either. "Let's find a place to camp where we can set up a watch for the night."

"It's not ideal, but at least we have some cover and Will

said the donkey has got plenty of hay to share with the horses.

"Jeremiah." Hattie said. Everyone looked at her and she shrugged.

"Who's Jeremiah?" Mark asked.

"The donkey's name is Jeremiah." Hattie laughed.

"Who the hell name's a donkey Jeremiah?" Caine belted out a laugh more contagious than the plague.

"Well, Jeremiah will be hosting our horses tonight and we'll hold up here." Will said. "We'll take shifts keeping watch in case he comes back. Everyone agrees?"

"No." Hattie and Mark said in unison.

"Yeah," Sarah said, "I'm not staying here either."

'Why do women always have to make everything more difficult?" Will complained.

Sarah swung her leg over her horse and sheathed her shotgun. "Oooh, just wait till I tell your wife."

Everyone had another good laugh as they mounted and prepared to leave without any further discussion. As always, The Maxwell Group followed Caine. And Caine always followed Sarah.

Mark pulled Hattie up onto his horse in front of him and wrapped his arms around her waist. As they followed the others down the hill, he watched the forest, expecting Travis to come flying at them with his knife drawn. "Don't worry. We'll find a place to camp tonight, and we'll get you back to the boardinghouse tomorrow."

Hattie nodded and seemed to shrink away from him. They rode for about twenty minutes in silence, and then Mark noticed Hattie rubbing her pocket again. "Have you got a weapon in there?" he asked. "Why didn't you use it on Travis?"

Hattie sniffled and smiled. She reached into her pocket

and pulled out a handkerchief-wrapped package. She peeled back the fabric to reveal the little soap buffalo. "It really did keep me safe," she said, with a tear rolling down her cheek.

"I told you it would." Mark reached into his pocket and removed the embroidered handkerchief she'd given him. He wiped her tears and then tucked his most treasured possession back into his shirt pocket.

Chapter Twenty-One

Memories of Travis were haunting Hattie's sleep. Every time she closed her eyes, the curtain rose on her own private theater of horrors. The scene was always different, but in each nightmare, Travis had her cornered and a deranged smile split his face. Malicious hunger gleamed in his eyes, ready to devour her.

But then Mark was there.

They'd made camp in a clearing and set up shifts to keep guard. The night was warm enough not to need a fire, so they'd just settled down somewhat close to each other. She'd hoped they might make it back to the boardinghouse to sleep, but everyone agreed that the trip would be safer in the morning. Hattie stared into the night sky, wishing on each star that she might have finally reached the end of her nightmare.

She turned over and studied Mark's face as he sat beside her. Every time she'd awoken in the night, he'd been there. He hadn't slept a wink. Mark returned her gaze with a soft smile. Hattie let his perfect features wash the ugly bitterness of Travis out of her mind. She scarcely believed he was real and had to repress the urge to touch or pinch him.

If she did something to stretch the boundaries of reality. Surely the dream she was in would distort, revealing itself for a nightmare like all the rest. Perhaps everything that had happened since Mark burst into the cabin was a dream, a figment of her weak and crumbling mind. At any moment, she would wake to find Travis before her.

But she could smell Mark, his clean pine scent even tinged with horse and sweat was like perfume. His body reclined against a boulder only inches from hers. He radiated warmth like a blanket over her, grounding her with a dose of reality. She smiled. It was the same warmth she'd felt the night he'd rescued her. Since that night, he'd always felt warm to her.

"Do you need anything?" Mark asked, interrupting her thoughts.

He was here, he was real, and she was safe.

"No, I'm fine. Thank you."

Hattie recognized his expression. Something was rolling around in his head. She waited for him to sort it out and say something, but the silence dragged out too long. She didn't want to go back to sleep, so instead she asked, "Is this what you meant when you said you could feel the sky on your fingertips?"

"I can't believe you hung on to that. Yeah, this is what I meant." He reached out his long arm as if to stroke the moon. A boyish smile crossed his face.

Hattie reached her hand out, too. When she returned her arm to the security of her blanket, she asked, "How did you find me?"

"Simon Oakley rode into Hope around noon." Mark

tugged the corner of the blanket over Hattie's shoulder and she snuggled deeper into the warmth. "He said you were missing and then ripped Paul and Daniel a new one." He laughed. "I wish I could have seen that." His smile faded, and he sighed. "He said that you'd sent letters asking for help, but we never received them."

Hattie sat up slightly and stopped him with a hand on his arm. "I can't believe I forgot." She dug into her pocket and pulled out the stack of letters and telegram cards. "I found these in the cabin."

Mark took the stack and wiped his sleeve across his forehead. "Son-of-a-bitch." He thumbed through the pile, but it was too dark to read anything. "That's why Simon thought we'd abandoned you and ignored your pleas for help."

Hattie nodded. "It's pretty clear what happened now," she indicated the stack in Mark's hand, "but I had no way to know that Travis was stealing my mail."

They grew quiet for a moment and Mark ran his hand over Hattie's hair and once again pulled up the blanket. He dropped his hand on her shoulder. The weight was comforting, like a hug. "I don't think Simon believed us until we were ready to ride out." He laughed again and stuffed the letters down into his saddle bag with his free hand. "The Maxwell Group can put together a posse faster than anyone, and he was sitting on a fresh horse before he knew what hit him."

Hattie smiled. "I can picture his face."

"We rode like hell to the boardinghouse and then had to stop to let the horses rest." Mark's thumb traced circles over Hattie's shoulder and tingles spread through her body. "Mrs. Oakley made us eat, even though I didn't want to stop at all." He rubbed his stomach. "I'm glad she did, because we won't eat again until tomorrow."

Hattie nodded, and Mark stared down at her in horror. "You haven't eaten at all today, have you?" The loss of his heavy hand on her shoulder made Hattie sad, but he had turned away so quickly that she couldn't stop him. "Mrs. Oakley said you hadn't had breakfast, and I hope to hell you didn't eat anything in that disgusting place of Travis's." He turned back to Hattie with a cloth-wrapped package. "I'm sorry it took me so long to remember." He handed the bundle to Hattie. "Here... Sit up."

He turned back to rummage through his saddlebag as Hattie sat up to rest her back on the boulder beside him. Hattie had never been so happy to see a biscuit in her life. She took a large bite and then choked on a crumb. Mark laughed and untwisted the cap from his canteen and passed it to her. "Slow down."

Hattie giggled, but swallowed and choked a few more times before she could breathe. "I didn't even realize how hungry I was."

Mark finished his story as Hattie finished the biscuits. "After dinner, Simon drew us a rough map of where he thought the cabin might be." He took the canteen from Hattie when she passed it and sipped. "The map wasn't very good, but he had all the major landmarks correct. We weren't even sure you'd be up here, but it's all we had to go on, so we followed it." He sighed. "We're lucky Hank's such a good tracker. We wouldn't have made it without him.

Hattie stared in the darkness at Hank's bulky silhouette. He sat on a rock, keeping watch over them as they slept. He was so big she'd been terrified of him, but as she looked at him in the darkness, he didn't seem quite so frightening.

Hattie finished and handed the napkin back to Mark. "Did Edna remind you of anyone?"

"A young Mrs. Fritz?" He said, not looking at her as he stuffed the napkin and canteen back into his bag.

"Yes, exactly!" Hattie bounced and clapped her hands together. "I nearly called her Mrs. Fritz a time or two." They both laughed. "They're truly decent people. I was lucky to enjoy their kindness and protection."

"I'm glad you found them. Who knows what could have happened if you hadn't had them," he said, his eyes wide and she suspected that he was imagining the awful things that could have happened to her.

"Travis met me at the stage. He knew I was coming because he'd stolen the letters from his brother." Hattie shivered. "I talked him into letting me stay at the boardinghouse until I sorted things out. He didn't like it, but for some reason he agreed." She pulled the blanket from her bedroll and settled it over her legs. "He thought that because his brother's money had paid for my ticket, I belonged to him. He said he had inherited me."

Mark wrung his hands together, "I'm sorry you went through that." He punched his knee. "I should have escorted you all the way here. I wanted to, I thought about it—I should have gone with my gut."

Hattie bumped his shoulder with hers. "You can't predict the future. It's not your fault."

Mark had a cute way of sighing when he accepted something as truth that Hattie loved. Nothing she could say would take away his guilt. He had a way of holding himself responsible for things that he didn't do, and she couldn't change that.

"It was so hopeless, sitting there with everything I owned in the world beneath me and this strange smelly man telling me I belonged to him." she shook her head. "I didn't know what to do." Hattie smoothed her dress. Her hand caught in the hole at her waist. Her cheeks flushed with embarrassment. "It was just plain luck that he let me go to the boardinghouse and didn't drag me up the mountain right then and there." She pulled the hanging pieces of her dress together and tied it. It would have to do.

"I don't even want to imagine what could have happened." He took her hand and ran his thumb over her knuckles. The light touch was thrilling.

"What will happen now?" Hattie stared at Mark's large hand. "Will you stay and track Travis down? There is some question about his participation in the death of his brother."

"Daniel will have a talk with the sheriff once we get back to town, and we'll sort everything out from there. The local guys are pretty good. They can probably handle it."

Night was full on them now, the darkness thick around them. Hattie could no longer make out the scenery. Crickets chirped somewhere just behind her and in the distance, an owl had much to say.

Hank stood and stretched his massive frame before gently tapping Daniel. The two of them held a brief, whispered conversation and then Hank went to lie down, and Daniel assumed the first watch.

Hattie watched Daniel move about. When he seemed to find nothing to do, he took to pacing about, hands held behind his back. She remembered seeing him like this back at The Rose Dunn House. It was strange to see him without Opal. With long strides, he maintained a steady rhythm. He walked with his shoulders pulled back and his head held high, exuding confidence and determination. It looked exhausting. He stopped pacing and directed his gaze at Mark and Hattie, who sat side by side across the clearing from him.

She braced herself, ready to be questioned.

Daniel kneeled in front of them and kept his voice low enough not to wake the others. "Do you mind if I ask you a few questions?"

There were a thousand things she would rather do, but Hattie nodded. "Not at all."

Three quick rifle blasts stopped the interrogation before it began.

Suddenly, there was nothing Hattie would rather do than answer questions.

∾

THERE WERE ANGRY VOICES IN THE DARKNESS AND THEN laughter.

"What the hell is wrong with you?" Daniel had sprinted to the edge of the clearing while Mark had tossed Hattie to the ground and covered her with his body. When he heard Will's amused laughter, he knew immediately what had happened. And from the round of groans at the campsite, everybody else got it as fast as he did.

Mark rolled half-off Hattie and stared over his shoulder. His heavy hand held her pinned to the ground until he could be sure that nothing was wrong. When he was certain that everything was fine, he helped her to sit up in time to watch Daniel cuff Will over the head. She deserved to witness that hit. The idiot should have known better than to fire a gun with all of their anxiety running so high.

Mark's muscles relaxed, and he righted Hattie. "Are you okay?" He hadn't considered that he might hurt her when he'd tossed her to the ground like that. He was a big man, and she was a small woman. He shouldn't have jumped on her like that.

"I'm fine." Hattie was a little shaky, but she seemed to be okay. She stared around for a moment and then asked, "What happened?"

Mark picked a few leaves and sticks from her hair and shrugged.

He didn't have to answer, though, because Sarah was pissed. "It's just Will being an asshole." Sarah said. "He can't help himself. Everything about him has to be a big show."

Will skipped into the clearing, proudly displaying three dead white-tailed jack rabbits. "Thought we could do with something hot to eat in the morning." He rubbed the back of his head but didn't drop his smile. Mark glared at his stupid brother and turned his attention back to picking debris from Hattie's hair.

Sarah threw something at Will and then rolled back into Caine's arms. Caine was the only one of the group who hadn't jumped out of his bedroll at the sound of gunfire. He'd merely rolled to his back when Sarah had leapt over him. Hank grumbled something and lay back down. When they'd been startled, he'd stepped in front of Mark and Hattie to shield them further from danger.

Daniel was the only one who had seen what was going on. He'd stood at the edge of the clearing and waited for Will to come close enough to speak to. After the commotion, he seemed to decide not to question Hattie because he settled himself on a large rock to keep watch.

The campsite didn't take long to quiet back down. A

few curses, a few threats of future violence—mostly from Sarah, and then everyone settled back into their previous postures. Mark waited a few minutes for Hattie to relax and start breathing normally again and then suggested she lay back down. Once she was comfortable, he resumed his seat beside her and threw his arm over her shoulder.

"Will's an idiot sometimes," Mark said. "He means well, it's just his nature to be a little theatrical."

Hattie yawned and took Mark's hand. "I'm glad you're here."

Mark squeezed her hand, feeling whole for the first time since he'd left her at the stagecoach. "I know," he smiled, not looking at her.

Hattie sat up and looked at him. "No, I'm really glad you're here."

He gazed into her shining eyes and moved almost imperceptibly to kiss her. Hattie's breath hitched, and she leaned in. Before their lips could touch, Mark remembered himself and turned his head. He cleared his throat to cover his embarrassment, but Hattie's blush proved that he'd been too late.

The moment was ruined. Hattie's smile dropped, and she lay back down. She pulled the cover back up to her neck and closed her eyes. Her breathing evened out and slowed followed by the fluttering of lashes on her cheeks. He hoped her dreams wouldn't turn ugly again.

Mark's thoughts ran a mile a minute. What was he going to do? He kept picturing the letter he'd sent to Boston. Could he get that back? So, he kept watch over her and wished life could be easier.

Daniel stopped in his walk and encouraged Mark to get some sleep. But sleep was impossible. He wouldn't sleep again until Hattie was safe.

Travis was still out there.

Chapter Twenty-Two

Mark twitched awake, his muscles tense. Trying not to disturb Hattie as she slept on his chest, he stared around the clearing. He blinked bleary-eyed in the gray, faint light, trying to filter out the sounds of his sleeping friends. Something had awoken him, a shattering sound somewhere outside, maybe.

Did he dream it?

A Meadowlark trilled and warbled in the distance—was that it? Or was there something else? He strained to listen as he stared into the morning sky. The sun was just beginning to rise, and it promised to be a lovely day.

He closed his eyes, listening for the sound that had awoken him, enjoying the weight of Hattie and her measured breathing. The peace of her sleep made him smile.

He must have fallen asleep and lay down beside her because they were twisted up together. One of her hands rested on his hip, her legs were wrapped around one of his and her head was heavy on his shoulder. Her scent and the warmth of her body surrounded him. He wanted nothing more than to wrap both arms around her and go back to sleep.

But he willed himself to focus, to listen.

It wasn't his imagination either, because when he turned his head, he saw that Caine and Sarah both had looks of deep concentration on their faces. Will looked the same. Mark shifted slightly to try to catch sight of Daniel and Hank, but he couldn't see either of them from his position.

Twigs snapped—could be a squirrel or some other critter scampering in the brush, but where did the birds go? The world outside drained of sounds, and an eerie quiet filled in the empty space. Through the silence, though, he heard another stick snap.

Repressing the urge to bolt to his feet, Mark gently shook Hattie's shoulder. She stirred awake, as innocent looking as a child, as her beautiful blue eyes sleepily opened. The corners of her mouth peaked into the slightest smile. At that moment, he would have given his arm not to have to destroy her happiness.

Mark shook her again, and when she saw his serious face, she stiffened. "Shhhh. You need to wake up." Mark pulled the blanket off of them and tossed it behind him. "Someone is out there," he whispered.

Hattie's face went ghost-white as she strained to hear what he'd heard. "I don't hear anything."

Mark nodded and helped her to sit up, motioning for her to hide behind the rocks.

A muffled song drifted through the morning fog and Hattie's eyes went wide. If possible, even more color drained from her face.

Fear flickered in her eyes and Mark was desperate to soothe her. "You're going to be okay. I'm here. I won't let anything happen to you." He moved the bedroll out of the way so he wouldn't trip over it and watched his brothers do the same. Sarah checked the chambers of her gun and then moved into position behind a boulder.

They should have stayed in the cabin the night before, at least it would have offered some protection. In the clearing, they had a handful of large rocks and a tree for cover. He spotted Daniel moving toward the horses, but still hadn't seen Hank. He just hoped the sharpshooter had taken his rifle when he'd wandered off.

The morning was humid. Moisture clung to their skin and pasted their clothes to their bodies. Fog blanketed the hilltop and obscured their view in every direction. Mark's heart raced as someone started singing. It was a wedding song and from Hattie's reaction, Mark knew Travis was singing it. After a couple of lines, his voice was joined by another, then another as the song made a circle around their camp.

They were surrounded.

Then the figures of eight lanky men with pistols drawn stepped through the haze.

"Thanks for coming to my weddin' boys." Travis spat on the ground. "But first, it's open season for yellow-bellies!"

"We don't want trouble." Mark shouted. "You can walk away now."

Hattie wanted to pull Mark back down behind the boulder. He was completely exposed standing there like that, but fear crushed her.

Travis scoffed, "You hear that, boys? The mouse is tryin' to bargin with the cat."

The other men rasped laughs as they closed in.

Hattie tugged at his pant leg, but Mark didn't budge. He stood tall in the clearing and faced down Travis. Hattie turned around and scooted up onto her knees so she could see what was going on, but Mark put his hand on her shoulder and pressed her back down. She had nothing to do, so she wrapped her arms around her knees and said a prayer.

Instead of praying for a hero, she prayed for strength. There was no mystery about what Travis wanted. He wanted Hattie, and her friends were in danger because of it. How could she hide behind a rock and watch her friends die for her? Then what? Travis would take her, and it would all have been for nothing.

She couldn't do that.

Spinning out of Mark's grip, Hattie stood. She tried to step away, but Mark yanked her into his arms. "What do you think you're doing?" He held her so tightly that she could hardly breathe.

Hattie turned in his arms and cupped his cheek, a sad smile rising and falling before she wiggled out of his grip again.

Hattie held up both hands to show that she had no weapon and stepped around the rock. "Travis! I'm here. Let them go. You can take me."

Mark's voice shook and if she'd been close enough, he would have grabbed her again. He stepped around the edge of the rock and reached for her, but Hattie side-stepped and avoided him. "Hattie, don't!" She wanted nothing more than to turn back into his safe embrace, but she couldn't sacrifice his life for hers.

Travis growled, "Oh, I plan to take you." He rubbed the front of his pants with one hand and thumbed the hammer of his revolver with the other.

Hattie's fingers splayed in the air, desperate to show Travis that she meant him no harm. She begged with her eyes as she slowly crept closer and closer to him. His friends, each one more disgusting and terrifying than the last, leered at her. Between the toothless grins and their filthy clothes, she was truly revolted. But she marched steadily on.

Travis was faster than she had realized and without warning, he'd fired a shot.

Mark yelped and disappeared behind a tree. Hattie screamed and froze in her tracks. She was paralyzed between giving herself up to save her friends and turning around to take care of Mark. The choice was taken away from her when gunshots erupted behind the miners.

They all turned toward the sound as one of their men fell to the ground.

Instincts took over and Hattie turned to flee the firefight. Before she could get away, though, she was tackled to the ground. She screamed for Mark as her face was pressed into the dirt. The metallic warmth of blood pooled on her tongue, and she whimpered. But Hattie had a reason to fight, and that's what she did.

Shots continued to fire around her as the man tried to drag her away. Hattie kicked at him, and he stumbled and slid a few feet down the hill. She inched backward with rocks digging into her hands as her feet fought for purchase. With a racing heart, Hattie searched for Mark in the chaos.

"Hattie!" Travis bellowed, running right for her.

She quickened her movements, pulling at her skirt as she tripped her way up the hill. She expected to be knocked to the ground again, but the strike never came. She circled the biggest boulder in the clearing and dropped to the ground behind it. No matter her intentions, she couldn't sweet talk a bullet, and they were flying from both sides.

MARK PEERED AROUND THE EDGE OF THE TRUNK AND SPOTTED Hank in the tree line. Hank took aim and two seconds later, one of Travis's men dropped to the ground. Turning up the hill, Mark saw Sarah and Caine holding their ground in the clearing. He scanned the hillside and counted four bodies.

There were still four men out there.

He couldn't see Hattie. Mark scouted for a new cover and decided to run for a rock several yards to his left. From there, he'd be able to see around the hillside.

The cacophony of gunfire rattled his head, intensifying the pain. He examined the finger sized gash in his arm; it stung and throbbed in the open air, but at least it was only a graze. As shots continued to ring out, he ran for the boulder.

He popped his head up from behind the rock, glad for the improved line of sight. Daniel had moved the horses further into the woods and stood with Will, ready to defend them. Two more bodies peppered the hillside, bringing their attackers down to just two.

Everything faded away when he saw Travis running after Hattie. Hatred and fear restored Mark's strength, and he took off. The last of the miners came for him, but Mark landed a shot in his flank. The man groaned and collapsed, then rolled down the hill.

As Travis closed in on Hattie, Mark lunged. He threw all of his weight at his enemy and wrapped his arms around Travis's legs. Hattie continued to scurry up the hill as Mark wrestled with the snake who wanted to hurt her.

Travis whirled around to face Mark; his pistol gripped with his finger on the trigger.

Mark took hold of his legs and flopped him back onto his belly and pinned a knee to his back, trapping the pistol beneath him. Travis thrashed, his body bucking and squirming, but Mark's strength was unrelenting. He kicked his legs as Mark freed his right arm.

Mark ripped the pistol from his grip and shoved it in the belt of his pants.

Travis growled and struggled, but beyond a bunch of grumbling, there was nothing he could do. "Get off of me! I'll skin you alive. Just wait until I get free."

Mark scoffed, but said nothing. He pressed more of his weight into Travis's back as muffled curses flowed from his mouth. He quickly surveyed the hillside, counting the dead men. *Only six bodies.* One of them must have recovered.

Silence ensued.

Where was everyone?

Mark scanned the hill and spotted everybody except Hattie, who he'd seen duck behind a boulder at the top of the hill. Hank was making his way up the hill toward Sarah and Caine. Will and Daniel were with the horses; everybody was accounted for except one of Travis' men.

A bullet blew by and Mark kicked his legs out and dropped to his stomach, bearing his elbow down on Travis. Travis groaned with his weight and let another string of curses fly. Another bullet whizzed by Mark's face, sending slivers of stone flying as it lodged in the earth. Mark winced as the shrapnel pelted his face.

Travis began fighting again. "Don't shoot me, you idiot!"

"Shut up." Mark jammed his elbow into Travis' ribcage, silencing him as he searched for the shooter.

"Where the hell are you?" he whispered.

He scanned up and down the hillside but saw nothing. Mark stretched to see Hank, but he had disappeared into the clearing at the top of the hill.

Mark spun too late. A heavy boot slammed into his chest, knocking the air from his lungs. He flipped backward off of Travis and crashed to the ground on his back. He gulped for air as he stared up into the barrel of a revolver.

"Toss your gun," he said through tobacco-stained teeth. The burly man nodded and flicked his revolver. Mark plucked the revolver from the holster and tossed it out of reach.

"You want to shoot 'im, or should I?"

"Get me up first, you fool!" Travis ordered.

There was something comical about the way the two men stumbled over each other in their haste to get Travis back on his feet. First one was off balance and then the other. The stranger's gun was always pointed somewhat in Mark's direction, so he couldn't get up, but it seemed that both of the men had forgotten about his brothers. They made little threatening statements back and forth to each other and seemed to delight in frightening Mark.

Unfortunately for them, they didn't know that he'd brought two dead-eye shots with him. He couldn't see them, but Mark was sure Sarah and Hank had already established some sort of competition for who could make the best shot.

All amusement was dashed when Mark saw Hattie bolt out of the woods. She was so light on her feet that the others didn't seem to notice, but Mark's heart stopped beating.

Hattie burst into view, her eyes darted back and forth across the hillside. Mark wanted to yell at her to run and hide, but he didn't want to give her away. He kept his eyes trained on Travis and the stranger. It seemed impossible for them to still be struggling together, but their distraction worked in Hattie's favor.

She crossed the twenty yards from the tree line without catching their attention. Mark's heart raced with dread as scooped up his pistol, drew in, and shot. The unnamed man collapsed with a gurgling rasp at Travis' feet.

Tears streamed down Hattie's face as she dropped the weapon to the ground and crumpled after it.

Travis immediately threw his hands in the air, giving Mark time to roll and collect his gun.

MARK APPEARED BLURRY IN THE CORNER OF HER VISION, BUT she couldn't bring herself to look at him yet. He sank to his knees and folded her gently into his arms. Her cries muffled in his chest. The sound of his heart steadied her.

Her grief ebbed, and she took deep breaths as he stroked her back.

"I thought you were gone," she whispered, breaking the quiet.

He planted a kiss on the top of her head. "I might have

been if you hadn't saved me." He smiled. "I was waiting for Sarah and Hank to come to the rescue."

Mark helped Hattie to her feet, and she noticed the blood on his sleeve.

He caught her gaze and shrugged, "It's just a graze."

She suspected he was downplaying the wound for her benefit, but let it go.

Staring into his eyes, she felt calm. Mark dipped his head toward her and she swooped in to meet him, kissing him long and deep. She'd waited for that moment so long, and she savored it. Everything inside her lit up and Hattie was home.

Cheers and whistles trickled down the hill, making her cheeks burn with embarrassment. But Mark pulled her close and gently kissed her again. It was the sweetest thing she'd ever experienced, and she never wanted to let him go.

Sarah beamed with her rifle propped on her shoulder, Caine and Hank beside her.

"Where the hell have you guys been?" Mark demanded with a smile.

"Covering your ass. Where do you think?" Caine barked and Sarah arched her brow in his direction, "Alright, they covered your ass. I sat like a pig in the mud." Everyone laughed, but the mood didn't last because Travis started complaining.

Hank stepped up to him and Travis shut his mouth in a hurry. "I'll bring him over and get him ready to ride out."

Caine and Sarah followed. Mark heard them discussing the scene as they walked away.

Sarah's voice carried over the wind. "I was sneaking around the clearing when that miner came up behind them. I would have got him, but then Hattie ran out and, well—you know the rest." Then they rounded the bend and were lost from sight.

Mark put his arm around her and pulled her into his chest.

Resting his cheek atop her head, he whispered, "It's over."

The moment was hardly romantic. They stood on the hillside, littered with dead bodies. Mark turned Hattie, and they followed the others toward the horses.

They'd moved the horses back into the clearing at the edge of the woods and Will had collected all of their bed rolls and camp gear. Their saddle bags were loaded up and Travis sat sullenly beside a tree.

Jeremiah wandered over untethered.

"I untied him and he just sort of followed." He reached out and scratched the poor donkey between the eyes. Jeremiah brayed happily and danced in place. "I think he's coming home with Hank."

Hank turned quickly. "Like hell."

Will wasn't as easily intimidated as Travis. "Just wait till I show him to Sasha."

Hank sighed. "Damn."

MARK'S ARM THROBBED, BUT HE HAD ONLY ONE THOUGHT ON his mind.

While the others finished tacking their horses, and Hank tied Travis to Jeremiah's back, Mark pulled Hattie to the side.

He stared into her eyes and tucked a piece of hair behind her ear. Laughing, he pulled a leaf out and flicked it away. She looked so sweet and serious as she stared up at him. Mark swallowed the lump in his throat and said, "I love you, Hattie." He took a deep breath and took her hand. "I've loved you for a long time. I should have said so before we left Boston." He kissed the back of her hand, encouraged by the quickening of her pulse under his fingertips. "Will you marry me?"

Hattie leapt into Mark's arms with a squeal and planted her lips on his. "Yes!" She squeezed him tightly and squealed again. "A million times, yes!"

"Well, shit." Sarah kicked the dirt. "I don't know how to get away without making an ass of myself."

Hattie giggled and threw herself at Sarah. The ladies embraced, and Sarah beamed at Mark over Hattie's shoulder. Her eyes were misty when she said, "I'm so happy for you." For all her bluster and bad language, Sarah was a sweetheart.

Caine led Blaze to his wife and grinned. "Congratulations."

Mark's heart soared until he saw Daniel's worried face. He left Hattie with Caine and Sarah and crossed to Daniel. He made a show of checking his girth while he spoke to his brother. He didn't want anything to bring Hattie down again. "What's wrong?"

Daniel swatted a fly away from his horse's face with a groan. "We know each other too well."

Hank stepped over and grunted a sort of agreement. "Uh-huh."

Mark looked between the two of them. He'd expected bad news from the look on Daniel's face, but now that he was so close, he had no idea what was on his brother's mind. "What's got your knickers twisted?"

He glanced around the clearing to where they'd collected the bodies of Travis's men and covered them with wood torn from Jeremiah's shelter. "They should be safe from predators until the sheriff can get up here. And I don't think we need to worry about Travis giving us any trouble with Hank leading the ass."

Daniel and Hank both shook their heads. What the hell?

"Did it somehow slip your notice that you now seem to be engaged to two women?" Hank asked.

Mark stopped breathing. His heart stopped beating. His brain stopped thinking.

Shit.

"Florence," he whispered.

His brothers didn't hide the judgement in their stares." How do you tell your fiancé about your other fiancé?" Daniel asked.

Will walked over and untied his horse with a lot of questions on his face. One look at the others and it was clear that they had all remembered the very important thing that Mark had forgotten.

Chapter Twenty-Three

T he July sky stretched endless and blue overhead. Birds sang their melodies, accompanied by the tromping of horse hooves. If it wasn't for the burning in his arm and the incessant whining from Travis, they'd have had a pleasant ride.

The group started back down the way they'd come, but the donkey turned into a hidden lane. Travis cursed and kicked at the poor animal, stopping when Hank sidled up beside him. His towering presence a silent threat.

The trek back to town was easier following the hidden route guided by Jeremiah. The new trail was clear and wide, and it solved the mystery as to how the cart had made it up the mountain.

The group was quiet as they traveled and from the looks they shot his way, Mark assumed most of them were considering his situation. He certainly couldn't think of anything else. He considered all the ways he could marry Hattie and provide for Florence, but there was no way he could get out of his situation without hurting one of them.

He thought about Bernie. He'd done the dishonorable

thing and never regretted it for a day. But his situation was quite different from Bernie's. Instead of another man being left in the lurch, a woman was going to travel across the country and be stranded in a town full of strangers. Of course, that wasn't exactly the case either. She would travel across the country and be taken care of by a clan full of strangers. No matter what, the Maxwell Group would still be there for her. She wouldn't be stranded.

Mark tried to bring up the topic several times, but each time he'd see Hattie's beautiful smile and decide not to do it. How could he throw a wet blanket over her happiness like that?

So, his guts twisted, and he kept his mouth shut.

Hattie, on the other hand, seemed happy as could be. She rode in front of him and rested her back against Mark's chest. Now and then, Hattie sighed contentedly, which always set off another round of questioning looks from his family. Halfway back to the boardinghouse, she fell asleep, and Mark cradled her in his arms.

How could anything that felt so right be wrong?

By the time they pulled up outside of the boarding-house Mark was fit to be tied. He squashed his emotions and gave Hattie a gentle shake to wake her up. She was so close, and her sleepy eyes were irresistible. Mark kissed her head as Edna, Simon, and an older couple he didn't recognize barreled out of the house to greet them.

"Hattie!" Edna and the older woman cried in unison.

Edna bounced a few times and clung to the older woman's hand. "We've been watching the road all night!"

Hattie stretched and smiled. "I can't tell you how happy I am to see you."

Mark dismounted and reached up to help Hattie down. As soon as her feet touched the ground, the two women embraced her. Like mother hens, they took her under their wings and swept her away.

Simon introduced his father-in-law Charles Coffey and waved after the ladies, saying his mother-in-law, Jennifer, was the older woman. "They'll take care of Hattie, and as soon as we get your animals settled, there is a hot meal waiting for you all."

"We need a doctor." Sarah said, poking Mark's shoulder.

Mark jumped and rubbed the makeshift bandage Hattie had tied over his wound. "What the hell."

Sarah shrugged and headed toward the barn with Blaze.

Mr. Coffey's eyes widened when fresh blood stained the patch. "I'll fetch Doc Anderson." He climbed onto a small wagon and set his horse in motion.

"Let's get these animals settled and give the ladies some time." Mark said.

"I'll be back soon." Daniel, ever the sheriff, even when he wasn't, climbed back on his horse. "I'm going to deliver this wretch," he tugged at Jeremiah's reins, "to the sheriff and then I'll be back."

They killed as much time in the barn as they could and then made their way into the house. As soon as they opened the front door, the aroma of gravy hit Mark like a ton of bricks, and his stomach growled.

As Mark climbed the stairs, he opened his mouth to call out for Hattie, but before he could form the words, she entered the hallway from a doorway at the end. His heart tripped over itself as it shifted from panic to relief. She wore a clean gown, and her hair hung in a damp braid down her back. She glowed like a star in the sky despite the dimness of the hallway.

"What's the matter?"

"Everything is fine. I couldn't find you and I got worried."

Her lips curled up. She blatantly enjoyed his suffering, but he smiled, too.

"You missed me that quickly?" She sauntered up to him and straight into his arms.

He draped his arms around her, enjoying the peace and quiet. He wanted to soak it in, but the food was calling for him. When her stomach growled, he laughed. Her face went bright red, and she tried to hide it in the front of his shirt. Mark kissed the top of her head and led her down the stairs.

Mr. Coffey arrived with Doctor Anderson before he could sit down, so Mark followed them into the kitchen and told Hattie not to wait for him. The doctor was a white-haired man with a heavily lined round face. He shooed everyone out of the kitchen and set his black case on the counter. Without much ado, he unwound the bandage Hattie had tied on Mark's arm. In no time at all, Mark was stitched up with a clean wrapping over his wound.

"Thanks, Doc." Mark held the door for the doctor, only to find the entire company sitting on the porch.

Edna invited the doctor to eat with them, but he declined. "Now, you all go have a seat in the dining room. I was so nervous I just kept cooking to pass the time." She laughed nervously and hoisted the hem of the dress as she made for the stairs.

The passive widow Mrs. Johnson sat glum faced in the dining room as they entered, not seeming to notice or care that they were there.

Mark and Hattie sat across from each other, following Mr. and Mrs. Coffey, who had sat that way.

Ten minutes into the quiet meal, Mrs. Johnson piped up. "Decided you didn't want to marry that other fellow then, did you?" Mrs. Johnson's voice was a bit garbled, like one who didn't speak often. "You want to marry this one instead?"

Hattie's eyes widened, and she looked at Mark, who didn't know what to say.

Mrs. Johnson didn't require a response, though; she just went on with her chatter. "I don't blame you. That other fella wasn't much to look at." The old woman stared at Mark, though she continued to speak to Hattie. "This one's a tall drink of water. My Jack was pretty, like him."

Hattie giggled and Mark chuckled too, despite the awkwardness. His brothers spent the next few minutes making comments about how "pretty" Mark was. It was a family joke that would live forever.

Mr. Coffey cleared his throat. "Is that your plan?" He glanced at Mark and then at Hattie.

"Yes." They answered together, and the company laughed.

Mrs. Coffey clapped her hands together. "How wonderful! God is good!" She threw her arms around Hattie. "Charlie can do it before you go home today!" She clapped her hands again. "Then we all get to be here for you."

"Ha-hey!" The men cheered; their deep voices reverberated off the walls of the small dining room.

Hank smacked Mark on the back. "Will, our little Mark is growing up!" He sniffed and pretended to flick a tear from his eye.

Mark rolled his eyes, but he beamed a smile dripping with pride at Hattie.

Daniel sneaked in during the cheer and his voice made Hattie jump. "What'd I miss?"

"Our boy is getting married." Will informed him.

"Well, I'll be. Congratulations!" He clasped his hands on Mark's shoulder, shaking him from side to side. "Opal's going to be so mad she missed it." He smiled and looked at the demolished remnants of food on the table. "Hey, did you guys save anything for me?" He sat at the open plate and picked through the leftovers.

Edna rose, "Don't fret, I never run out of food."

HATTIE'S EYES WELLED AS SHE STOOD BEFORE THE FULL-length looking glass in the gown she'd brought from Boston. Sarah, Edna, and Jennifer had helped her prepare just as Mrs. Fritz, Elizabeth, and Sophia had done not so long ago.

Jennifer rubbed her back and stared at her in the mirror. "What's the matter, dear? Why are you crying?"

"I just have so many feelings. I keep thinking of how happy I am and how far I've come." Hattie went to sit on a stool but thought of wrinkles and instead chose to lean against a bedpost. "Do you think it is bad luck that Mark saw me in this dress once?" She accepted a handkerchief from Edna and wiped at her face. "The last thing I need is more bad luck.

"Oh, sweetheart." Jennifer hugged Hattie tight, and a vision of her mother flashed through Hattie's mind. "God has a plan for you. Mark is part of that plan."

Hattie smiled as tears rolled down her cheeks. "You remind me of my mother."

Sarah pulled Hattie up straight and turned her back to the mirror. As she placed little flowers into Hattie's hair, she said, "I've never seen Mark so happy."

Jennifer excused herself to check on the men, and Edna took her place beside Hattie. Edna and Sarah took turns primping and fluffing Hattie's hair and gown.

Edna pointed to the handkerchief in Hattie's hand. "Dab don't rub, you don't want Mark to see you all puffy."

Sarah chimed in, "I've seen the way that boy looks at you, rub all you want."

Before she knew what hit her, Hattie was holding onto Daniel's arm at the end of the church aisle. Butterflies fluttered in her belly and her heart pounded with excitement. The church was beautiful, with a high vaulted ceiling and stained-glass window above the altar.

The organ player began, and Daniel whispered in her ear, "You nervous?"

But then Mark turned around, and the smile that broke across his face took Hattie's breath away. She couldn't help but return the grin.

"I'll take that as a no." Daniel laughed under his breath and gave Hattie's hand a squeeze as he led her down the aisle.

Reverend Charles opened with a prayer and in no time at all, he'd escorted them through the "I dos," and asked for the rings. Hattie was startled, but Mark pulled a little box from his pocket and handed it over. Mark stared into her eyes and winked.

Time stopped. Hattie floated through the ceremony, lost in Mark's eyes.

"You may kiss the bride."

Nobody else existed after those words were spoken. The entire world faded away, and Hattie was blind to everything but Mark. He slowly raised her veil. With one hand on the back of her head and one at her waist, Mark pulled Hattie close.

Her breath hitched, and her heart skipped. Hattie took a small breath and then Mark's soft lips pressed down on hers. She'd kissed him a few times before, but nothing like that wedding kiss. Every nerve in her body hummed and the butterflies in her belly went wild.

When Mark's tongue softly traced her bottom lip, Hattie opened and welcomed him into the warmth of her mouth. She ran her hands up Mark's strong arms, feeling the shape of his muscles in a way she had never had before. At his shoulders, she paused, then as he deepened the kiss, she slid her hands into his hair.

His neck was strong, and his hair was soft. She breathed in his clean scent and let her hand trace the line of his jaw. Hattie lost herself in the moment and clung to her new husband. All of her dreams came true with that kiss.

When the church erupted in applause, she reluctantly pulled back.

Mark's smiling face was mere inches from hers, and she beamed back at him. They were wed. Mark brought his mouth down on hers once more, but this time softer and only for a second.

Mark rested his forehead on hers. "I love you, Mrs. Webb."

"And I love you Mr. Webb."

Chapter Twenty-Four

When Edna's attempt to get them to stay the night failed, she insisted on packing them a giant hamper of food for their journey. Though she'd already fed them a large meal, and they would all arrive home in time for dinner, she could not be put off.

Everyone was eager to return home, but none quite so eager as Mark. He just wanted to be alone with his wife. Of course, when he'd mentioned it in the barn, his brothers had jumped down his throat. After endless promises that he did not intend to force his bride into any sort of marital relations against her will, his brothers let him be. There was no offense taken. His brothers were protective of his bride, and that would never be a bad thing.

The group made quick work of tacking the horses for the ride. They tied most of their supplies to Jeremiah, but Hattie's luggage would have to come by coach and train through the local shipping depot. She packed a few things to tie her over for a few days, and Mark arranged the rest with Simon.

Mark's family rode ahead of them on their journey back to Hope and gave the couple as much privacy as could be managed. Their conversation drifted on the wind and Mark and Hattie caught pieces here and there. They laughed over long-standing family jokes, stories of the good old days, business on the ranch, and teasing the new couple who rode a little way behind. Mark was content to let them have their fun.

The newlyweds fell into their old familiar rhythm. Hattie rode double with Mark, so they had no problem speaking privately together. They talked and laughed, but at times, they rode together in silent companionship. Hattie's happiness was everything.

His own happiness would have been complete if not for the secret that he kept. During their quiet times, he considered telling her. But every single time she would sigh contentedly, and he couldn't bring himself to say the words. So, Mark wrapped his arms around his wife and prayed that God would help him find a way to make things right for Hattie and Florence.

The road grew increasingly familiar and soon the group emerged on the stretch leading to their respective homes. One by one, they waved and shouted their good wishes as they dispersed toward their own homes. Then it was just Mark and Hattie trotting down the dusty lane as the sun set behind them.

MARK STOPPED AT THE TOP OF A SMALL RISE AND POINTED out the cabin below. Hattie sat up straight and studied the charming scene. With the sun setting behind them, the landscape glowed, and everything was warm and welcoming.

She couldn't wait to get closer. She wanted to inspect the cabin before it got too dark, but by the time they arrived, the sun would set. So, as they rode toward their home, she did her best to memorize everything as it was.

Mark pointed out the barn and chicken coop. Hattie was delighted that she would have fresh eggs every morning to feed her husband. He seemed to hesitate when he pointed out the outhouse, but she was happy to see that it was well built and far enough from the house that she wouldn't be bothered by unwelcome smells. She wondered if he'd carved a crescent moon into the door.

When they arrived, Mark dismounted first and then reached up for Hattie. With his strong hands on her waist, he lowered her slowly, sliding her body down his until her feet hit the ground. In a bit of modesty, Hattie shifted back to allow her skirt to drop, but immediately pressed back against him.

Mark leaned in and pressed his mouth to hers. Hattie didn't hesitate to open her mouth at the first tap of his tongue, and she wound her arms around his neck so she could pull herself closer to him. They clung to each other at the hitching rail and burned the last of the daylight.

Mark pulled back and huffed a few long breaths. Then he led Hattie to the house, pointing out a hole in the path that he said he'd been meaning to fill. He let Hattie inside and then promised to return quickly after settling the horse.

Walking around the cabin by herself felt odd. It was her home, but it wasn't yet. The cabin was beautifully built and rustic. The rugged charm of it reminded her of Mark.

She ran her finger against the smooth wooden logs forming the walls into the kitchen.

Entering the kitchen, she marveled at how tidy Mark kept the place. The pantry was well stocked and organized; the cupboards were neat, and everything was in good repair. Even the stove seemed to have been blackened.

Hattie's eagerness to look around bubbled inside of her, but the cabin was quickly growing dark. She discovered a lamp on the kitchen table and scanned the room for matches to light it. It didn't take her long to locate the matches on a table with a stack of old mail and telegram cards. She snatched them up and lit the lamp.

There was a small sitting area with a fireplace, and she imagined all the quiet evenings she would spend there with Mark. A warmth of longing spread through her. He'd made a point of speaking to her about the consummation of their marriage, but Hattie wasn't afraid of her husband. Nobody had ever made her feel as secure as Mark did, and her body warmed when she thought about being his wife.

Moving to the bedroom, the sight of the bed made her giddy in a way she had never known. The long ride with his body pressed against hers had left her aroused and excited. Hattie brought her hand to the bodice of her gown. Her nipples responded just to the thought of Mark's attentions. That was no surprise, though. She'd been thinking of him for months while she pleasured herself in the dark. Hattie dropped her hand to her waist. If he weren't about to come in at any moment, she might have dropped down on the mattress and relieved the building tension in her body.

The door opened behind her, so Hattie left the bedroom

to meet Mark in the main room. He toed off his boots and set them neatly beside the door, then turned and smiled.

"I see you're finding your way around."

Hattie lifted the lamp to show that she'd managed just fine. "Yes, I love it already." She set the lamp on the table and crossed her arms. "You're so tidy."

He laughed. "I'm afraid you're giving me too much credit." He turned the wick up on the lamp a little. "Iris has been here just about every day to check on me. I'm sure that the other ladies were probably all here while we were gone." Mark stepped over to the pantry and opened the door. "Yup, none of this was here when I left."

How could she ever repay such kindness? "That's very sweet."

"Hungry?" He asked.

"No, lunch was enough for me." Hattie seemed to have too many arms all of a sudden, and she didn't know what to do with them. She stood in the middle of the kitchen, wishing she had something to do. There was nothing though, no dishes to wash, no socks to pick up from the floor, nothing. Thanks to the July heat, she didn't even have a fire to feed.

Silence fell between them as the darkness grew. Mark shifted from side to side and scanned the room for something to do. It put Hattie at ease a little to know she wasn't the only one struggling to figure out how to proceed.

Hattie decided that it would be her job to break the tension. She took Mark by the hand and led him to the sofa. They sat together and stared into the empty fireplace.

They spoke of simple things. The weather, plans for the garden, and where the others lived in relation to the cabin. Mark shared the story of the cabin. He called it 'Scott's Place' and told her how Jeni had come as a mail-order bride years ago. He told her about Iris and how the rescue house had come to be named after her twin sister, Rose.

The stories were all interesting, and Hattie wanted to know them all, but with every passing minute the house grew darker and Hattie grew more anxious.

Then Mark cleared his throat. "I just want you to know, there's no hurry, to uh—you know," he was so cute when he was nervous. "I can sleep in here if you prefer."

"Oh, Mark. I'm not afraid," she said. "I understand why I should be, and with anyone else, I would. But I'm not afraid of you."

He smiled, "Not at all?"

Hattie stood and pulled Mark to his feet. "I'm nervous. I guess anyone would be." She turned and walked toward the bedroom. At the doorway, she turned back to him, full of courage. "I'm more excited than nervous."

The surprise on Mark's face was comical. He was so sweet.

Hattie led Mark to the bed, and he sat down on the edge. She kneeled in front of him and pulled off his socks. He watched her every movement with such concern. But his Adam's apple bobbed and his breath slowed when she finished and stood in front of him.

Hattie took both of his hands and put them at her waist. "I won't break, Mark." Hattie stepped forward between his legs and stood in front of him. She lowered her mouth to his and ran her hands through his hair.

Mark rose to his feet in front of her and slid his hands around her back. The kiss deepened and Mark's hands slid downward. He cupped her butt through her dress, and Hattie gasped with pleasure.

Mark pulled back, and they both worked to catch their breath. Hattie stared into his eyes as she unbuttoned his shirt. Inch by inch, his chest was revealed, and Hattie ran her hand over his warm skin. His taunt waist delicious to touch. She ran her hands up and down his side, and he did the same to her.

She quivered, rising to the tips of her toes, and she kissed him with a delicate sear. A throaty moan escaped him, making her toes curl with pleasure. She wanted to elicit that sound again. She untucked his shirt and slid it down his arms. She tossed the shirt onto the floor and ran her hands over the warm silk of his skin, loving the soft patch of hair on his chest.

His eyes were glazed as he stared at her. "Mmm."

Oh, that moan did her in. Hattie moved her hands to the front of her gown and began to work open the buttons, but Mark's hands stopped her before she'd opened the third button. "Let me." He stared into her eyes as he lowered himself back to the side of the bed with her standing in front of him.

Every inch of Hattie screamed to be touched as he opened her dress in torturously slow movements. A hundred years after he'd started, he slipped Hattie's shirt down her arms and tossed on top of his own. Hattie breathed heavily as he ran his hands up her body and cupped her breast through her chemise. Mark swallowed and turned his face up to Hattie. She brought his mouth down on his and pressed against his palm.

"Mark," she whispered. The slight roughness of his hands was intoxicating. Hattie reached behind herself and unbuttoned the hem of her skirt. She untied her petticoat and let the two pieces slide to the floor together. Bracing herself with her hands on Mark's shoulder, she stepped out of her skirts and kicked them to the side.

Hattie stood in front of Mark in her undergarments.

Mark stood again and removed his pants. She stifled a gasp with her hand at the size of his erect manhood. They both knew she'd seen naked men before, but Mark was magnificent. He didn't shy away from her gaze, but he didn't press for her to go on.

Hattie took a deep breath and finished disrobing. Mark rewarded her with another of those delicious moans. Then his hands and mouth were on her again. He lowered her to the bed and lay on top of her with his weight supported by one elbow. As he ravished her mouth, his free hand molded to the curves of her body. Everywhere his hand passed, fire ignited.

Hattie squirmed with need for him. "Please, Mark."

She stroked his chest. He shivered and moaned again. Hattie bit her lip, relishing his throbbing hardness against her belly. He let her set the pace, and she was ready to go.

She spread her legs, welcoming him. Then moved her hands to his hips and guided him into position. Mark paused and stared into her eyes. Hattie smiled. He would never stop worrying about her.

He kissed down her neck while massaging her breast. A moan escaped her as he rolled her nipple and she arched her back.

"I'm ready," she whispered, hot in her ear. "I need you."

He gazed into her eyes, then kissed her firmly as he gently slid inside her. Pleasure forced a moan from her as his moan answered hers and he worked slowly, thrusting his hips in a gentle rhythm with hers.

His hands skimmed over her, moving from her breasts to between their bodies. He found the little spot she rubbed when she was in bed alone and thumbed it. Hattie's eyes fluttered as electricity shot through her body.

He rubbed the little spot over and over, in quick small circles as he thrusted and she lost all sense. The intensity mounted until she couldn't take it anymore.

Hattie panted and moaned, clutching the sheets and his shoulder while wave after wave of pleasure over-whelmed her. Mark thrusted faster, and she gripped him with both hands as Mark moaned his release.

Mark wrapped her in his arms and they laid together naked, just as she had dreamed.

"I love you." She whispered in the darkness. His measured breathing and steady heartbeat were the last things she remembered before falling asleep.

Chapter Twenty-Five

Since Hattie and Mark had visited the other families, Hattie was more comfortable being left on her own while the men moved cattle. Mark kissed her sweetly and whispered loving words in her ear, then mounted his horse and rode out to join his brothers. The sight of him on his horse made her heart throb.

She was looking forward to being naked with him again. Hattie laughed at her own gratuitous imagination as Opal carried a tray of tea and cookies out to the porch where Hattie sat, watching the men on horseback become little black dots in the green expanse.

"I'm so happy you're here! I just can't believe it!" Opal beamed, setting the tray on the table a little to harshly, sloshing tea everywhere. "Oh my," she said, dabbing at the spill with a napkin.

Hattie giggled. Some things would never change. "I'm overjoyed to be here! I was pleasantly surprised when Mark gave me a tour. Everything is tidy and well-prepared. He has truly thought of everything, leaving me with nothing to worry about."

"I wouldn't expect anything less from our Mark." Opal said, plopping in the rocker beside Hattie.

"And everything is okay?" Opal raised her brows and Hattie caught her meaning.

Embarrassed, yet not surprised by Opal's way of cutting to the heart of a matter, she said, "Yes," and let the subject drop.

Hattie and Opal were preparing lunch when a knock on the door pulled them away.

Hattie smiled at Paul. She looked around, hoping to see Angela, but he was alone.

"What brings you out here, Paul?" Opal said, wiping her hands on her apron and joining them at the door.

"Uh, Hattie, is Mark around?."

"No, he and the others are out herding the cattle and moving them to the east pasture." Paul sighed and then nodded slowly. Hattie didn't like the unease he wore on his face.

"What's wrong Paul? Don't keep us in suspense?" Opal demanded, and Hattie was grateful.

"Um, it's a bit delicate." He said, removing his hat.

Opal dragged him inside and pushed him into a chair. "Sit down and spill it." She pointed to the sitting room beside the entryway, and Paul obeyed.

Hattie closed the door and followed them into the front room. Paul breathed deeply and Hattie's mind raced, trying to fathom what was wrong.

What trouble could Mark have been in?

"This morning a woman came in on the first stage. She's settled over at Elenor's place now." Paul rubbed the back of his neck and shifted in his chair.

He hadn't said anything shocking yet. What was he getting at? And what did it have to do with Mark?

"Come on, Paul." Opal gasped in exasperation. "Get to the point before we die of old age."

Paul groaned. "Her name is Florence Campbell—"

Hattie interrupted "From The Rose Dunn House?"

Surprise crossed his face. "Yeah, how'd you know?"

Hattie shrugged. What was the big deal about Mrs. Campbell coming to town? "She arrived at the house on the day we left. We met briefly in passing."

Paul listened attentively, his concerned expression deepening by the minute. Drops of sweat formed on his forehead, and he took a breath before speaking. "Hattie, let me be frank with you. I have something to share, and it may not be easy to hear."

Hattie wanted to scream for him to just say it already, but she remained composed, bracing for whatever was to come.

"Mark sent for a bride."

Opal and Hattie both gasped and covered their mouths with their hands.

He crinkled his brows and pressed on. "He was working with Mrs. Phillips and corresponding with Mrs. Campbell. She has letters from him. He paid for her tickets to Hope as a mail-order bride."

"But we're married." She said, even though it didn't need to be spoken.

"I know." He paused before blurting, "This won't change anything for you, but we're going to have to make things right for Mrs. Campbell."

"Where is the poor woman now?" Opal asked.

"She's up at the boarding house with Elenor and Angela. She was quite upset when Mark failed to meet her. I told her I would come looking for him and explained about having been called away on an emergency for a couple of days."

"An emergency that he married!" Hattie wasn't just mad, she was hurt. How could Mark have married her knowing this woman was on her way west to marry him?

Paul looked away. She shouldn't have yelled. It wasn't Paul's fault.

"We need to help her." Hattie declared as she rose to her feet.

Paul blew out a long breath and then nodded.

"Mark's a good man, but it's going to be hard to wiggle his way out of this mess." Opal followed Hattie out the door. "Hattie wait! I'm coming."

Hattie turned, arms crossed, watching as Opal slipped on boots and ran through the door.

"Lace your boots, Opal." Paul said, smirking.

Hattie tapped her toe as she waited. Opal bent over. "Paul, fix up the wagon. I think we're going to need to get the other ladies' help for this one."

Paul looked uneasy, but it was quickly overshadowed by the daggers Hattie was shooting from her eyes. In no time, Jeni, Maggie, Abigail, Opal, and Hattie loaded up in the wagon, always eager for adventure.

Dropping the babies off with Minnie, Maggie's nanny, the whole crew headed to town. Paul's discomfort was a prime topic, and the woman teased him until his ears were bright red.

Then the tone shifted. "I can't help but feel like we had a hand in this," Jeni said, rubbing her nail against the splintering wagon.

Hattie shot her a quizzical look. "What could you have done?"

"Well, Caleb said Mark was looking glum, and I may

have encouraged Caleb to prod Mark about taking a wife." She bit her lip. "I'm sorry, Hattie. I didn't know your story. I still don't, but I know Mark and he's a good man."

Hattie frowned. She had thought him a good man, too. Why would he have kept the secret from her, and put this poor woman through such an experience? Her stomach churned with jealous fire. The image of the beautiful redhead standing in the doorway flashed through her mind. And Mark had written to her. He'd proposed marriage to her.

What if everything had been a lie?

Her resolved wavered a bit.

"Hattie?"

She'd be silent for too long. "He should have told me. I wouldn't have married him if I knew he was engaged."

Maggie jumped in. "But you still love him. And he loves you. That wouldn't have been different. He'd just have been married to the wrong woman."

"Of course, I love him." Hattie felt tears pricking at the corner of her eyes, but she was determined to keep them from falling. "I'm just angry. And disappointed."

Abigail scooted closer to her and touched her hand. "The important thing to remember is that no matter what happens—whatever the truth is—you will get through it. And you'll do it with all of us by your side."

Jeni leaned forward and clasped Hattie's other hand. "You're one of us, now. We adopted you. But for the record, I'm sure it'll turn out to be okay. I mean, it's Mark."

Their words strengthened her, but the only thing that would make her feel better would be to get to the bottom of the story.

The boarding house was more chaotic than she'd expected. Elenor Bix loudly greeted all the Maxwell women, hugging them and demanding they sit down for a bite to eat.

As they were all filtering toward the dining room, Mrs. Campbell came down the stairs. All noise and activity in the room ceased, and Hattie watched Mrs. Campbell turn red as an apple under their scrutiny.

Elenor made a quick introduction and then shoed everyone into the dining room where she'd set out a fairly impressive spread of cookies, pie, tea, coffee, and milk. Mrs. Whitfield entered from the kitchen carrying another tray of cookies and set it on the table.

Angela was a sight, waddling to embrace Hattie, "You look wonderful, Hattie!"

Hattie stepped back and held Angela at the end of her arms. "Me? Look at you," she touched Angela's belly.

The group settled down and filled themselves with deserts. They talked of the children and weather, anything but Mark and Hattie. Throughout the snack, Hattie watched Mrs. Campbell. The poor woman looked like a kite with no wind, drifting along with no power.

When everyone settled, Hattie introduced herself again. "Mrs. Campbell, I am Hattie Webb."

"Please, call me Flower." Then Mrs. Campbell's head snapped up. "Webb?"

Hattie's brow creased. "I married Mark Webb after he came to my rescue four days ago." She shook her head. "I didn't know he had written to you."

The last of the wind left her sails, and Flower wilted.

"He married while I was on my way to meet him?" Flower spoke with such a tender voice, Hattie had nothing but compassion for her.

"What he did was wrong. I'm here as a friend. I want to get to the bottom of this and help you get settled."

Hattie reached for her hand and Flower reluctantly gave it. "I know what it's like to be stranded in a town without friends. You don't have to worry about that here."

After accepting Hattie's friendship, Florence shared a glimpse of her story. "And then, I found myself at The Rose Dunn House. Everybody was nice enough, but I knew I wasn't meant to stay there." She wiped her mouth and set her napkin on top of her plate.

Hattie said nothing and Florence continued. "I presume you're familiar with Mrs. Phillips?"

Everyone nodded.

"She's the reason several of us are here," Jeni said.

"She came to the house in search of a wife for Mr. Webb. I saw it as an opportunity if the match proved favorable. I'm a widow, you see, and my heart still belongs to my husband. I needed a husband to accept me knowing this. We corresponded a few times, and I discovered that his heart also belonged to another. I didn't come here expecting a love match, but I had hoped we could become good friends."

Hattie wiped a tear from her face. "Like you, I arrived in the town where I was to be wed and did not find my groom. He was not wed to another, though. He was killed while I was traveling to him." She tried to hold back tears, but they ran down her face. "What a pair we make. Both stranded and without husbands."

Jeni laughed. "When I arrived, my groom was the handsomest man you ever saw." She smiled. "He took one look at me and flat-out rejected me. I also found shelter in Elenor's house. I'll have to tell you the rest of my story another time, though."

Hattie shook her head. "Who knew this was such a popular situation to find oneself in?"

***

Mark and Daniel strode up the steps, hungry and ready to sit down.

"Opal?" Daniel called, but the cabin was silent.

"Hattie?" Mark called, panicking.

"They're probably at Sarah's house." Daniel looked around. "Your wagon is gone and Sarah's got some new fangled doodads that Opal has been wanting to see."

"Doodads?" Mark laughed as he mounted his horse again.

"I don't know, some sort of machine to help with the washing, I think."

The women were up to something, because they weren't at Sarah's, Jeni's, or Abigail's houses. At Maggie's place, they found all the children running wild in the yard. Minnie sent them to town, telling them to look at Elenor's place.

Daniel shrugged, and they turned their horses toward town. The boardinghouse was all lit up, and it looked like some sort of party was going on in there. Mark tied his horse to the hitching post and climbed the steps.

He entered with Daniel at his heels, and the first person he saw was Florence Campbell. He would remember her flaming red hair and clear blue eyes anywhere. Then his eyes landed on his wife, and his pulse spiked when she turned and fled into the kitchen.

Mark followed her through the house and out the back door. "Hattie, please let me explain."

She looked at him so coldly, he'd never seen such disdain on her face before, and it gutted him. "How many wives do you need, Mark?"

"I thought you were married to Quinn when I wrote to Mrs. Phillips." He reached for her hand, but she pulled away. "Hattie, I thought I'd never see you again. You were married." He shoved his hands in his pockets and paced a few steps away before turning back. "I didn't know how to get over you. I was a wreck for ages. Everyone thought I should write to Mrs. Phillips, so I did.

He stepped forward again. "But then you needed me, and I learned that you weren't lost forever. I always meant to telegram Mrs. Campbell, but it slipped my mind."

"It slipped your mind?"

He nodded, hoping she could see the honesty in his eyes.

"How do you forget something like that? This poor woman came here expecting to marry you, only to find herself groomless in a strange town, with no friends?"

Guilt washed over him. "Hattie, I'm so sorry. Of course, I'll help Mrs. Campbell, and she won't find herself friendless in Hope."

"Why didn't you tell me?" Her hurt was worse than her anger.

"I didn't mean to keep it from you. Believe me. You can trust me."

"Can I? I'm not so sure." She turned her back, and he saw her hand come up to wipe a tear from her eye. He'd rather take a bullet than see her cry.

"Hattie please." He melted into a puddle at her feet. She could ask for anything and he'd do it. "I didn't mean to hurt anyone, least of all you. I would never. Please, Hattie, you've gotta believe me."

She was silent for a moment, but then her gentle hand touched his cheek.

"I love you, but I need to know that I can trust you. Do you have any more secrets?" He took her hands in his and gazed into the blue pools of her eyes. "I promise, no more secrets."

"You don't have another prospective wive scheduled to arrive next week?"

He half smiled. "No, you're the only wife for me. And I promise to help Florence. Whatever she needs."

"We've already taken care of it." Hattie said confidently. "Flower was very understanding, all things considered. She would've made you a good wife."

"But she's not you. She could have never been you." He wrapped his arms around her.

Mark leaned back and looked into her eyes. "Do you mean to say this was all sorted out before I even arrived?"

Hattie shrugged. "Pretty much," she said. "But you still owe Flower an apology, and you're paying for her accommodations for as long as she needs it."

"I love you, Hattie."

"I love you too."

Chapter Twenty-Six

Mark threw his pillow at the window and shouted, "Shut up, Doodle!"

Hattie laughed from the other room and he blinked his eyes to let in the light.

Mark woke every day to the joy of Hattie. His morning ritual with the damn rooster seemed to amuse her, and so her laughter was the second thing he heard every day. He was going to put that damn rooster in a pot, but then Hattie's laughter wouldn't be the second thing he heard in the morning.

He climbed out of bed and stretched. Then collected his pillow from the floor and tossed it onto the bed. He pulled on his pants and grabbed a clean pair of socks from his drawer. He reached for a shirt but decided against it. Hattie got turned on by the sight of his naked chest, and if he was lucky, she'd drag him back to bed.

"You're burning daylight," Hattie called.

Mark chuckled and left the bedroom. He took Hattie in his arms from behind and helped himself to a handful of her breast and a nibble at her neck. Hattie moaned and leaned back into him, then she swatted him away. "Go sit down. Breakfast is almost ready."

He could watch her all day. She moved around the kitchen with a confidence that he loved. She'd stir this, and then flip that, and then somehow, she'd pull everything off the stove and set it on the table all at the same time. It was magical.

He lived to make her smile because life was easy with Hattie. She filled each day with love and made their home peaceful. When he was a little boy, his mother had made their home feel like that, and he'd missed that sweet comfort since she'd died.

He'd offered to make any changes to the cabin that she might like, but she'd declined. Whenever he'd bring it up, she had insisted that the house was perfect, and that she wanted for nothing. Finally, he asked the other women for suggestions. Most of them had lived in Scott's place, at least for a little while, so he thought they would have ideas about how he could make his wife more comfortable.

Maggie suggested a bookshelf in the sitting room. No surprise from their resident bookworm, but Mark couldn't believe he hadn't thought of it himself. Maggie helped him gather volumes from Hattie's favorite authors, and he surprised her with the collection about two weeks after they'd moved in.

Her delight was so moving that he couldn't wait to do something else for her. So he set to work building a bathroom like his brothers had for their wives. He had to enlist the help of Caleb and Hank, but they had it ready to unveil in no time.

Mark held Hattie's hands over her eyes and led her into the new bathroom. It had been a monster sized chore to keep her out of there until he could complete the construction. But her surprise was well worth the effort. She'd marveled over the tub at Abigail's house several times, and he knew she would love it.

Mark wrapped his arms around Hattie's waist and whispered in her ear. "Ready?"

She leaned back into him and hummed. Mark laughed and pulled her hands from her eyes. Hattie gasped at the sight of the claw-foot tub and stood in awe at the pumping system they'd rigged. Mark walked her around, showing her the drain and explaining how they'd set it up to drain down into the garden. He showed her the taps and water heater.

"You mean we can have hot water right in the tap?" She circled the tub, fingering the shiny pipes.

Mark beamed, "Sure. You just have to light the fire early to warm it." He pulled Hattie close and nibbled at her neck. "Or, when it's hot..." He kissed her mouth. "like today..." His nimble fingers worked the buttons at the front of her dress. "we can fill it with cold water."

Hattie slipped his buttons from their holes and then dropped his shirt on the floor. "That's a big tub. We could probably fit together."

Mark's jaw all but hit the floor when she lunged for him. He lifted her up, and she wrapped her legs around his waist. Between kisses, he said, "That was the idea."

Hattie gave him one more long, burning kiss and then slid back to the floor. "Let's get it going now."

She pulled the levers like he showed her and after a moment, water gushed in bursts, then streams. She dropped the plug into place and watched the water fill the bottom of the tub.

Her lips found his again. He could never quite get his fill of her. No matter where he was or what he was doing,

Hattie was on his mind. If he could stop what he was working on and come into the house for a moment throughout the day, he did. If he could find a reason to sneak away early, he did. Sometimes he even woke in the middle of the night and reached for her.

They made love on the bathroom floor while the tub filled. Afterwards, they soaked long until their fingers wrinkled. Then they climbed out of the tub and went to bed together.

~

HATTIE'S FIRST SUMMER ON THE RANCH WAS GONE IN A FLASH. Before she knew it, the trees were burning with yellows and oranges as October came to an end. Hattie and Mark worked together to bring extra firewood into the house. She needed to finish canning the last of the vegetables from her garden, and then Mark would turn the soil and let it rest until spring.

When they'd shifted enough wood to get her through the day, Hattie sent Mark off to the barn and she returned to the house. She was just finished washing the jars when Opal arrived to help.

Hattie went out on the porch and watched Opal tie the horse to the hitching rail. "Wait till I tell you the news from town!" Opal said as she hugged Hattie. With Opal it was always "news" never gossip.

Hattie looped her arm with Opal's. "Ok, but we have to work while we talk." She laughed. "Last time we didn't get anything done, and I had Mark in the kitchen making jam with me until the wee hours of the morning."

Opal huffed but laughed. "Sure, but you got a good

story out of it." Opal elbowed Hattie in the ribs. "I bet you got an even better story out of it that you won't tell."

Hattie blushed as she remembered that late night in the hot kitchen. Mark had lifted her onto the counter and slid his hands up her skirt. He'd taken her there, standing beside the sink. Her face heated, and she covered it with her hands.

"Told ya." Opal squealed and then turned to the table loaded down with cucumbers. She wilted. "I hate pickles."

"Well, Mark loves them." Hattie said. "And so does Daniel."

Opal shrugged.

Hattie elbowed her friend and then handed her a knife. "Nice neat little slices, and tell me what's going on in town as you chop." She pumped water into a pot and set it on the stove to boil.

Sometimes it took a minute to get Opal going, but once she started, there was no stopping her. She was five cucumbers in before she started her news. "Old Crow-pepper died," she said as she aggressively sliced. "Good riddance. His sweet wife won't lose any sleep over it." She scooped slices up on the side of her knife and dropped them into a jar.

"Should we do something for her?" Hattie asked.

Opal shrugged. "I don't think she'll stick around long. She never liked living in the West." She chopped and scooped. "I bet she's out of town before winter."

Hattie nodded. She didn't really know Mrs. Crowpepper, but she couldn't imagine anyone being relieved with the death of their spouse.

Opal seemed to be unbothered by the thought. She charged forward with her news. "Doris Sand's oldest girl is determined to be a doctor. No matter how much they try to convince her that she should be a nurse, she won't go for it."

Hattie giggled. "I suppose you didn't have anything to do with that."

Opal shrugged again. "Well."

"Uh-huh."

"Anyway." Opal shifted the jar aside and pulled another close. "The oldest Pilot girl is due soon. She looks like a twig that swallowed a watermelon."

"Poor thing, doesn't she still have a while to go?" Hattie swapped Opal's full jar for an empty one. "What did you say her name was?"

"I can't think of it. Every time I see the girl, her name just flies out of my head." Opal had a tendency to talk with her hands, and the way she flung the knife around as she chatted made Hattie's hands itch to take it away. "It's probably because every time I see her, she asks me when I'm going to have a baby and I just want to get away from her as fast as I can."

Hattie turned to watch Opal. "You don't want children?"

Opal either didn't hear the surprise in the question, or she didn't care. "No, I've never wanted children." She filled another jar and slid it to Hattie.

Hattie stuffed the pickles down and poured saltwater brine over them. She set them aside and reached for the next jar. "Don't you like children?"

"Oh, I love them." Opal stopped and rested the back of her hand on her hip with the knife still in her grasp. Hattie just waited for Opal to cut herself. "I know it's not what everyone else expects. I just don't want children."

"Is Daniel ok with that?" She'd never met a woman who didn't want to be a mother.

Opal shrugged. "There are plenty of children for us to play with already." She turned back to the table and resumed her chore. "What about you? You two going to have little ones any time soon?" She caught Hattie's eye. "You know you don't have to if you know what you're doing." Opal said, her tone taking on a more serious note, the way it did when she wanted to get her point across swiftly. "I learned some tricks from the ladies down at Cooper's saloon."

Hattie blushed. She sipped at a cup of tea to buy herself time. Opal had a way of throwing her off balance. "Oh, I would love to be a mother. Mark would be a wonderful father." She smiled and Opal seemed satisfied.

"And Auntie Opal and Uncle Daniel are always here to lend a hand." With a flourish, Opal returned to her task.

The ladies worked all afternoon together and put up enough pickles to stock their own pantries and share with the others on the ranch. After the long day, they cleaned up and Opal headed out.

Hattie set herself to the task of making dinner and wondered what had been keeping Mark. He was later than usual, and she hoped he would be home soon. She'd just slid the biscuits into the oven when she heard a commotion outside. She dropped a tea towel on the counter and untied her apron.

As she stepped out into the beauty of the late afternoon, she saw Mark scurrying across the porch. What was he doing? She laughed as she watched him run, hunched over with his hands out in front of him. He grunted and groaned. Hattie would have given anything to have Abigail's talent for recreating a scene on paper. She watched him for a while, but then realized he was chasing some sort of rodent and she jumped clear out of her skin. Hattie climbed on top of a chair and squealed.

A flash of black and white fur piqued her curiosity. It wasn't a rodent.

"Get over here." Mark said as he scooped up the ball of fur and put it behind his back. It whined.

"What are you doing up there?" Mark smiled, "It was supposed to be a surprise, but he turned out to be more mischievous than I realized?"

Hattie arched her brow. "He?" Since Mark had the critter well in hand, Hattie climbed down from the chair and fixed the cushion she'd knocked askew.

Mark brought his hand out from behind his back and revealed a small black and white Border Collie puppy chewing on his finger. It snapped its head up and barked at Hattie. Mark passed the puffball to Hattie, and she cuddled him close. The sweet thing was all fluff and no substance. Hattie cradled him on his back, rubbing his pudgy belly.

"I thought he'd be good company for you on your walks, and maybe he'd keep those foxes away from the hen house." Mark put his arm around Hattie and scratched the little dog's head.

"Oh Mark, he's beautiful!" Hattie kissed her new companion. The puppy licked her face and nibbled her nose. "He's a rambunctious little fellow. Does he have a name?"

"Whatever you decide."

Hattie held him away from her and looked into his inky eyes. He tilted his eye to the side and examined her as well. She laughed, "I think he looks like a Duke."

Mark smiled and scratched between Duke's ears. "Good choice. Welcome to the family, Duke."

Hattie turned into Mark's arms and gave him a kiss. "We've started a family."

Mark's slow smile spread across his face. "So, we have."

Hattie watched his face, hoping to memorize his reaction to her words. "And in a few months, we'll add another."

It took a second, but then Mark whooped and swept Hattie off her feet.

Sophia

finds

faith

KRISSYANN
GRANGER

Sophia Finds Faith

THE MAXWELL BRIDES SERIES: BOOK EIGHT

The pump whined, resisting each rise and fall before releasing a sputter of water. The arm needed to be greased. Sophia grumbled about it to herself, but she would never tell Elijah. The house was in disrepair, with the number of things in need of fixing growing every day, but she could never say a word. Sophia was not a complainer, anyway. She worked hard to keep the home as pristine as was within her means. The leaking roof, cracked windows, uneven doors, and ever-growing drafts were issues out of her control.

She tried not to think about these things and let the thoughts pass through her mind unheeded. Her eyes found Elijah splitting wood near the house. Her heart raced as she tried to assess his mood. She knew it was silly to think that he could read her mind, and of course he couldn't, but somehow, he always seemed to know when she had bad thoughts. But the axe hit the chopping block without more flourish than needed to split the wood. It was when he started really throwing things around that she needed to worry.

Sophia raised and wrestled the pump arm down again.

Elijah would not like her telling him how to take care of his home. It was not her place. A good woman does as she's told. She doesn't do the tellin'. That's what Elijah always said, anyway. She thought about this vaguely, her eyes falling from her husband to the slowly filling bucket. The fiery leaves had come and gone. The vibrancy of summer was a mere ghost in the sea of brown vegetation. It was an unseasonably temperate morning following days of rain. She stood numb to pleasure. The blue of the sky and warmth of the sun were lost on her. She tried not to think, tried to keep her mind empty and pure, but in the rhythm of their work, her mind drifted.

Squeak, gush, chop—Today I will be better.

Squeak, gush, chop—I will remember to be grateful.

Squeak, gush, chop—I will be a good wife.

Sophia wanted nothing more than that, but no matter how hard she tried, she just kept failing. Elijah did his best; he was a good husband to her in this way. He didn't want to hurt her, he just wanted to make her better. Her tongue probed the split in her lip. This is how he loves me. Her arms ached, more from the bruising than from pumping. Images of the night before flashed in her mind, but she would not think about it now. Pain only means you're doing something wrong. She used the discomfort to bring her out of herself to focus on the task at hand. She repeated these words over and over in her mind, forcing herself to push through the pain. After all, she'd been through worse.

One more pump should—Sophia was suddenly yanked off her feet and dragged away. Hands were wrapped around her mouth and waist, dragging her away. She tried to fight, to get to her feet, but they were fast and strong. Scruff bristled on her cheek as a face pressed against hers. She tried to scream for her husband but couldn't. What would he think if he saw her in the arms of another man like this? A wide, calloused hand stifled her meek cry, only allowing a soft squeak to escape. She squirmed, kicking over the water bucket as he pulled her backward. Sophia dug her feet into the ground, her heals carving ruts into the damp autumn earth.

A soft Irish lilt whispered in her ear, "This is a rescue, love. Yer safe with me."

She wasn't safe with anyone but Elijah.

Sophia fought to free herself, but he was too strong. He pulled her to the edge of her house and pressed her up against the wood siding. Splinters pricked her palms and snagged at her dress. The stranger pinned her to the wall with his body. He was big and she couldn't move. She could see around the corner of the house and into the yard, though.

She searched for Elijah when she noticed a tall man skirting along the front of the house. Elijah's back was to him. He swung the ax, ignorant of the danger, as the blade glided seamlessly through the log and deep into the chopping block. Elijah stopped with both hands on the ax handle and put one boot on the block to free the trapped tool.

The tall stranger took his chance. He drew a gun and shouted for Elijah to get down on the ground. Elijah—always the chance taker—ran without so much as a backward glance toward Sophia. He disappeared behind the house with the assailant at his heels.

Sophia wriggled in the vice-like grip. She had to do something. What, though?

"I'm not goin' hurt ye. We're gettin' ye outta here.

You'll be safe with us." Her abductor repeated these words over and over, promising safety.

Safe? If you don't kill me, surely Elijah will. With the thought of what Elijah would think of her, a full body sob overtook her. She shook so violently that she almost freed herself.

Who was this man? And why did he think she needed saving?

Yet something in his lilting voice made her want to trust him. Each syllable rolled from his lips in a wave, falling on her ear like a note from a forgotten lullaby, shining a light on a dark place deep inside her. The feeling clashed with her equal need to fight for her freedom. How could the voice of a man taking her hostage elicit such a response?

His touch wasn't violent. He didn't squeeze her like a vice, growing tighter and tighter, until she complied. He didn't strike her or even threaten her. Instead, he restrained her in nothing more than a firm bear-hug. In fact, the more she struggled, the gentler he seemed to hold her.

Why?

Glass shattered somewhere inside the house and voices raised, but she couldn't make out their words. She stopped resisting when a single gunshot rang out. A flock of birds took to the air, and then everything went silent. The sound stopped the very air inside her lungs.

The stranger chose that moment to whisk her away. He pulled Sophia to a waiting carriage and pushed her inside.

His hands were warm on her back through her dress. The intimacy of his touch was a betrayal to Elijah, causing another powerful surge of tears. But what could she do? She had never been much of a fighter. It was always easier to do as you're told. So she gave up the fight and climbed inside.

Was Elijah okay?

The man climbed in and sat across from her. It was her first chance to get a look at him. Afraid to make eye contact, she stole glances at him as the carriage rattled into motion. They rounded the house and then stopped. Sophia searched out the window, hoping to lay her eyes on her husband. Did they shoot him? Why would they attack a man in his own yard like that?

What did they want with her?

Read the rest of Sophia's story here https://amzn.to/3M4hpEU

* 9 7 8 1 9 5 5 6 0 9 2 7 2 *